TIME FOR SHERLOCK HOLMES

TIME FOR
Sherlock Holmes

A NOVEL BY

DAVID DVORKIN

DODD, MEAD & COMPANY

NEW YORK

Copyright © 1983 by David Dvorkin
All rights reserved
No part of this book may be reproduced in any form
without permission in writing from the publisher
Published by Dodd, Mead & Company, Inc.
79 Madison Avenue, New York, N.Y. 10016
Distributed in Canada by
McClelland and Stewart Limited, Toronto
Manufactured in the United States of America
Designed by Judith Lerner
First Edition

LIBRARY OF CONGRESS CATALOGING IN PUBLICATION DATA

Dvorkin, David.
  Time for Sherlock Holmes.

  I. Title.
PS3554.V67T5   1983   813'.54   83-8918
ISBN 0-396-08175-4

to the spirit of Arthur Conan Doyle

TIME FOR SHERLOCK HOLMES

1

A Trip to Sussex

IT HAS BEEN, if I remember correctly, about sixty-five years since last I wrote about the adventures of my friend Mr. Sherlock Holmes. At that time, I told how he had retired to the Sussex countryside to raise and study bees and to await gracefully, if with his usual intellectual energy, the inevitable end of a long and eventful life. That this end has not yet come is but one of the remarkable facts my friend has at last given me his permission to tell to the public.

When Sherlock Holmes informed me, toward the end of his long and brilliant career as a consulting detective in London and its environs, of his intention to remove himself to the countryside and devote his declining years to the study of bees and to the compilation of a casebook which would at once illustrate and expound his justly famous methods of criminal detection, I in my turn informed him of my desire to spend the rest of my life in the city.

"Country air and country food are certainly better for one's constitution, Holmes. I'll grant you that. But old age is dull enough without adding the enforced dullness of the countryside. No, I think I shall prefer the bustle of London to the end."

He shook his head and sighed. "Well, old friend, there may be more than ordinary health involved. But we shall see what we shall see."

This conversation took place shortly before Holmes removed himself permanently from the city. In the years that followed, our contacts were perforce limited. The necessity of obtaining supplies having to do with the study of bees—supplies not available in rural areas, due to the abstruse nature of his scientific studies—occasionally brought Sherlock Holmes back to town, despite his recently acquired and frequently expressed aversion for London. Then, too, his work on a book about crime detection, a book which depended heavily upon his own past cases for the elucidation of various points, required that he consult my notebooks, which provide, if anything, an even more complete record of Sherlock Holmes' career than do the notebooks of Mr. Sherlock Holmes himself.

The years passed, and on each of his trips to London, I observed how relentlessly and unceasingly Nature worked to destroy even so vigorous and active a man as Sherlock Holmes. On every visit, my old friend was thinner, more wrinkled, and his hair, if anything, even whiter than on the previous visit. That parallel changes were taking place in myself, I was well aware; but since I saw myself every morning in the shaving mirror, the steady, gradual effects of age were not so striking in my own case.

In the summer of 1925, when I was in my early seventies and my prognosis for myself was a gloomy one—indeed, I felt I had little chance of surviving until the following spring—I received a telephone call from Holmes. I had not heard from him for months, and I feared the worst, so you will understand my pleasure at hearing his well-remembered voice. (In spite of all the outward signs of the deterioration due to age, by the way, Sherlock Holmes' voice had remained as hale and firm and strong as ever.)

"Watson!" he greeted me cheerfully. "I have a duty for you, just as in the old days. There is a train leaving Paddington for Brighton in three hours. Get off at Hewisham, as usual. I'll have my man pick you up, and you should be at my rural retreat in time for tea."

"Really, Holmes, this is too much," I protested. "Considering my age and my condition, how can you expect me to gad about the countryside like—like—a young goat in the spring?"

"My dear old friend," he replied gently, "it is precisely because of your age and condition that you must come. I shall expect you by tea time." And before I could utter another word, he had hung up his telephone.

It has long struck me as more than a little curious that a single command from Sherlock Holmes has always been enough to set me off, against my better judgement, on expeditions both tedious and foolhardy. I followed his instructions to the letter, taking the specified train from Paddington Station and getting off at Hewisham, one of those small, insignificant villages still so common in England in those days and at which one could easily imagine the trains were reluctant to stop and impatient to leave. Indeed, I had scarcely alighted on the platform when my bag was rudely thrown from the train to land beside me and the train began to move again, quickly gathering speed as it fled south to Brighton.

I looked about and found myself in a pleasant enough spot, if a deserted one. The abundant greenery, clear skies, and clean air of the country afforded me a welcome change after the noise and smells of London. I breathed deeply, glad already that Holmes had persuaded me to come to this charming place. A voice suddenly interrupted my reverie.

"Doctor Watson, aren't ye? This way, this way."

I turned to see a tall man in the dress of a farmer, a wide-brimmed, floppy hat shading his face from the sun. He seemed an interesting specimen of rural life, and I inspected him carefully. My steady gaze and lack of other response seemed to anger him.

"Come along, then, Doctor—if doctor ye be!" he snapped.

Offended as I was by this boorish behaviour, I nonetheless held my tongue and, picking up my travelling bag, followed him to a small, horse-drawn wagon of a type one still saw quite frequently on farms in those days. The horse turned its head and favoured me with a long, hostile stare. Returning it, I climbed painfully into the wagon and seated myself between two bales of hay. Holmes' man climbed on at the front of the wagon, took up the reins, and cursed the horse into motion. Those were the last words I was to hear from him throughout the trip.

The drive from the station to the old farmhouse Sherlock Holmes had purchased took above an hour, and in all that time I was unable to elicit a single word from my unpleasant companion. He said not a further word to the horse, either: the beast seemed to know its way, following a faint but discernible track across quiet, rolling green meadows. After a time, I was obliged by the steady heat of the afternoon sunshine to remove my jacket, but my driver gave no sign that the heat affected him in any way.

At last, to my great relief, we arrived in the yard in front of the old farmhouse where my friend now lived. The driver stopped the wagon, leaped down from it, and with still not a word, began to wander away.

"Here!" I shouted, my patience and politeness alike stretched to the breaking. "Here, my good man! Tell your master immediately of my arrival."

He stood still, his back insolently toward me. "He already knows," he grunted.

"Does he, indeed? Then where is he? Where *is* Sherlock Holmes?"

"Right here!" The man spun around, straightening his back and whipping off his hat as he did so, and I beheld the familiar features of Sherlock Holmes—the hawk nose, the penetrating eyes, the latter now twinkling merrily at the joke he had played on me.

"Holmes!" I cried, amazed at his skill and audacity. "All this time—the entire trip from the railway station—and I never suspected."

He laughed in delight. "The old skills remain, my dear fellow. Forgive me for deceiving you, but you know my old love for such tricks. Now come into the house, and we'll call for tea." And he led the way, as straight of back and quick of step as ever, striding to the door quiet as though he were a man fifty years younger than his actual age.

"Slower, Holmes," I called out to him. "Remember old Watson, who has not the advantage of clean Sussex air to keep him young."

He apologized and promised to control his impatience thenceforth. We strolled together into the house at a more leisurely pace.

2

The Secret of the Sussex Wine

IT WAS A LARGE, rambling old place, built more than fifty years
earlier by a gentleman from South Africa who had, so Holmes
informed me, later met his death in a most peculiar and awful
manner in this very house. The house commanded a dramatic
and beautiful view of the Channel, but because of the nearness
of that great body of water, the site was subject to frequent mists
and cold drizzle. It must have been a gloomy place indeed at the
time of the first owner's death, but Holmes had bought his own
electric generator and had had electric lights installed throughout the building. Thus it was cheerful enough that evening as
we sat drinking tea in the well-lighted library after supper, a
pleasant sea breeze coming through the window along with the
droning hum of insect life and the fragrance of flowers.

"It's pleasant enough, Holmes. I must admit that."

He looked at me keenly. "A nice change from the noise and
smells of a summer evening in London, Watson?"

"Indeed!" I laughed. "It's almost enough to make me wish to
spend my remaining years—or months, perhaps—with you here
in the country."

"And you would be welcome, of course. But . . . months, you
said?" His normally unreadable face betrayed his distress.

I shrugged. "I fear so. But let us not discuss so dreary a topic
as death. What luck with your bees?"

He pressed a button set into a small box on the table beside
his chair. "I want you to taste something, Watson. Then I'll answer any questions you may have concerning my bees."

When Mrs. Hudson answered Holmes' electrical summons, he
said to her, "A fresh bottle of *the wine* from the cellar for our
guest, if you please, Mrs. Hudson." I raised my eyebrows at this
strange emphasis upon those two words, but with the faintest of

smiles he placed his finger upon his lips to forestall any questions. So we sat in silence for perhaps five minutes, until the housekeeper returned with a bottle of *the wine*.

I must confess that, while we waited, the generous portion I had eaten earlier combined with the warmth of the tea, the mild breeze, and the insects' hum to induce in me a pleasant drowsiness. I was awakened by the sound of the tray with the bottle upon it being placed on the table next to my companion's chair; Holmes was regarding me with a look of compassion and concern, an expression he quickly masked, when he realized I was awake, with a bright-eyed joviality. "Well, Watson!" he cried. "Here we have *the wine*! I'll be interested in your opinion of it."

I stifled a yawn. "Perhaps it would be more prudent of me to retire than to indulge in wine."

"Nonsense, Watson. I'll not have that. I must insist."

"Oh, very well," I said resignedly.

"Good, good." He extracted the cork and poured two generous glassfuls. Since the bottle was of a dark green glass, only then could I see that the wine was of a deep golden color, between that of honey and golden syrup. I noticed also that Holmes was looking at the wine with what I could only regard as an unhealthy fascination. I was tempted to ask him whether this precious wine of his contained some extra ingredient—cocaine, perhaps—but I forebore, knowing that he had, after my years of gentle pressure and both friendly and professional counsel, turned away from the use of the addictive substance.

When he handed me my glass, I sniffed it, and its sweet, almost sickening odor finally told me what this mysterious wine was. "Why, this is mead!" I exclaimed.

"Indeed it is. Fermented and bottled on this very farm, from honey produced by my own bees. Drink up, Watson!"

"After demanding of me that I behave like a young goat in the spring," I grumbled, "you now wish me to be a Viking." However, I drank first a mouthful of the mead and then the rest of the glass. "By George!" I exclaimed. "Holmes, this is quite good! However, it *is* a bit sweet for my palate, and I should not care to drink it with any regularity."

Wearing an ambiguous expression that I hoped indicated

amusement but which I feared denoted hurt feelings instead, he murmured, "On that score, Watson, we shall see what we shall see."

I slept more soundly that night than I had done in years and woke greatly refreshed. "Holmes," I said to him over breakfast, "country air is indeed beneficial. I feel positively ten years younger."

"That much!" he marvelled. Then he bent his penetrating gaze upon me. "An improved prognosis, Doctor?"

"It's surely too soon for that," I replied shortly, sobered by thoughts of the future. The rest of the meal passed in silence.

But during the succeeding days, my health continued to improve dramatically. I fancied I could taste food better, smell the many smells of the countryside (not all pleasant!) more keenly, and hear the sounds of insects and animals far more clearly than I had been able to in years. One evening, while Holmes and I were sitting down to our evening tea, accompanied by the inevitable glass of Holmes' honey wine, I mentioned as much to him. "I'm forced to conclude," I finished, between reflective sips of the sweet, amber wine, "that London air, water, and food do indeed contain noxious substances that age one prematurely, and that I would be well advised to remove myself to the country, to increase the number of years remaining to me."

I swallowed the remaining mead quickly and poured myself another glass, ignoring Holmes' amused glance. He had insisted on my drinking a generous glass of the honey wine every evening. At first, I had acceded only to humor him and to atone for any insult I might unintentionally have given him on my first evening, when my opinion of the mead had been perhaps too frankly expressed, but I had in time become quite addicted to my evening glass—and often two or three glasses—of it.

"I notice, Watson, that you now speak of remaining years, not months." When I was seated once more with my mead and my tea, he continued in a quiet, reflective tone, "While it is certainly true that London air and London water are foul while both are pure here in the country, and while it is also true that country living will prolong one's life when compared with city living, nonetheless it is also a fact that each man is allotted only a certain span. Healthy living will enable him to come nearer to attaining that span of years than will unhealthy living, but the span itself is not increased. Only *the intervention of Man* can do that."

This odd speech left me quite puzzled, but before I could comment, Holmes spoke again, in a voice that rang out in the quiet of the evening. "That wine you are drinking so eagerly—that wine, Watson, that is somewhat too sweet for your urbane palate—is rejuvenating every cell in your body, just as it has made and kept both me and my housekeeper, Mrs. Hudson, young!"

Silence reigned for a few moments following this extraordinary outburst. *Good heavens!* I thought. *He has gone mad!* The brilliant analytical mind had at last succumbed to senility. Knowing from my years of medical practice how carefully one must deal with a man in the throes of severe delusion, I seized upon the very last of his words and said cautiously, although not without a tremor in my voice, "Surely this middle-aged housekeeper of yours is not the Mrs. Hudson of Baker Street, but rather her daughter?"

His eyes blazing fiercely, Holmes declared, "She is indeed the Mrs. Hudson you knew so long ago in Baker Street. Nor is she middle-aged: like me, she is physically young but disguised to appear old, so as not to arouse suspicion and superstitious hostility amongst the villagers and to avoid shocking you while you were still in a weakened condition."

I opened my mouth, intending to offer some soothing words, but before I could speak, he continued in a calmer tone. "I realize I cannot expect you to believe me without proof, Watson, so to prove that I am neither insane nor senile, I want you to perform a detailed and complete physical examination upon me. I have taken the liberty of having your own medical instruments brought here from London; along with the equipment I have here for my own biological work, they should enable you to satisfy yourself that what I say is the simple truth."

As always, Sherlock Holmes was proved correct. After a careful examination, I was forced to admit that he appeared, physically, to be in his mid to late twenties. I next examined myself, insofar as that was possible, and was both astounded and delighted to discover that, after only one week of daily ingestion of the miraculous wine, the aging process had reversed itself in me and I was detectably younger and healthier than I had been a week earlier. How could I doubt any longer the extraordinary assertions of my friend? After all those years of unravelling the twisted misdeeds of men, that great analytical mind had at last succeeded in unravelling one of the most profound mysteries of Nature! Sherlock Holmes had discovered the true Elixir of Youth. And he now offered me a full share of it, provided that I agreed, first, to move down permanently from London, and second, never to share our secret with anyone else.

"To the first condition, I was almost ready to agree even before you told me of the secret of the wine, Holmes. But your second proviso—! Why not share this wonderful discovery with the world?"

But on this point he was immovable. "The world, Watson," he said firmly, "is an ass." He went on in a sombre tone, "After the terrible war we have just seen, the world will have to attain a far higher level of reason and social maturity than it has ever yet displayed before I will even consider giving it my secret. Were I to share this knowledge now, the results, I am convinced, would be social upheaval on a catastrophic scale, and that second Great War, which I am convinced is coming in at most another fifteen years, would be even more calamitous than it will in fact prove to be.

"I have shared my secret with Mrs. Hudson," he continued, "simply because she is a superb housekeeper and I lacked the patience to train another; also, she can be trusted to keep the knowledge to herself. I offer now to share it with you because of our old and fruitful friendship and because I trust *your* ability to keep a secret as well. Oh, and I have included Mycroft in my secret, of course, for obvious reasons. But I will share it with no one else."

When further argument proved ineffectual against his determination to keep his rejuvenation secret from the world, I at last gave in and acceded to his second condition as I already had to the first. Although I reopened the matter upon occasion in later years, I had no more success in changing his mind than during the conversation just described; indeed, from one decade to the next Sherlock Holmes would insist that mankind continued to deteriorate rather than to improve.

The extent of his withdrawal from both his fellow men and all memory of his previous life can be demonstrated by one incident I recall vividly. Holmes and I were walking in the nearby countryside one day when we happened to pass a large, handsome house, the front gates of which bore the name *Windlesham*. Beyond the gates, a pleasant spread of lawns and trees was visible. A tall, powerfully built man of late middle age stood upon the lawn, gazing about him in pride of ownership. He noticed us passing by and, with an expression of bluff good-fellowship, started toward us as if to begin a conversation. But Sherlock Holmes hurried me on, despite my expressed intention to meet the owner of the imposing place and request a tour of the grounds. I thought Holmes' manner inexplicably rude, and I told him so in a most frank and forthright manner.

"That fellow," he replied testily, "is a writer of detective stories. You should have realised by now that I do not desire any contact in any form whatsoever with my old profession, with those who practice it or with those who are so foolish as to attract the attention of those who practice it, or even with those who make a living by chronicling the adventures of fictitious practitioners of it."

"But surely," I said timidly, "the man must write other things as well?"

"Historical romances and spiritualist treatises," he said scornfully. "And those are even more frivolous than stories about made-up detectives!" And with that, he strode along, puffing furiously at his pipe and rebuffing my further attempts at conversation.

And so the decades passed and the world roiled and rumbled about us, changing in a variety of ways I could never had predicted, while we three, in our little enclave on the Channel, lived on unchanging. I had long ceased taking the London papers, even though the *Times* had once been such a major part of my day, and the only sign of change in the outside world of which I was aware was the way, year by year, the aeroplanes passing overhead and the ships gliding up and down the Channel in the distance increased in size and how the use of sail diminished and eventually disappeared on all but the smallest boats. Conversation, reading, bees, and scientific investigations occupied the time of Doctor John Watson and Mr. Sherlock Holmes as the decades slipped by and the outside world went largely unheeded. Then came that terrible crime that penetrated even our shell, pulling us back willy-nilly into the turbulent activities of the rest of mankind and marking the true beginning of my tale.

3

A Death in Downing Street

"GOOD HEAVENS!" Sherlock Holmes exclaimed.

It was shortly after breakfast on a mild summer day in the early 1990s, and we were sitting in the library, reading. I was engrossed in a book, and I will admit to you what in those days I would have tried to conceal from my companion, that it was an historical romance, one of the products of the fertile imagination of that neighbor of ours upon whom Holmes had showered such contempt during our walk. And a fine, ringing tale it was, replete with bowmen and medieval rulers both evil and noble. Holmes was studying a small local newspaper, the *Daily Mirror*, published in Hewisham. He steadfastly refused to read the London papers, insisting that they recalled to him in a particularly unpleasant way that hurried and eventful metropolitan life he so wished to forget. The Hewisham *Daily Mirror* concerned itself in the main with local doings—pig farming, fishermen's catches,and cricket matches—and allocated but a single page at the very back of the journal to news of London and the rest of the world. Meager as it was, the news in the *Daily Mirror* had at least the virtue of timeliness.

At Holmes' exclamation, I looked up from my book to find that he was staring at his newspaper with a horrified expression on his normally impassive face. He read hurriedly to the end of the item that had so upset him, and only then did he meet my gaze. "Watson," he said in a voice scarcely above a whisper, "the Prime Minister has been murdered in a locked room!"

"Good heavens!" I exclaimed in my turn.

"You may well say so," he agreed. "Listen." He began to read aloud from the newspaper.

" 'The Prime Minister was found this morning when her private secretary, unable to open the door to the Prime Minister's office and obtaining no response to his vigorous knocking, summoned the police. When the police had broken down the door and discovered the Prime Minister slumped over her desk, they at first believed she had suffered a stroke. It has since been disclosed, however, that she had been shot at close quarters.'

"It goes on to say that her secretary, a young man named Wilford, was the last person to see her alive. That was yesterday evening, the third of June, when Mrs. Chalmers told him she had some urgent work to do and did not wish to be disturbed. She entered her office, locking her door behind her. Somewhat later, Wilford, who was working late himself in his adjoining office, thought he heard Mrs. Chalmers' voice, raised as if in anger. He then knocked at her door and enquired whether she needed help, but she replied that she did not, so he thought no more of the incident. Shortly after this, Wilford went home. It was not until he returned to work at Number Ten Downing Street this morning and obtained no response to his knocks upon the locked door that he at last became alarmed."

He threw the paper to the floor in anger and rose to pace over to the window, where he stood staring out over the rolling fields to the broad blue waters of the Channel, sparkling in the sunlight. "One would think, Watson," he said in a tone of disgust, "that Britain's Prime Minister would be more securely guarded, and that her whereabouts and state of health would at all times be known to the appropriate security officials." After a pause, he muttered, "There are certain elements to this case, however, that intrigue me."

Meanwhile, I had cast my book aside and recovered Holmes' paper from the floor. I quickly scanned the news item, gazing with interest at the accompanying photograph of the Prime Minister, taken some years earlier, after her party had first come to power. She stared at me from the newspaper, a grey-haired lady of early middle age, with the black skin of the West Indies and a thin, determined face; an iron-willed woman possessed of a penetrating intelligence not unlike Sherlock Holmes' own. How curious to reflect that, in terms of years alone, she could have been my great-granddaughter! By a strange twist of fate, the photograph had been taken in the very office at Number 10 Downing Street where the Prime Minister had been found murdered that morning.

The paper was suddenly snatched from my hand. I looked up in some annoyance to find Holmes staring at the photograph in fascination. He turned to a small table by the window, opened a drawer and rummaged about in it. Finally he found what he was looking for—a small magnifying glass—and with it he studied the newspaper photograph intently. "How remarkable and suggestive!" he exclaimed. "Watson, a terrible foreboding has seized me. We must travel to London immediately."

"London!" I said in astonishment. "Holmes, we haven't been to London in well over fifty years. What reason could we possibly have for going there now?"

"If I told you my suspicions now, you would think me mad," he said gravely.

If it were not for Holmes' longstanding insistence on cutting himself off from the outside world, we would have had a television set in the house, or at the very least a wireless, and we would have received the news from London all the sooner. In a similar vein, Holmes now insisted that, despite the unexplained urgency of our trip to London, we should take the train rather than fly.

However, when we arrived in that great, noisy metropolis late in the afternoon of the same day, I discovered that Holmes had not been quite so cut off from the outside world for all those years as I had supposed. We took a taxicab from the railway station to the huge, gleaming white building that housed the headquarters of the Metropolitan Police. (The headquarters had only recently been moved to this new building, which as yet had no name. City wags had already taken to calling it "New New Scotland Yard.") It was immediately obvious to me that Holmes was remarkably familiar with the building and that he had some particular destination in mind. We soon found ourselves in a small office containing a large desk, behind which sat a very large man whom I recognised instantly.

He rose ponderously from his chair and extended a mammoth hand. "Sherlock!" he exclaimed in delight. "After all these years! But I did believe that this case was possessed of those bizarre, *outré* elements so beloved by you in the past, and that you might as a result emerge from your rural retreat."

"Indeed, Mycroft," Sherlock Holmes laughed, for the man in the office was none other than Holmes' older brother, "you were correct, as always." He turned to me. "Watson, you will recall my telling you that Mycroft was one of the three persons to whom I had disclosed the secret of my wine. You will also remember my telling you long ago of the major role Mycroft has long played behind the scenes in the British government."

I nodded. Mycroft Holmes had always eschewed any high office that might have brought him to public attention. Nonetheless, despite his lack of high official title, Mycroft had been a cornerstone of government policy and action. I could readily understand that, with the advantage of that Elixir of Youth discovered by his younger brother, Mycroft must over the years have cemented his position and increased his influence in the government all the more. From what Sherlock Holmes had told me of his older brother, I had long ago learned to respect Mycroft's intellect and importance; however, on the few occasions when I had chanced to meet him, I had always found that I did not care for the man personally. What he had to do with the present case, the assassination of the Prime Minister, I could not imagine. Sherlock Holmes quickly illuminated this point.

"Mycroft," he explained, "has for some years worked in closed cooperation with that special branch of the Metropolitan Police whose duty it is to safeguard the Prime Minister. It is as a consequence of that assignment that he has an office in this building. You can see, I hope, why Mycroft, of all people, can tell us what is known in this case."

Mycroft had seated himself again while his brother spoke. Now he sighed gustily and said, "I fear not much *is* known." He gave us a short account of the case, which differed only in minor detail from the article carried in the Hewisham *Daily Mirror* that morning. "I must confess myself thoroughly stymied," he concluded.

"You have no hypotheses at all, then?" Sherlock Holmes asked in the most innocent tone imaginable.

Mycroft was clearly deeply wounded. "Good gracious, Sherlock! Of course I have an hypothesis. However, the hypothesis itself partakes of elements which are most bizarre and *outré,* so much so that I have hesitated to mention it to anyone. This in spite of that old maxim of mine I have long urged you to take to heart, that one must adopt that hypothesis, no matter how improbable, that remains after all the impossible hypotheses have been eliminated."

"Ah, yes," said Sherlock Holmes shortly, *"your* maxim. I assume that, since the body was found, the carpet in the office has been trampled flat by many a policeman's large feet."

Mycroft nodded. "I was one of the first on the scene, however."

"Ah! Commendable foresight and vigor in one normally so lethargic, my dear Mycroft. Did you find two parallel grooves . . . ?"

"Yes!" Mycroft cried in delight. "In the carpet near the desk."

"Perhaps four feet apart and five long?"

"Approximately." Mycroft looked pleased. "Then you think it plausible after all, Sherlock?"

"Oh, indeed. What of the third book from the left, on the fourth shelf from the bottom, in the bookcase behind the desk?"

Mycroft smote his desk with the palm of his hand. "Good heavens! I forgot to look. Sherlock, sometimes I suspect that that wine of yours, even while it preserves the body so miraculously, allows the mind to decay! How *could* I have forgotten such a detail as the book?"

"Never mind, Mycroft," Sherlock Holmes said soothingly. "You may be immortal, but you are still human and therefore imperfect. Can you arrange for Watson and me to examine the scene of the murder?"

Mycroft of course acquiesced immediately to this request, and he arranged the matter with a quick telephone call to a subordinate stationed in the Prime Minister's residence. Soon afterwards, Holmes and I were in a taxicab *en route* to Downing Street.

Holmes puffed on his pipe and gazed out of the window beside him at the greatly changed streets of London. I, meanwhile, pondered the impact the assassination would have upon this city and the nation it governed. History had not been kind to England during the many decades of my seclusion in Sussex; the murder of Mrs. Chalmers was but the latest of many cruel blows. "It is indeed a tragedy," I said with a sigh.

"Tragedy?" Holmes remarked, turning from the window. "Hardly a tragedy, Watson. This is the first time in all my life that *I* have perceived a detail that *Mycroft* had overlooked. No, no," he said in smug self-satisfaction, turning back to the window, "it is a triumph I have longed for since boyhood."

4

Speedier than Sound

WE WERE PASSED without challenge by the policemen on guard at Number 10. Obviously, Mycroft's telephone call to the men's superior had done its work; I was impressed anew with the man's influence. We walked down a long hallway toward the anteroom of the office in which the murder had taken place. My eyes were riveted upon its closed door in fascination. Holmes, meanwhile, stared about at the hallway, his penetrating gaze missing not a detail.

"Observe, Watson," he murmured, "how many shadowy nooks and crannies this hallway contains. Hiding places, all of them, whereby a would-be assassin could elude watchmen. No supernatural means would be needed for the crime." He shook his head in annoyance. "Perhaps Mycroft's mind *is* failing."

We were met at the door to the office by a tall young man, a thin and nervous fellow whose face and demeanour suggested immediately to my professional eye that he had recently suffered something approaching a nervous breakdown. I speculated that he was either a relative of the dead woman or else someone who had been charged with her safety and was therefore on the verge of professional ruin. Fortunately, I did not mention these speculations to Sherlock Holmes, for both guesses were wrong; the young man introduced himself as Wilford, the late Mrs. Chalmers' private secretary. "I assume," he said, in a voice that was still trembling, "that you are the two men Scotland Yard called to say would be here."

"Precisely, Mr. Wilford," said Holmes. "May we see the room?"

Wilford produced a key and unlocked the door. "I was instructed, by an enormously fat man who came here with the police, to keep it locked so that the room would be undisturbed," he explained.

"Excellent," said Holmes. "More than I had any right to expect."

I engaged Wilford in conversation by the door while Sherlock Holmes examined the room in minute detail. Wilford repeated essentially the same story we had already heard twice. However, my conversation with him disclosed immediately a fact not mentioned in the newspaper report, that he was extremely hard of hearing. That, I realized, explained why he had not heard the fatal shot (the gun used, moreover, had been of very small calibre), and it also implied that the angry words he had heard must in fact have been spoken at rather high volume. Our conversation was interrupted when Holmes called me over to the desk. I was surprised to see that his earlier ebullience, that fierce gleam in his eye and the colour in his normally pallid cheeks that were the marks of Sherlock Holmes embarking on a fascinating case, had faded, leaving him drawn and anxious.

"It is as I feared, Watson," he said in a low voice so that Wilford, who was still standing uncertainly by the door, should not hear. "The very worst has happened. A thousand small details confirm it, but no examination of those details is necessary, for the villain has left his calling card. See!" He pointed to a book that lay open upon the desk.

I peered at it dutifully. It was a small volume, old (older than I!), and bound in red morocco. The exposed page was covered with the abstruse symbols of mathematics and astronomy; equation followed equation, linked only by such phrases as "therefore," "it therefore follows," and "it is thus clear that." The page was titled "A Sufficient Approximation for the Many-Body Problem," and that meant no more to me than did the symbols which followed. I said as much to Holmes, adding, "It might as well be written in Greek, as far as I'm concerned."

"Much of it is," he replied absentmindedly. "Watson," he said suddenly, "the very worst has happened, and the consequences may be fearful. Let us hope we will be in time to forestall the working out of this evil. Come along!" He rushed from the room, nearly knocking over the bewildered Wilford.

[19]

I managed to catch up with him in the hallway. "For Heaven's sake, Holmes," I demanded, "where are we hurrying off to this time?"

"New York, of course," he replied in an impatient tone. "And this time I *will* make a concession to modern transportation."

Mere hours later we were aboard a new Concorde II, that magnificent man-made eagle, soaring more than eight miles above the sparkling blue surface of the Atlantic, speeding toward New York almost four times as fast as sound. It was a remarkable experience for a man of my age and background, who had never flown before; in fact, after so many decades of country solitude and calm, the last day or so had seemed an unrelieved confusion of dashing and scurrying about, and this latest mad hurry, aboard the latest and speediest of the supersonic passenger aeroplanes, was but the finishing touch.

At that time, British Airways still permitted smoking on its aircraft, and Sherlock Holmes lost no time in stuffing his huge pipe full of shag and lighting up. He settled back in satisfaction, huge clouds of smoke billowing up about his head, on his face that look of otherworldly concentration that signified an absorption in the intricacies of a particularly complex problem. He was utterly unaware of the angry glances and mutterings of our fellow passengers, just as he resolutely ignored my own questions: What was the evil we must prevent? Did he know who had murdered the Prime Minister; and, if so, who was the culprit? What would we do in New York? Only one of my questions did he deign to answer, and that one had nothing to do with the mysterious adventure in which we were involved. How, I asked him, had his brother Mycroft managed to keep secret his immortality, when he had come in contact every day for so many decades with a succession of government officials?

"Ah, Watson," he explained between taking in and expelling great mouthfuls of smoke, "there are two reasons. First, there is the very fact of the succession of ministers. A man might take over an office, say as part of a new government, see Mycroft there—another minor civil servant, remarkable only for his girth—and leave the office a few years later, leaving Mycroft behind him, still apparently a minor civil servant. The fact that

Mycroft had not been observed to age in that period would not be noteworthy, first because many a man does not age visibly in so relatively short a time, and second because your senior minister is given to ignoring the great crowd of faceless civil servants who in fact do all the work of the ministries and whose careers of quiet diligence are all that keeps so vast a structure as modern government functioning. Mycroft, especially, because of his sedentary habits, soon takes on the appearance, to any casual observer, of being but an extension of his desk."

I listened with great interest; as far as I could remember, this was perhaps the first time I had heard my old friend speak in praise of government officials of any level. He had forgotten his pipe during the latter part of the above speech, and it had consequently come perilously close to going out; this was always a hazard with Holmes' smoking, for he had the bad habit of keeping his pipe going hot and furious, puffing on it regularly and too frequently, rather than smoking at the leisurely, gentle pace that is one of the marks of the truly civilized man. Now he puffed madly at it until it was once again producing its hot smoke copiously, and only then did he resume his explanation.

"The second reason to which I referred is Mycroft's importance. I told you long ago that Mycroft, more than any other civil servant, *is* the British government. Now, not all senior ministers are oblivious to his importance. However, those who realize that they are supernumerary and that Mycroft runs their ministries for them, understandably prefer to keep this fact to themselves; they certainly will not draw the attention of others to Mycroft, for example by referring to his curious seeming agelessness, for that might also draw attention to his vital importance and, as a consequence, to the ministers' irrelevance."

After this burst of speech, he lapsed into silence, staring thoughtfully at the back of the seat before him, although now his absorption appeared to be of a less pleasant nature than it had before. His worried expression and his even more resolute puffing seemed to indicate that this matter upon which we were engaged, whatever its identity, was of a most distressing nature.

I, meanwhile, had much to occupy my own thoughts.

Sherlock Holmes, during the many years we both lived in

London, had been a difficult companion—difficult both in his odd habits and his difficult manner. Retirement in Sussex, however, had changed him vastly; he had become a pleasant man, even chatty at times, as if our rural retreat had brought out in him the spirit of his country squire ancestors. The change had delighted me. In early days, our friendship had been more than a little one-sided. Indeed, the relationship was more on the order of that between knight and squire than that between friends who are social equals. But during our decades of peaceful seclusion, I had managed at last to break through Holmes' wall of reserve, to perceive some of his deeper feelings and to learn much of his personal history, to see the remarkable depths of the unique soul that hid behind his cool exterior—in short, to become at last and in fact his friend. To my great distress, I had been obliged to watch helplessly while his active involvement once again with crime, in the matter of the murder of Mrs. Chalmers, had caused Sherlock Holmes to revert to his older self—brusque, withdrawn, and sarcastic. That this crime seemed to him to embody some terrible though yet unnamed evil beyond the fact of the murder itself, was obvious, and I was ready to admit that this unspecified sinister danger must be playing a part in his emotional relapse. Nonetheless, the whole process saddened and even disheartened me.

There was another matter which occupied my thoughts during that trip. There were old memories for me in America, many of them painful; going back to the United States after the lapse of so many decades was bringing those memories suddenly to life. During those years when I was recording Sherlock Holmes' adventures for publication, I had often considered concocting a romance based upon my own youthful experiences in San Francisco and my great affair of the heart in that lovely city; maturer consideration had soon convinced me of the unwisdom of that idea.

"Calm yourself, Watson," Holmes broke into my reverie, "we shall certainly not have to go so far as California." Then he relapsed again into his abstracted silence. Was it my imagination, or did his puffs of smoke take on an air of smug self-satisfaction? He had repeated his old trick of divining the pattern of my thoughts from a number of small clues, but this time I refused to give him the further satisfaction of expressing surprise or admiration at his feat. I thought it noteworthy that he penetrated only to a knowledge of my thoughts about San Francisco and not to my thoughts concerning him and the change of nature he had recently exhibited.

Holmes finished his pipe just as the aeroplane dropped below the speed of sound to begin its approach to New York. The cabin, by this time, was so filled with the smoke from Holmes' pipe that I could scarcely see the glowing red meter at the front of the cabin that showed the craft's speed in multiples of the speed of sound. The other passengers were sneezing and coughing and casting upon us such looks as made my blood run cold. I am convinced that it was not coincidence that British Airways enacted its rule against smoking in its aircraft only days later.

5

Time and New York

NEW YORK! My heart thrilled as our great craft slipped in over the harbor. It had been far too long since I had visited this second greatest of the world's cities. From the window by my seat, I could see the vast array of neon advertising signs flashing their commercial messages out over the water in a vain attempt to ensnare the passengers on the now-vanished ocean liners. I had looked forward to seeing again that marvellously ludicrous statue, for so long a world-famous symbol of the United States. However, due to my long isolation in Sussex, I was quite unaware of the explosion of a ship carrying liquefied natural gas that had destroyed the Statue of Liberty only the year before.

Our trip through the city from airport to hotel in a taxicab was a sheer delight to me, although I could well imagine that it would take mere days for the crush of people and vehicles to unnerve and oppress even so inveterate a lover of the urban life as I. Still, it was late spring, often a pleasant and hopeful time in London and New York alike. In the country, spring can be seen as part of the great annual cycle, slow, majestic, inevitable; but in the city it comes all at once, rushing down the streets and alleys and bringing with it greenness and a relief from the dreary dullness of winter.

"You will observe the changes in this city, Watson," Holmes remarked pragmatically. "One could surely write a book, or perhaps a whole series of volumes, on the intricate relationship between the changing face of a city over the years and the changing nature of the crimes planned and committed within it."

"No doubt," I replied shortly. I could not resist adding, "I suppose you are planning to produce such a series of volumes?"

He sighed. "I foresee that I shan't have the time. A monograph, perhaps; no more than that."

Among the changes that time had wrought was the disappearance of the Hotel Taylor, that wonderful refuge and home away from Home for travel-weary Englishmen. I discovered, however, that Holmes had found a fair substitute and had reserved a room for us; this he must have accomplished during our last day in London, although when he had found time to do so, I could not imagine.

It had been early morning when we left London. By the time we reached our hotel and settled in, it was suppertime. We ate well at an excellent nearby restaurant and then retired to our room. I had picked up some cigars on the way back to the hotel and had ordered brandy sent up; the availability of this service reconciled me all the more to the absence of the Hotel Taylor and convinced me that our present hotel was a more than adequate haven for Englishmen. I settled happily into a large, overstuffed armchair, a cigar in my mouth and a glass of brandy near my left hand. In my right hand, I held that novel of stirring adventure in mediaeval Europe which I had been reading in Sussex when this adventure started. As a consequence of our rushing about—first across southern England and then across the North Atlantic—I had been able to make no more progress with it, and I was most eager to see how the company of stalwart mercenary bowmen who were the heroes of the tale managed to escape from the fearful predicament in which the news of the Prime Minister's murder had left them. But if I thought I was to be allowed to thus refresh myself after our hurried voyage, or that Sherlock Holmes planned to relax in some manner himself, I was much mistaken.

Before I could even discover *whether* the mediaeval bowmen escaped from their sinister enemy, Holmes had snatched the book from my hand. "Watson," he said in a tone of disgust as he examined the cover, "I told you that man wrote foolish nonsense. We have so little time. Do not waste it. Now, this," he produced a slim book and handed it to me, "this might be more rewarding. You have probably read it before. Reread it."

I took it from him with ill grace. It was *The Time Machine*, by H. G. Wells; I had indeed read it, years earlier, and I had no desire to read it again just then, engrossed as I was in the other novel. "Really, Holmes," I grumbled, "this is simply too much. Surely a man of my years deserves some relaxation after these last trying days."

"Watson," he said in great earnest, "we have many more trying days ahead of us if my fears are correct, and far too little relaxation. Now I must leave you for some hours. Reread that book, and while you are doing so, remember this name: Moriarty." He left the room, moving with that feline quietness and grace of which he, more than any other man, was capable.

Moriarty! That, more than any other word he might have spoken, filled me with fear and trepidation. I was now prepared to follow Sherlock Holmes' instructions once again without protest even when, as in the case of the Wells romance I held, the instructions seemed pointless and frivolous.

What could Holmes have meant by using that evil name? When Moriarty died in the Reichenbach Falls, that had marked the beginning of the end of the criminal organization he had built. Sherlock Holmes had once referred to the professor as "the Napoleon of crime"; and like Napoleon's, Moriarty's empire had not survived his reign. Or was there another Moriarty about, perhaps a relative of our erstwhile enemy, who wished to play Louis Napoleon to the dead professor's Bonaparte? Feeling far less comfortable and relaxed than before, I put my cigar out and started reading the Wells novel.

"The Time Traveller (for so it will be convenient to speak of him) . . ." Once again the strange story cast its spell over me. Along with the narrator, I listened as the Time Traveller expounded his advanced theories to his skeptical friends; with them, I watched the demonstration using the small, working model of the Time Machine; and I was there with the rest of them in the house at Richmond, later, when the Time Traveller returned from his trip to the distant future to tell his fantastic story. I was surprised and amused to notice from the few descriptive details supplied by Wells how great was the physical resemblance between the Time Traveller and Sherlock Holmes. I vaguely recalled that Wells had known Holmes, even visiting him once in Sussex to seek his help on some matter; could the brilliant novelist have used the master detective as the model for his fictive traveller in time?

It was an interesting speculation and, along with the brandy and the novel, it beguiled my time for the next hour or two. Finally, the combined influence of jet lag, brandy, and the supremely comfortable armchair overcame the stimulus of speculation and Wells' imagination, and I fell asleep, only to be plagued by a horrible nightmare in which strange apelike, or perhaps spiderlike, creatures with pale flesh and hair and vaguely humanlike faces chased me through endless horizontal and vertical corridors.

I was awakened by my shoulder being shaken roughly. It was Sherlock Holmes. I rubbed the sleep from my eyes and drew my watch from my pocket; it was 2 AM. "Aah, excellent," he said briskly. "You're awake at last." His cheeks were glowing with rare color and his eyes were bright: it had never ceased to amaze me how Holmes' nocturnal adventures seemed to refresh and revitalize him better than would a full night's sleep. "Did you finish the book, Watson?"

"I'm not sure," I said honestly. "I fell asleep while reading it."

Holmes laughed in delight. "Poor H. G. would be mortified!" He flung himself down in a chair and began to fill his pipe. "But never mind that. It's only the gist of the story that matters in the present circumstances."

"That's all very well, Holmes, but unless you have something of importance to say to me, I'm going to bed." I stood up, stretched, and headed sleepily for my bed.

Holmes emitted a great puff of smoke. "If you can keep your eyes open, Doctor, I'll tell you just what we're doing in America."

Of course, he had my full attention with that, and I sat down again and listened without demur.

With his pipe going well, he plunged into his explanation. "You probably remember," he said, "that I was acquainted with H. G. in his youth, long before he became a well-known writer. The acquaintance was purely social, and the meetings were infrequent.

"However, in the autumn of 1927, when you had already joined me on the farm, Wells paid me a visit in Sussex. I recall that you remarked upon his appearance at the time: your professional attention was drawn to his distraught manner and exhausted appearance; you diagnosed overwork and recommended a vacation. As he wished to speak to me in private, you retired from the room and left us alone."

I indicated that I remembered the incident, but only vaguely.

"It developed from what he told me after you had left the room that his sufferings were more mental than physical, although it was in fact the case that his health was not good, for he was suffering from one of the relapses which had plagued him throughout his life. His wife had died of cancer only shortly before, and his grief, combined with the debilitating effect upon the whole family of her protracted and painful final illness, certainly was the major cause of his apparent fatigue and depression. But there was more.

"Wells' romance, *The Time Machine*, which I gave to you earlier, had been published thirty-two years before his visit to me in Sussex. He now revealed that that intriguing romance was not entirely an invention! He had changed the names of the actors and embellished the Time Traveller's report from the future so as to make it more readable for the general public, and he had invented the ending in which the Time Traveller climbs upon his machine and disappears just as the narrator is entering the room; beyond that, however, he insisted he had changed nothing and had simply recorded a true story."

"That's preposterous," I interrupted. "Surely he was joking. Or perhaps his recent grief had unbalanced him."

"I must confess," Sherlock Holmes replied, "that my own initial reaction was identical. He was able, however, to convince me of his perfect sanity and lucidity and to offer sufficient proof of his veracity.

"He went on to tell me," Holmes continued, "that in reality his friend the Time Traveller, rather than vanishing aboard his machine, had been murdered and his machine stolen."

"That is certainly sad, Holmes. But I cannot see why a tragedy of more than a century ago should send us flying across the Atlantic."

"Oh, but there is much more," he said, wagging his long index finger at me. "Have I not told you in the past, Watson, to gather all the pertinent facts before leaping to conclusions? H. G. had managed for thirty-five years to keep from the public the true story of the fate of the Time Traveller and his machine. His wife's death and the recurrence of his own old illness had suddenly brought him face to face with the fact of his own mortality, and he had decided it was past time to inform some trustworthy friend that the device was in the hands of a murderer."

I felt the skin at the back of my neck prickling. "And this murderer was . . . ?" I whispered.

"Excellent, Watson!" Sherlock Holmes cried. "You have penetrated almost to the core of the matter. By the way, what time is it?"

I drew my watch from my pocket. "Past three o'clock," I told him, feeling my weariness returning suddenly.

Holmes uttered an exclamation of annoyance. "There is no such thing as punctuality left in the world, I fear." He rose and paced over to his coat, which he had thrown across his bed when he had returned earlier. "As you may remember," he said, speaking hurriedly, "I was always careful, in the old days, to maintain contacts in the criminal world on both sides of the Atlantic and on both sides of the Channel. Unfortunately, during the last fifty or so years I have allowed those contacts to lapse. Most of the men I knew then are of course either dead or retired; however, I spent some hours earlier tonight reestablishing contacts with those few who are still alive and active in their profession and, through them, with the successors of the others." He smiled faintly. "I told them I was Sherlock Holmes' grandson Henry, trying to follow in the old man's footsteps. These are the smaller criminals, their crimes too minor to attract Sherlock Holmes' attention in a dangerous way, and they used to help him so that he would keep the greater criminals from gobbling them up. They have decided to help his grandson for the same reason."

He drew from his coat pocket a revolver; after checking it, he slipped it into the pocket of the smoking jacket he was now wearing. "The man we are chasing is in America; I had been almost sure of that and brought us both here on the strength of that conviction; tonight, my new associates have confirmed it. They have promised to send a messenger with word of the man's location, if they could determine it, or else with the news that they could not. He was to have been here at three AM." At that moment, there came a soft knock at the door.

"Aha! This must be he," Holmes said loudly. Then he strode quickly over to me and turned off the lamp by which I had been reading earlier and which was the only light in the room. "But just in case it isn't . . ." he whispered. He grasped my arm and pulled me over to the wall beside the door, next to the handle, and he drew the revolver from his pocket again. Carefully he reached over and, without making a sound, unlocked the door. Again there was a knock. "Come in," Sherlock Holmes called out.

The door was flung open. There was an explosion of staccato noise and flashes of light, and I instinctively closed my eyes. Through it all, I heard Holmes' revolver fire twice, calmly, deliberately, and then all was still. All the way down the hallway, I could hear the sound of doors being hastily locked as the largely foreign clientele emphatically dissociated themselves from the violent doings of the natives.

The light coming through the open door showed a body sprawled halfway into the room, a machine gun lying on the floor near the dead man's convulsively clenched fist. "I must resume marksmanship practice at the earliest opportunity," Holmes remarked conversationally. "I had not intended to kill him."

I looked around at the holes riddling the furniture and walls. "Was this your messenger?" I asked in a shaking voice.

"No doubt my messenger is dead. No, this is proof that our quarry, while he may not yet realize who we are, is aware that we are after him and knows where we may be found. Let us pack our belonging quickly and leave. You have your revolver? Good. Keep it with you."

I needed no urging to hurry. Ten minutes later, we were paying our bill at the front desk, making no mention of the destroyed room and the body upstairs. We were able to find a taxicab in front of the hotel and once again we were off. I was surprised to find that my heart was racing with excitement and I was filled with an emotion I had not felt for two normal generations: the thrill of the chase.

6

Two Headquarters

THE ADDRESS Holmes had given the driver turned out to be that of an abandoned warehouse near the harbor. It was a gloomy, deserted area of dingy buildings and dark streets. The driver looked about and muttered, "Cheez!" He turned around and asked, "Hey, Mister, you sure you wanna get out here?"

"Quite," said Holmes.

We paid, got out with our suitcases, and watched the taxicab leave. Privately I thought the driver's trepidation justified and wished we had remained in the vehicle. "Come along, Watson," Holmes said briskly, and he set off for the rear of the warehouse. There we entered the building through a concealed door and, after many a twist and turn along dusty and cobwebbed passageways, during which I made the most strenuous efforts to keep close to the light of my companion's electric torch, we found ourselves suddenly in a well-lighted room, dust-free and furnished like the parlor of a fashionable home. This, indeed, was what it was, as I understood a short time later. Holmes leaned toward me and murmured, "Listen carefully to everything, but do not speak unless it becomes absolutely necessary."

We had to wait for only a few minutes, and then two grim-faced young men appeared, each holding a pistol aimed at us, and motioned us through the doorway by which they had entered. This led into a large room, well furnished and tastefully decorated, in the centre of which was placed a handsome desk of some dark wood. The man behind the desk, short, stocky, black-haired, balding, and somewhat garishly dressed for my taste, rose hastily and gestured to our two armed escorts that they should retire from the room. They did so, and he walked around the desk and approached Holmes with his right hand outstretched.

[31]

"Mr. Holmes," he exclaimed as they shook hands, "why did you come here? I'm delighted to see you, of course," he added quickly, "but I thought my messenger would give you all the information you needed." Try as he might to be cordial, his urgent desire to see us gone was evident.

"Your messenger never reached me, Mr. Silvestre," Holmes replied. The name was one which even I recognized as belonging to one of America's most notorious criminal bosses. Holmes related what had happened in our hotel room. "All too obviously, Moriarty's men intercepted him and sent their own . . . message . . . in the place of yours."

Our host uttered a string of oaths, most in English but interspersed with words in a Romance tongue. "Has he penetrated my own organization, that he knows my plans?" he wondered aloud. He shuddered. "This is frightening!"

"All the more pressing, then, that you help me find him," Holmes urged.

Silvestre hesitated for a moment, then arrived at a decision. "He is too powerful. I can't take any more risks. I'll do this much, however: I'll tell you where Moriarty's headquarters are, I'll let you have a car, and I'll give you the name of a contact. But after that, I will not be involved."

Holmes smiled sardonically and said nothing. Subdued before this open contempt, our host drew from a drawer in his desk a road map of the State of New York. He spread it before us and pointed to a small town in the northern area of the state, near the place where the great St. Lawrence River empties into Lake Ontario. "Moriarty has a temporary headquarters here," he explained. "How long he will be there, I don't know. And I also don't know how many men he has there, or weapons—anything like that. This is the best way to get there." He traced a route on the map; then he mentioned a name and address. "That," he explained, "is your contact up there. Now, goodbye." Suddenly he glared at Holmes with a fierce hatred born of his sense of inferiority to the calm, even supercilious, detective. "Don't ever come here again!" he hissed.

"You promised me a car," Holmes said mildly. He held his eyes on the other man's face until the latter lowered his gaze.

Silvestre pressed a button on his desk and a door opened, revealing the two young men who had earlier conducted us there. "Show them out," he ordered in a hoarse voice. "Let them have the Jag."

I have no idea where or when Sherlock Holmes had learned to drive an automobile, but the operation of the vehicle we had been given certainly seemed to present no mysteries to him; his driving was secure, confident, and only slightly faster than I would have preferred. The magnificent car purred northward along the dark highway like one of the great cats whose name it bore. As we had a trip of some duration ahead of us, Holmes chose to finish the explanation which had earlier been interrupted at the hotel by gunfire. He took up the narrative at the point where he had stopped before as if the intervening events had never happened.

"Shortly before his murder, however, the Time Traveller had told Wells of a most curious visitor he had recently had. This was a tall, thin man of late middle age who had in some manner learned something of the Time Traveller's experiments. He professed a great interest in the Time Traveller's work and in his machine, which he was particularly insistent upon examining, and he displayed an enormous breadth of scientific knowledge. It was, however, a physical peculiarity, a habit, of this visitor's that struck the Time Traveller most forcibly, and that was the way his visitor had of leaning forward slightly and continually moving his head from side to side—much, the Time Traveller remarked to Wells, like a lizard."

"Good heavens!" I muttered.

"Indeed," Holmes nodded. "As I am sure you have realized, that visitor was Professor Moriarty. I have not a doubt that it was his agents who murdered Wells' friend and stole that amazing machine of his, so that it might later be used in some evil work of the professor's."

It was a curious sensation to watch the cars on the other side of the highway, now visible in the lightening dawn, as these old ghosts of nineteenth-century London crime suddenly emerged from my memory and the past. "Thank heaven, at least, that we don't have that particular evil to worry about," I remarked.

"Whatever evil plans the Time Machine might have figured in surely died with Professor Moriarty in the Reichenbach Falls in 1891."

There was silence for a few minutes, before Holmes responded. "Watson," he said quietly, "we cannot be sure Moriarty died in the Reichenbach Falls."

"What! How can that be?"

"You will recall that when I returned to life so miraculously in 1894 after seemingly dying with Moriarty at the Reichenbach Falls, I told you that Moriarty had tottered on the edge of the cliff for a few seconds and then fell over it, and that I had then leaned over the cliff and had seen him fall for a long way, strike a rock, bounce off it, and finally splash into the water below the falls. Note, however, that for a moment after he toppled off the cliff, he was out of my sight. Suppose that during that moment a mannequin, dressed in clothing like Moriarty's, were substituted for him and Moriarty himself was drawn to safety. I could thus have easily been misled."

"Impossible, Holmes," I protested. "How could such a thing have been accomplished?"

"To a man in possession of a device that enabled him to travel in time, I fear that such a feat would present few difficulties. He might, for instance, travel back to the remote past, before there were any but the most primitive of human settlements in the vicinity of what we today call the Reichenbach Falls, and install in the cliff face, above the water, a retractable net of some sort, into which he could have fallen during his fight with me. By the time I was able to reach the edge and look over, his followers could have drawn him in and flung out the dummy. Any clumsiness or inefficiency in the execution of this scheme could have been compensated for at leisure by the use of the Time Machine. Convinced that he was dead, I would have ceased to search after him."

"But why should he bother with this subterfuge? Surely he could merely leap forward in time to a date such as the present one, when he could safely assume you were long dead of old age."

He nodded. "No doubt that was precisely his intention. I as-

[34]

sume that the Time Machine was damaged in the struggle when Moriarty's men took it from its proper owner, and the result was that the device was able to travel into the past and then return but was not able to move forward in time from its present. That being so, Professor Moriarty would have needed time to repair the machine, and he would not have wanted me bothering him during that time. Convincing me that he was dead would have ensured him such a respite. It is true that the evidence I had accumulated was used by the police, after the incident at the Reichenbach Falls, to break up Moriarty's organization and convict most of its principal members, but that must surely not have occasioned the professor himself any loss of sleep, first because there is truly no honor among thieves, as you and I have learned so well during our long careers, and second because he did not need his former associates to effect repairs to the Time Machine. I might also point out that, once he journeyed into the future, not intending to resume his operations in nineteenth-century London, he would have no use at all for the organisation he was leaving behind. Remember that the Time Machine, as described by Wells in his novel, had room for only one passenger."

"Surely you are not saying that Moriarty was successful in his work on the machine, and that he then came forward to our own time!" A chill ran through me at the thought that the terrible professor, whom I had believed dead so long ago, had returned to the world as if from the grave.

Holmes sighed. "I'm afraid that I *am* saying so, Watson. I fear that Moriarty once again stalks the land, even more dangerous than he was a century ago, for now he has in his possession a device that provides him with a perfect means of escape, should we seem to be drawing too close in our pursuit of him, and also because he is, I believe, thoroughly deranged.

"One hundred years ago, he attempted the assassination of the Prime Minister of Great Britain, hoping that the confusion attendant upon the shock of that murder would cast the economies of the Western world into disarray, thus presenting an opportunity to him and his new allies on the Continent and in North America to greatly increase their power. Had it not been for our intervention, he would have succeeded. It was immediately clear to me when Mrs. Chalmers was assassinated that the murderer was Professor Moriarty, hoping to put into effect in this century that plan which failed in the last. He could not have realised in time that the immense political and economic changes during the decades over which he had jumped had deprived Britain of her once preeminent position in the world, so that the murder he has committed has accomplished nothing from his point of view."

"But how did he manage the deed?" I asked in bewilderment.

He shrugged. "Nothing simpler. What served him at the Reichenbach Falls could have served him just as well in Downing Street. He could have travelled back to very ancient Britain, moved his machine to the point that would later become the Prime Minister's office, and then come forward to our time, murdered Mrs. Chalmers, and escaped once more into the past. Again, he moved his machine to what would become a safe place and returned to our present. It is only the movement of the machine in space that presents a remaining difficulty: Did he somehow transport some of his supporters in time, or did he, with the strength of a madman, manage the moving of the machine by himself? In any case, he is here now, in our own time."

"Why, then, is he in America?" I asked. "Good heavens," I gasped as the answer suddenly struck me. "Now the fiend plans to murder the American President!"

"Precisely. It must not have taken Moriarty long to realise his mistake and to discover which world leader it is whose murder would indeed cause the chaos Moriarty desires. One life, two lives—little enough the number of victims means to that man whom you so properly termed a fiend. You know well the history of my ancient feud with Moriarty; that and the danger he represents to all of mankind demand that I do all in my power to stop him."

I watched the passing landscape as I digested this new remarkable information. For the first time I paid attention to the highway markers as they flashed by. "Holmes," I observed, "this is not the route Silvestre recommended."

"Indeed it is not," he smiled. "The automobile, as I may have had occasion to remark to you before, like most of Man's other inventions, can be a powerful tool of either Good or Evil—or, of course, of neither." Of this suggestive hint, I could make nothing, and silence reigned for the rest of the trip.

It was not long afterwards that billboards advertising a variety of services and products alerted us to the nearness of our destination, while causing me to reflect once again upon the many changes America had undergone since the far-off days of my youthful sojourn there. Once we had entered the town, whose roads were now full of sleepy drivers on their way to work, we stopped to buy petrol and obtain directions to the address of our contact. Holmes also obtained a road map of the town, and once back in the car he perused this for a few minutes before starting off. "Excellent," he murmured. He pointed at a place on the map. "Here," he said, "is where our contact lives. Note that there is a park across the street from him. We will drive to the park first, avoiding that street."

"I don't understand, Holmes. If he is our contact, why do we not contact him?"

"For the same reason we did not take the route recommended by Silvestre."

The park was a small one but pleasant and, at that early hour, almost empty of other visitors. There was a small zoo in the park, and Holmes left me there while he went off on a mysterious errand. "Stay here and watch the monkeys, Watson," he said. "They are remarkably instructive beasts."

Now, monkeys may perhaps be instructive, but I have always found watching them to be most boring, and before many minutes had passed, I was considering leaving the vicinity of the cage to try to find Holmes. Before I could do so, however, he returned, saying, "Good, you are still here. I feared I might find that you had foolishly left to go in search of me. I have been using one of the public telephones to call up our man and arrange a meeting here in the zoo in a half hour. Now come along." He set off quickly down the winding, tree-lined paths of the park, stopping in a grove which, while concealing us from view, enabled us to watch the houses on the other side of the street from the park.

"Now, Holmes," I demanded, "tell me *why* we did not go to the house as we were supposed to do."

"Because I have the strongest suspicions that Silvestre has thrown in his lot with Professor Moriarty, at least to the extent of betraying us to him. That, I believe, was why he recommended a particular route to us, so that Moriarty's men might intercept us along the way, and that was why I took a different route. Moriarty will surely have allowed for the failure of that plan by stationing men in the house we are expected to visit. Now let us watch for the response to my telephone call."

After perhaps five minutes had passed, a group of a half dozen men suddenly emerged from one of the houses across the street. They entered the park, walking hurriedly and conversing in low whispers, and continued down the path in the direction of the zoo. "You see?" Holmes murmured with a cynical smile. "Our welcoming committee. They will wait for us in front of the monkey house—an appropriate place—for another twenty to thirty minutes, which should give us all the time we need." We waited until the men were all well out of sight; then Holmes motioned me to follow him, and he set off through the park in yet another direction.

He led at a very rapid pace, crossing streets and leading me down an alley behind some houses. I was breathing heavily by the time we stopped, some ten minutes later, but Holmes seemed invigorated, his eyes glowing and a spot of color on each cheek. He drew his revolver from his pocket and gestured for me to produce my own. He pointed at the house we were nearest to. "That is the rear of the house from which those men exited. *Now* we will pay our contact a visit."

I was afraid that some neighbours might see us advancing upon the house with revolvers in our hands—it was, after all, broad daylight—and notify the police. In the event, this did not happen, and we gained the rear entrance apparently undetected.

The house seemed to be deserted. As quietly as possible, we moved from room to room trying to find some useful information or someone we could question. Holmes kept glancing at his watch, obviously worried that the group of men would return and discover us. We had just finished with the rooms in the upper storey and were descending the staircase again for one last quick search of the ground floor before giving up. Suddenly

Holmes yelled, "Down!" As much from surprise at his shout as anything else, I stumbled and fell down the stairs. I felt a rush of air on the back of my neck as something whipped by me; had I not fallen, the bullet would have shattered my skull. Another shot, this one from behind me, and the danger was past. I looked up from my position on the floor at the foot of the stairs to see Holmes pass by me and kneel down by a figure which lay half in the doorway of a nearby room.

"Watson!" Holmes snapped. "Come here!" He turned to the man on the floor. "Moriarty! Where is Moriarty?"

Holmes' bullet had caught him in the middle of his chest and he was bleeding copiously; he stared up at Holmes dully with eyes from which the light of intelligence was already fading. Holmes put his mouth near the man's ear and said loudly and distinctly, "My friend is a doctor. He will save your life if you tell me where Moriarty is."

The dying man struggled to speak, coughing up blood, the effort and motion making the blood flow all the faster from his chest. Finally he managed to mutter, "Detroit. Grosse Pointe."

Holmes stood up. His face was suddenly worn and old. "The chase continues. Come, Watson."

"But what about this man? I must try to help him!"

Holmes made a gesture of dismissal. "It is too late. He is beyond your help, and we have no time to spare. Come along."

7

Grosse Pointe and Points West

IT WAS NOT until we were once again upon the highway, driving steadily toward the city the dying man had named as Moriarty's location, that I asked Holmes how he intended to find his quarry once we reached Grosse Pointe.

"I have not yet fixed upon the best method," he admitted. "Perhaps it would be best to let him find us."

I pondered this unsettling idea for a while in silence. Then Holmes spoke again. "Indeed, Watson," he sighed, "the whole tenor of this adventure is not what I had anticipated. I have always been able to accept the necessity of engaging in rough-and-tumble and of travelling when one is in pursuit of criminals, but in this case, those elements are the dominant, almost the only, ones to the near exclusion of intellectual method, of deduction. What opportunities have been available for the application of my old deductive methods have not been entirely satisfactory to me. In the old days, as you well know, I used to depend heavily upon my extensive knowledge of cigarette tobaccos, bicycle tyre treads, and so forth. A man smoking a tobacco supplied only by a certain tobacconist, or riding a bicycle whose tyres he must have purchased at a certain shop, or perhaps carrying upon his shoes a type of mud found only in a certain section of a certain city—such a man may be easy to track down. Now, however, such products are mass-produced and shipped to markets throughout the world. Furthermore, the items are mixed without regard to individualized craftmanship; for example, a man's cigarette may contain tobaccos from many locations, mechanically blended, and identical cigarettes may have been sold to perhaps a few million other men in the same week. Modern building construction techniques have made the identification of soils, to a degree sufficiently precise to be of use in detection, virtually impossible. Finally, television and the cinema, the mobility of populations, the collapse of the class structure, and the sad inadequacy of what passes for education now, have combined to level accents and usages into a uniformity which badly hampers the detective."

"In short," I concluded for him in what I intended as a sarcastic tone of voice, "the world is going to the dogs and we will never see the lamps lit in Europe again."

Holmes laughed. "Why, not at all; you quite misunderstand me. No, Watson, the most salutary effect of immortality is that it enables one to view the drab sameness of the present as merely a momentary aberration in the history of mankind. With all of time left in which to explore the works of Man, the mighty wonders he will perform in the distant future, we cannot, we *must* not, lose hope because of the meanness we see about us now. A thousand years from now, Watson, you and I will still be here; can we really believe that this," he waved his hand toward the streets of the small, anonymous factory town through which we were passing, grey buildings, dreary little houses, squalid, identical streets, dying trees, "that this will still be here then?"

"Then you are hopeful for the future."

He snorted. "Of course I am; otherwise, why wish to live forever? Rather, let me say that I will be hopeful after we have defeated Moriarty. If we fail in that, eternity may not be worth having."

"Holmes," I asked cautiously, "you are quite sure, are you not, that the man we're pursuing is indeed the same man you battled a hundred years ago in England?"

Holmes cast upon me a gaze so penetrating that I squirmed under it, fearing that he could divine the doubts I had been entertaining as to his sanity. "I am utterly convinced of it," he said shortly, returning his gaze to the road.

"In that case," I pursued doggedly, "how can we be sure that Moriarty is indeed planning to murder President Wolff? Perhaps he is working on some other plan entirely, some more mundane or pedestrian criminal undertaking. Perhaps—"

"You are not in possession of all the facts, Watson," he inter-

[41]

rupted. "Two days ago, an attempt was made upon the life of President Wolff. One of the White House maintenance staff was apparently subverted and attempted to shoot the President. He failed and committed suicide before he could be captured. In my view, the incident reeks of Moriarty. The American government authorities have tried to keep the matter silent for reasons known only to them, but the matter is known throughout the underworld of the East Coast. I can assure you, my friend, that we are on the right track."

I still had serious doubts concerning the reliability of his information and the accuracy of his conclusions; even more troubling, I still wondered whether my old friend was as sane as in earlier days. Was it possible, I wondered, that Holmes' immortality elixir preserved the body but not the mind, and he was now displaying the mental effects of extreme age? However, I kept these thoughts to myself. I would continue to cooperate with him—it was, after all, certainly the case that we were in pursuit of a dangerous criminal who had already attempted to murder us—and let events prove or disprove Holmes' contentions.

Once we had arrived in Grosse Pointe, we checked into a motel and waited. I should rather say that I waited, for Sherlock Holmes disappeared a few times during the next two days on his customary mysterious errands.

Late in the afternoon of the second day, I was sitting alone in our motel room, reading that historical novel I had been trying for so long to complete, and making a manful attempt to forget where I was and pretend I was still in Sussex, when Holmes burst precipitously into the room and switched on the television set.

"Holmes!" I exclaimed, trying to hide my historical novel, for I knew how strongly he disapproved of that branch of fiction. "It is not for nothing that Americans term that device 'the idiot box.' Please turn it off."

In the meantime, the television had been shouting at us. "Hush, Watson," he said. "The evening news. Watch it with me."

I considered this request to border on the incomprehensible, but I complied, as I always had with even the most unreasonable of Holmes' orders. After the newscasters had run through the day's depressing developments throughout the world, the nation, the state, and, of course, Detroit, they turned to more light-hearted matters.

"Our city was honored today," said the young man on the screen, displaying a great array of white teeth in a charming smile intended to signal the humorous nature of this news item, "by a visitor from England who claims to be descended from the famous detective, Sherlock Holmes. He certainly looks a lot like drawings of Sherlock Holmes, as you can see in this interview, which we taped earlier today in our studios." Then, while I goggled in amazement, the aforementioned young man disappeared from the screen, to be replaced by a film of an interview with Sherlock Holmes. Holmes replied with utmost seriousness to the interviewer's obviously facetious questions; he also made a point of mentioning our motel by name at least twice. After the short film segment was over, the young newsman returned with a humorous remark or two, concluding, "So there you are, folks. If you want to talk to a real, live, modern version of Sherlock Holmes, just visit the Ottoworld Motel in Grosse Pointe and ask for him by name. And now we have Harry Brown with the weather. What's it look like out there, Harry?"

"Blimey, mate, a lot better than it does in Baker Street, *I* can tell you, old chap, by Jove!" quoth Harry, with a twinkle in his eye. Chuckles from offscreen greeted his sally.

"Holmes," I cried in exasperation, "what *now*?" I turned about to discover that he was engaged in examining both our revolvers' magazines. He handed mine to me, saying, "We must leave quickly. I have no idea how much time we have."

I pulled on my jacket, for an evening chill was descending, and followed him outside. He led me to a battered, nondescript automobile parked not far from the door to our room. When Holmes put his hand to the handle of the car's door, I looked over the parking lot in a vain search for the magnificent Jaguar in which we had arrived. I asked Holmes what had become of it. "Too conspicuous," he replied. "It's in a used car lot in Detroit." We entered the vehicle, Holmes seating himself behind the steering wheel and inserting a key in the ignition. It was growing dark rapidly, but even so he evidenced some concern at the possibility of our being seen. He reached over to the back seat and brought forth two hats, both of brown leather and both possessed of wide and somewhat floppy brims. One of them he placed upon his own head; the other, he handed to me.

"Am I to *wear* this object?" I said plaintively. "I would look like an art student from Rome!"

" 'An art student from Rome'!" Holmes repeated with a laugh. "Watson, you betray your century. Now, be silent and watch for a visitor."

There was quite a coming and going at the motel at that time of night. This elicited a soft curse from my companion, for it seriously complicated our task. In time, though, a car arrived whose driver and passenger were not casual visitors.

Three men got out, and beside me Holmes drew his breath in sharply. They looked around quickly, then approached the door to our motel room, one directly from the front and the other two from the sides. As they drew near to the door, they all drew guns and rushed into the room. A few moments later, the three of them came out again more slowly than they had entered, muttering to each other, and even in the gathering dark I could see that their faces were darkened with anger. I glanced at Holmes; his lips were drawn back in a feral grin, and he murmured, "Now is the hunter become the hunted."

We watched as the three men re-entered their car and drove off. He started our own car and we followed them. Only then did I realise that this had been his design all along. "By Jove, Holmes!" I exclaimed, quite unaware that I sounded like Harry Brown's, the weatherman's, imitation of an Englishman. "You plan to follow them to Moriarty's hideout. How utterly ingenious!"

Holmes glanced at me in surprise. "Really, Watson," he said scornfully. "Have you never watched any American gangster films? I have borrowed an extremely common plot element."

Common the plot element might be, but in our case when we had followed our unwitting guides to their destination, the man who was our true quarry had fled. This must have surprised the men we had followed as much as it did us.

They had led us to a small men's clothing shop in a quiet neighbourhood of shops and flats. When they stopped in front of the shop, we drove by without slowing down, but instead turned a corner and stopped on another street. Holmes told me hastily to wait at the corner with my pistol in my hand and my eyes on the door through which the men had entered the shop, while he circled the block and approached the shop from the other direction. Fortunately, the street was dark and no police were about; I peered around the corner at the silent shop front, wondering if this were appropriate behaviour for a retired doctor well into his second century.

At last I saw Holmes approaching from the other direction, and I emerged from my hiding place. Together, guns at the ready, we entered the shop. The place seemed deserted at first sight. We moved forward cautiously at first, then with increasing confidence. Finding no one in the rear of the building, we returned to the front and stood indecisively among the racks of clothing. Suddenly, Holmes exclaimed sharply and darted forward. He drew aside the pairs of trousers hanging on a nearby circular rack, disclosing a body. I must say I was struck by how well and tastefully the dead man was dressed—befitting, perhaps, a gangster whose base of operations was an expensive men's shop. Holmes, however, had been attentive to other details: He muttered a curse and said, "It's one of the men we've been following. Look around for the others."

We found them, both just as dead as their comrade, both hidden under racks of clothing.

"Hidden," Holmes remarked, "but not so well that we could not find them after a short search. Moriarty does not tolerate failure."

I looked nervously over my shoulder. "Perhaps we'd better look for their killer," I whispered.

"If he were still here," Holmes replied briskly, "we'd both already be dead. I fear that, by circling the block instead of entering the building immediately, I gave the murderer time to escape. If you did not see him exit through the front, then he must have done so through the back, and that shortly after I had passed by." He searched the bodies quickly. "Well, well," he muttered, holding up for me to see a slip of paper he had found in the jacket pocket of one of the dead men. "Lily Cantrell," he read aloud, "followed by a street address in Chicago." He sat back upon his heels. "On the road once again, Watson. We must of course visit this lady and discover what her connexion might be with Professor Moriarty."

"Since time is of the essence, perhaps this time we might fly."

Holmes smiled faintly. "Indeed, Watson, we shall fly to your Miss Cantrell."

I hid my annoyance. By a most unpleasant coincidence, Lily Cantrell was a name from my past, a detail of which Holmes but no one else knew. A far more distressing thought had intruded, however. "Is it not remarkably fortuitous that we are provided with the next step in our pursuit?"

"Bravo, Watson! Remarkably fortuitous, indeed. One is obliged to speculate, in fact, that the course of events is not under our control but is rather being controlled at will by the ubiquitous Moriarty." The ebullience he had displayed before and the sharp, intense, eager concentration which had always characterized Sherlock Holmes the pursuer had both drained from his face. "I feel," he said, "like some character in a Greek tragedy, controlled by the gods and driven about at their whim, yet unable to do otherwise, to take control of his own fate or actions. We must play out this drama, following the implicit directions our enemy has given us. We must be careful, but nonetheless we must go to this address in Chicago; no other course is available to us."

8

The Name from the Past

BY THE TIME we arrived in Chicago, I was suffering from a confusion of time and place which, I have since read, is a common
effect of modern travel. I believe I suffered from it even more
acutely than might a younger man who is used to the hurly-
burly of late-twentieth-century life. For so many decades, I had
lived in isolation on the farm in Sussex, a turn-of-the-century
island in the midst of a changing world, that I still viewed the
modern world from the perspective of the late nineteenth century. I was obliged to remind myself that this was Chicago and
that it was a Thursday.

While Sherlock Holmes arranged the renting of a car, I pondered what I had come to regard as the central problem of immortality: While physically I was as a man in his twenties, and
indeed looked much that age, mentally I reflected my chronological age. I surprised myself upon occasion with my mental rigid-
ity, my stodginess, and my querulousness. Simply, I viewed myself as old; I could not bring myself to realise that I was in fact
young and hale.

Yet another curious consequence of my extreme age occurred
to me. I had lived to see my earlier chronicles of the adventures
of Sherlock Holmes and Doctor Watson become world-famous;
and yet, since copyright does not last forever and cannot be renewed indefinitely, I was no longer earning royalties. (Indeed,
were that not the case, I would have been obliged to disclose the
fact of my continued existence in order to collect royalties so
many decades after my presumed death of old age.) This extrav-
agant voyage to America was being financed, not by current royalties, but rather by the interest being earned by earlier royalties,
wisely invested long ago.

As soon as Holmes returned with our car, we set out for the

address we had found on the dead man. This involved a long and tedious drive from O'Hare Airport, but at last we found ourselves in front of a large block of flats at the edge of the lake, near the city's northern border. This was an area which clearly had once been quite grand and expensive. Now it was decaying badly, and only the relatively high property prices imposed by the nearness of the lake had so far kept it from deteriorating the last few steps into slumhood. It was the curiously bright light of early summer evening; we had just avoided the crush of evening traffic, which was only now beginning to filter into those side streets.

Entry was gained by pushing a button next to the name "Cantrell" in the foyer. This rang a bell in Miss Cantrell's flat, and she could then, if she chose, unlock the interior door of the foyer for us by pushing a button of her own, which would cause a buzzer to sound near us, alerting us that the door had been unlocked. Before she would do this, however, she asked us our names by means of a two-way electrical speaking device set in the wall of the foyer near the button. The names Holmes gave—Henry Holmes and James Watson—meant nothing to her, of course, and she was most reluctant to admit us; this was, as I have said, a deteriorating part of the city. But when Holmes said we had got her name from Professor Moriarty, she gasped and said hastily, "Just a minute"; and indeed it was only a second or two before the buzzer sounded and we were able to open the inner door of the foyer.

She lived on the third floor. During the time it took us to climb the stairs, she had apparently had second thoughts about allowing us into her flat. The door was open but secured by the chain, and she peered out at us through the slight opening the chain permitted. "What do you want?" she asked in a timid voice.

I could see that she had pale skin and light blonde hair; for the rest, I could tell only that I wished to see more, even while I was disturbed at the degree to which her colouring resembled that of the Lily Cantrell I had known in my earlier life.

Sherlock Holmes was clearly uninfluenced by any such disturbing feelings as those which afflicted me. "We want to find Professor Moriarty," he said in a firm voice.

"But you said he sent you," she responded uncertainly.

"No, I did not. I said only that we had got your name from him. Moreover, I do not know if he is aware of the fact, since in actuality we obtained your name and address from one of his underlings, who was dead at the time. Perhaps," he continued, "we can be of help to one another."

She hesitated no more after that, but opened her door and let us in. "I thought he had grown impatient and sent you for me," she said simply.

While Holmes questioned her as to her meaning, I observed her carefully and wordlessly. She did indeed resemble the Lily Cantrell I had known so intimately 120 years earlier in San Francisco, although not so closely on keener inspection as my first glimpse of her through the partially opened door had led me to expect. What resemblance there was consisted of certain gestures and certain mannerisms of speech and hearing. And yet such things are not superficial, for they can be said to go much deeper than the truly superficial resemblance of outer appearance; and it was eerie indeed to sit there in a lakeside flat in late-twentieth-century Chicago, listening to the faint sounds of evening automobile traffic floating up from the street, watching the freighters and barges barely visible on the dim horizon of the great expanse of grey water I could see through the broad window before me, watching and listening to a young woman who brought back so vividly and so painfully that other Lily Cantrell and that other window overlooking a great body of water—my long-dead love of another place and an ancient time.

What were my fickle body and mind doing to me? I was no modern young man to react physically to a young woman I did not know; I was old, old John Watson, twice widowed, older surely than any other man alive. This accidental similarity of name and manner had unmanned me in one way even while it reminded me of my physically young manhood in another.

With an effort, I forced myself to attend to the meaning of Lily Cantrell's words rather than to the manner in which she said them. She told Holmes that some years before, she had been so unwise as to take some money from the bank in which she was then employed. She had not been caught, but her conscience had so troubled her that she had never repeated her crime; she had returned the money as surreptitiously as she had taken it, but she was nonetheless convinced that a careful audit of the bank's books would reveal her guilt. One year ago, she had been contacted by a man whom I recognised immediately from her description as Professor Moriarty. He had told her who he was and he had displayed a minute knowledge of her theft, threatening to expose her to the police if she did not do just as he told her.

"One moment," Holmes interrupted. "Did you say that this happened *one year* ago?"

"Yes, a year ago," she repeated, not noticing the glance Holmes and I exchanged. "I was terrified," she continued, "and I agreed right away. He told me to quit my job at the bank and apply for a clerical position in the city government's offices. That's where I work now. Every month, an envelope arrives in the mail, stuffed with money." She trailed off at this point and sat staring out at the lake.

"And what has he required of you in return?" Holmes prompted, far more gently than I might have expected.

"Nothing," she replied. "Or almost nothing. Occasionally I have been ordered to mail him some documents I take from work, or give him other information about the city administration. But it's never anything important; he could get most of it from the Chicago newspapers."

"Then you have an address to which to send these papers?" Holmes asked, leaning forward slightly in his chair.

"A post office box in Kansas City."

"And he contacts you occasionally? By the posts—that is, by mail?"

"No. Telephone. Last time he called . . ." She hesitated as if unsure whether to trust us any further. She looked at me appealingly, and I said earnestly, "My dear girl, we want to help you." At that, she smiled in gratitude and continued.

"Last time, he hinted that he would soon have something more important for me to do. I would have to go to Kansas City and meet him there, and then he would tell me more."

Sherlock Holmes stood up abruptly. "Thank you for confiding in us, Miss Cantrell. It's growing late and we must leave you now and check into a hotel I have in mind. I believe we will be able to help you escape from Moriarty's clutches; if you have no objection, we will call upon you again tomorrow."

Downstairs, once we were headed toward the hotel Holmes had chosen, he asked me whether I believed all that Lily Cantrell had told us. "Yes, of course," I replied instantly. "She is obviously yet another of the Professor's innocent victims."

"Not quite innocent, by her own admission," Holmes remarked. "Perhaps your history has prejudiced your judgment. You trust her, then?"

"Utterly," I said, my annoyance showing. "Absolutely. With my life, if need be."

Holmes raised his eyebrows at this extravagance, but all he said was, "It may yet come to that."

Later, in our hotel room, he said, "Watson, I want you to see a great deal of Lily Cantrell. I am sure this is an assignment which will not strike you as onerous. You may choose to trust her; indeed, it will be easier for you to follow the order I have just given you if you do trust her. I, however, am filled with doubts as to her truthfulness and reliability. Also, she is a woman, and therefore inherently unstable."

"Come, Holmes," I protested, "that is monstrous!"

"Aah, Watson, Watson," he said in an indulgent tone, "monstrous I may be, but grant at least that I am consistent over the years, just as you are yourself. Your remarkable faith in the so-called fairer sex has diminished not one whit in your long life, any more than your susceptibility to women's charms has faded with age. Just as well: I have further investigations of my own to pursue, and your dalliance with Lily Cantrell will at least serve to keep both of you out of my way."

I chose to ignore the insult implicit in his words and asked him, "How could Moriarty have contacted Lily a year ago? Has he been in our own age longer than we assumed?"

Holmes had settled into a chair and lit his pipe. "Yes," he said between puffs of smoke, "that is one possibility, and probably the least disturbing one. It is also possible that he made his trip to the present in stages, stopping at various points along the way, until he reached—ah—this point in time. The third possibility that springs to mind, and this is the one that disturbs me the most, is that Moriarty has used the Time Machine to travel back one year and subvert Lily Cantrell, presumably doing so only after we had arrived in America and made our existence known to him, thereby causing him to decide that he needed a well-prepared subordinate in Chicago to meet us. If that is so, then the device is still operating with at least some success, and that may mean that Moriarty will be impossible to capture. Without being ourselves in possession of a means to travel in time, how may we hope to capture a criminal who can move into the future or past at will?"

"Surely," I observed, "even if he is now able only to travel forward into the future, as you had earlier surmised, he can escape from us with ease."

"Yes," he said reluctantly. "That has crossed my mind. I must admit that I am going on faith to a large extent—faith that the Time Machine is not working. If it is able to transport Moriarty in either direction in time, for any distance, then he is quite simply beyond our grasp. More than that: We are at his mercy, for he may lay for us any trap he wishes, or he may use time travel to enter our room at night and murder us. Since this has obviously not yet happened, perhaps it is safe for us to assume that Moriarty, if he can travel in time at all, can do so in only one direction. The faith I mentioned is my fervent hope that he cannot so travel at all, and that this pursuit of him in space in which we are engaged will be successful in the end. If he were free to move in more dimensions than we, the matter would be hopeless."

The grim picture he painted, as much as the tired, pessimistic look upon his face, filled me with chill foreboding. In my mind's eye I saw Moriarty moving at will in both time and space, while we were limited to the three familiar dimensions, and I lost hope.

While Holmes busied himself with errands whose nature he would not disclose to me, I assiduously performed the duty he had assigned to me.

This was a curious matter, my squiring about town a woman who was in truth so many generations younger than me. However, she was unaware of this age difference, and soon enough, under the influence of my young and ageless body, I became unaware of it, too. My assignment was simply to keep her company, to be available when Moriarty contacted her again and told her where in Kansas City to meet him. Also, I was to keep both Lily Cantrell and myself out of Holmes' way. Perhaps I might have accomplished all this without spending quite so much time with her, but I have always been a thorough man, and I was most diligent about my assignment.

She was charming, intelligent, with a mind that was both penetrating and endlessly inquisitive. These, too, were traits she shared with the Lily Cantrell of long ago. It was inevitable that my feelings for the present Lily Cantrell should become identical to those I had entertained toward the earlier Lily Cantrell. Whatever distress these unfamiliar feelings might have occasioned me was pushed utterly out of my awareness by Lily's disclosure that her feelings toward me were much the same as mine toward her.

Among the aspects of modern life which I had long found shocking in the extreme was the habit of young people of living with each other in the manner of husbands and wives, but without the sanction of either Church or State. I myself had been married twice, properly, in a church, and although I had been romantically involved upon a few occasions, I had never, with one exception, even attempted physical intimacy with the ladies who were the objects of my affection. That one exception was the original Lily Cantrell, and in that case it had been as if an external force, powerful beyond the ability of either of us to resist, had driven our bodies together to match the union of our hearts. It was an incident which had long bothered my conscience—the conscience of a nineteenth-century man—and now, once again, as if Fate were playing cruel jokes on me like those played by the gods in the plays of ancient Greece, the very same thing happened all over again.

I had not slept with a woman since the death of my second wife. The physical and emotional closeness elated me and made me behave, for once, in accordance with my physical, rather than my chronological, age. Reality quickly intruded itself, however, with a telephone call from Professor Moriarty. When Lily hung up the bedside telephone and turned back to me, her face was drawn and pale.

"That was him—Moriarty," she said in a strained voice. "He gave me the address in Kansas City and told me to come there immediately."

I telephoned the hotel, but Holmes was not in the room. I tried again an hour later, but he was still away, and I decided I could wait no longer. Lily and I booked seats on a flight to Kansas City that was scheduled to leave early the next morning, and then we tried to get what sleep we could before it was time to leave; needless to say, the prospect of running Moriarty to ground at last precluded much sleep. (So did certain other matters, but I am still too much a product of the nineteenth century to refer to them in any more detail.)

Before we left in the morning, I tried one last time to contact Sherlock Holmes, but again without success. All I could do was leave a message with the hotel clerk, including in the message the address Lily had been given.

Filled with trepidation no less than excitement, we boarded the plane for the short flight to Kansas City. It occurred to me that I might pull off my greatest coup if I could capture Professor Moriarty by myself, with no help from Sherlock Holmes.

All of this, however, was driven from my mind when, during the flight, Lily remarked that her grandparents had moved to Illinois from San Francisco, and that she had been named after her grandmother's great-grandmother. I was cast into mental turmoil by the horrifying thought that I had been sleeping with my other Lily's great-great-great-granddaughter. Before I could question her about this ancestor of hers, the aeroplane began its descent, and I forced my attention back again to the upcoming confrontation with Professor Moriarty.

9

True Colours

WE RENTED a car at the airport and asked the young lady behind the desk at the rental agency for directions to the address Moriarty had given Lily. Perhaps the term "lady" is not appropriate in this case, but its use is yet another habit which remains to me from my nineteenth-century origins. She was popping her chewing gum at us between sentences—an unspeakably execrable habit—and simultaneously looking us carefully up and down. This scrutiny made me uneasy. I imagined that my clothing, far from blending in with that of those around me, was hopelessly old-fashioned and marked me as a relic of the previous century; was this gum-popping creature, I asked myself, mentally condemning me as a cradle-robbing old goat?

"Green Hills, huh?" she said between pops. She had a street map before us and marked a route on it swiftly and heavily with a ballpoint pen. "See this Interstate? This is the one ya want." The terminology and the map combined to confuse me, but Lily seemed to follow the girl's directions. At last, with the marked-up map in our hands, we were in the car and on our way. Now, for the first time, we discussed what we would do when we arrived.

Lily was of course unaware of my desire to gain Sherlock Holmes' approbation by capturing Professor Moriarty on my own. "Now, James," she said, "I want you to drive past the place before you stop. You can let me off and wait for me. I'll be in no danger. Moriarty could have had me killed long ago, if he had wanted to. Obviously he hasn't wanted to, so he won't harm me now. If you came with me, it would be a different matter."

I was about to protest vigorously and to insist that indeed I would accompany her into Moriarty's presence. On the verge of speaking, however, I thought better about it. Beyond a doubt,

Lily would be difficult or perhaps impossible to convince, should I argue for the merits of my accompanying her. A more powerful argument in favour of my acquiescing to her request, however, was Moriarty himself: When Lily showed up at his door as he had ordered, and alone, he would have no reason to suspect that she had travelled with a companion. Thus, while Lily occupied his attention, I could infiltrate the premises undetected.

"You're sure you'll be safe?" I asked anxiously. Yet I am forced to admit that my object, the glory of single-handedly capturing Professor Moriarty, was so great that, despite the increasing affection I felt for Lily Cantrell, duplicity had influenced my asking of that question. Concerned as I certainly was for her safety, I was also determined that she should be unaware of my intentions, for if she were convinced that I was waiting for her in the car, then her manner would not be such as to arouse Moriarty's suspicions. There would be no furtive glancing about on her part as she looked for her companion, and if she were asked if she had come alone, she could answer without hesitancy or prevarication that she had. She was, I knew, such a pure soul and so incapable of wrong deeds or thoughts, that she would be incapable of not betraying the truth to Moriarty. Better, then, to make sure that the truth so far as she knew it was such that she could tell it without doing harm either to herself or to me.

She smiled sweetly and warmly at me. "Oh, James, that's touching! I'll be okay—especially knowing that you're waiting for me." In view of the deception I was practising upon her, her sincere and affectionate response, as you may well imagine, made me feel a thoroughgoing cad.

Our destination proved to be in a secluded area only now becoming integrated into the sprawling twin metropolises of Kansas City. We drove for some distance along a winding, narrow, hilly road past unspoiled stands of trees and fields in which new corn stood fresh and green. I was put in mind of English country scenes of my youth, although the heat was somewhat more oppressive than I remembered from those long-gone summers. Had I seen corn growing on farms in England well over a hundred years before? I was no longer sure. Perhaps, I thought, there is a limit to the brain's capacity to hold memories; perhaps this would provide the final barrier to my longevity, as my brain ceased to function due to an overload of old thoughts and memories and I slipped into a unique form of senility! Such thoughts as these, I longed to share with Lily; once this adventure was over, I must disclose the full truth about myself to her and hope she would not be repelled by my age.

The pastoral nature of the area was broken in many places by large complexes of flats, many of them still under construction: a harsh and jarring note, this extrusion of the city into what must once have been in idyllic rural retreat.

I was driving while Lily, holding the map before her, gave me directions. We passed a sign announcing the proximity of a lake, and Lily's tension increased. "We must be almost there," she muttered. She leaned forward and stared at the postboxes and address signs we passed. "There!" she exclaimed, pointing to an entrance on the right, almost hidden by trees and bushes. "No, don't turn in there," she cautioned as I slowed down. She pointed at a building complex across the street from the entrance. "Go into that apartment parking lot." When I had done so, she leaned across and kissed me. "Now, just wait here for me, James. Really, I'll be okay." Then she was gone, walking quickly across the street and disappearing down the shaded drive.

I waited for some minutes in a quiet, unthinking revery, feeling the warm, moist air on my skin, listening to the faint, distant sounds of birds, children, and lawnmowers. At last, thinking that surely enough time had passed, I checked my revolver to assure myself that it was fully loaded, replaced it in the pocket of my trousers, and left the car.

Once I had crossed the road, I found that the house to which the drive presumably led was invisible, obscured by trees. I therefore decided that it would be impractical to cut across fields and sneak up on Moriarty as a Red Indian might, since I would be too likely to lose my way amidst the thick, confusing forest. Steeling my nerves, I walked down the gravelled drive, hoping there would be nothing in the way of a lookout. After I had taken but a few steps into the calm shadows, the sounds of urban civilization, the highway noises and lawnmowers, disappeared. Beyond a fence to my right, a horse moved slowly through sunlight-dappled shade. It was as if I had entered another world, secluded, peaceful, and secure from the jarring clamour of the twentieth century. It was such a place, I realised, as I had been unconsciously seeking as a refuge ever since leaving the farm in Sussex, and the house, when it suddenly came in view, meshed perfectly with that feeling. It was a large, rambling place built in an old style, largely of grey native rock, most of the walls covered with ivy and other climbing vines. How, I asked myself, could this quiet, cool, delightful place be no more than a facade for the evil of Professor Moriarty?

Still my luck held, for, as I approached the house, I remained unchallenged. Nor did this change as I turned from the drive where it passed by the building. I mounted a few steps, crossed a small porch and entered through a door that stood ajar. Not a sound had yet disturbed me, neither from the world I had left behind nor from the house itself or its environs. If my faith in a Supreme Being had not been destroyed years earlier by the horrors of two world wars and threats of a third, I would have thought my success thus far sure proof that God was on my side.

The door opened into a short and very narrow hallway, which in turn led into a sitting room with a stone fireplace and a window that looked out onto the porch I had just crossed. The room was empty. However, the far end of the room was a wide archway, beyond which was a dining room with a large, ornate table set as though for a banquet, and standing next to the table, her back to me, was Lily. She was quite alone and seemed to be absorbed in an examination of something on the table. I experienced a rush of relief at her obvious safety, and I called out her name in a low voice.

She turned to me and smiled, but it was a troubled smile, and her face bore the signs of tension and worry. I thought, too, that she seemed sad, as though aware of a loss of something important to her. "Come here, John," she said. "Everything is all right, you see."

A multitude of feelings were jumbled together in me as I stepped up to her and took her hands in mine: relief, still, but also puzzlement at the sadness in her tone, matching the look upon her face; disappointment, I must confess, at the realisation that, if indeed all were well, then Moriarty must not be here and so I could not hope to capture him after all; and only last of all, sudden surprise of her use of my correct name, John, rather than James. It was this as much as the faint sound behind me and her involuntary glance over my shoulder that made me turn around. But my response was too late. I felt a terrible blow on the back of my head, a momentary crashing, splitting pain, and then all sensation disappeared, but for a momentary floating feeling and then the hard smack of the floor against my cheek.

Before consciousness left me entirely, I heard a dry, soft, well-remembered and much-hated voice say, "Well done, Lily. Now that the pilot fish is in our nets, the shark must soon follow." Then all faded away.

10

Moriarty Speaks His Mind

A LONG, dreamlike period followed in which I would occasionally regain only partial consciousness—that is, I was aware of some physical sensations and could hear and partially understand conversations being conducted nearby but was unable to awaken fully or to move my limbs—and would then lapse again into a deep sleep. In retrospect, it is clear that I was being kept in a heavily drugged state, that the torpor of which I was so unable to rid myself was chemical in nature rather than an aftereffect of the blow I had suffered. At the time, however, I was aware only of the profound peril in which I had placed myself and of the urgent need to awake.

I said the period was dreamlike; I had better said nightmarish. During my short stretches of awareness, I could tell that I was being loaded into an automobile; that this was followed by a long trip, first in the car, then in an aeroplane, and then in a car again; that at last I was somehow supported, unmoving, in an upright position. Throughout this time, I struggled desperately and in vain to gain control over my body. I was surrounded by those who were my enemies and the enemies of Sherlock Holmes. Now and then I heard Lily's voice, and I experienced great anguish at my inability to protect her from these men who were surely her enemies as well. Thus does the mind, even in moments of the most extreme danger, delude itself as to the true colors of those it loves!

At last the haze that shrouded my senses and my mind thinned. A sharp prick in my arm indicated that I was being given some substance to counteract the drugs in my bloodstream, and then a sudden violent slap upon my face roused me fully.

I was seated in a chair, bound to it tightly so that I could not move my arms or legs and in fact could breathe only shallowly. Standing before me was a tall, slender, middle-aged man with grey hair and a thin, lined, ascetic face. The high forehead of genius combined with the hate-filled glare of the deep-set eyes and the slow, almost imperceptible, reptilian motion of the head to create a preternaturally chilling effect. It was of course Professor Moriarty, virtually unchanged from my last sight of him so many decades earlier. To my shame, I realized that my manhood had deserted me and I was weak and shaking with terror— as though he were a reptile indeed and I his avian prey!

He looked down at me, leaning forward, his head protruding, as it were, from his hunched shoulders. Affecting a calmness I most certainly did not feel, I said, "Well, Moriarty. You've cooked yourself up a sorry mess of trouble by kidnapping me!"

My bluff certainly did not work, for he laughed—a harsh and grating sound. "Doctor Watson, do not delude yourself. You are a small fish, indeed, but you will serve my purpose. Far from making trouble for myself, I have ensured that the illustrious Sherlock Holmes will soon grace my nets just as you, in your far less illustrious fashion, do now. Thus I can hold you both here, alive, to witness my final victory over you—more, over all the world. The world," he muttered, no longer speaking to me, "that used me so ill." He paced from side to side before me. "Yes, the world, the *whole* world. I will give it an object lesson."

He continued in this strange manner for some time, behaving and speaking as though his mind were unbalanced. Since he required no reply from me, and in fact seemed to be paying me no attention, I took the opportunity to observe my surroundings more closely. We appeared to be in a large factory building, for through the window of the small office in which I was seated, I could see a great expanse of machinery and conveyor belts. None of it was in operation, however, and dust lay thick upon the desk and other furniture in the office, leading me to conclude that the place had been closed down and perhaps abandoned until Moriarty's advent. Faint sounds of hammering in the distance, however, indicated that the professor was making use of the facilities for some purpose of his own. What that purpose was, I most assuredly could not have guessed; I was to discover that both the audacity and the horror of his intentions certainly exceeded anything I might have dreamt of.

[61]

My attention was drawn back to the man himself. He had stopped speaking and was staring at me. Once again, I was struck by something of the lunatic in his face. Evil he might have been since his youth, but he had given me, when last I had seen him, the impression of a perfectly sane man, with an immensely forceful will and the utmost self-control. His genius and his evil had both been expressed in ways that, in a good man, would have excited admiration: His sanity, self-control, strength of will, and ceaseless industry were all characteristics that we had professed to admire in the previous century. Now his nature had changed into bizarre and hate-filled insanity. If anything, this made him an even more fearful figure than before, for he now struck me as unpredictable.

He had spoken obsessively of the world as though it were but one person, and that one his enemy. He had raged at some length about imagined injuries and slights the worlds had visited upon him. And yet this was the man to whom the world he reviled had granted great and richly deserved academic honours at an early age, only to see him cast his position and his honour aside at the same time and take to a life of debasement and evil; the world had raised him up, and he had spurned it and harmed it in return, and yet now he complained bitterly of all the hurts *it* had done to *him!*

His silent stare was a demand for a response, so, keeping my voice steady with some effort and hoping to induce a return to sanity in him by my words and manner, I said, "By kidnapping me, Professor, you have only made it certain that Sherlock Holmes will make it his business to track you down and destroy you. Had you chosen to dwell in this century in quiet and obscurity and without dabbling in any crimes, we might perhaps have been able to ignore you. Now, that is impossible."

He uttered an exclamation of annoyance. "Can you be so stupid," he said harshly, "that you still do not understand that you are merely the bait? That I am holding you captive precisely to bring Sherlock Holmes here, within my reach? I had always assumed your intelligence to be greater than implied by your foolish manner and adolescent writings about Sherlock Holmes, but now I see I was mistaken. Perhaps I should have expected as much, for you are after all only a doctor of medicine, and it has always been obvious to me that true intellectual ability is to be found only in some physical scientists and great criminals."

"And," I said rashly, stung by his words, "certain consulting detectives?"

He grew flushed with sudden rage and struck me violently upon the face. "You fool!" he hissed. "You idiot! I arranged with ease for you to fall in love with one of my agents, who delivered you to me as neatly as if you had been a package in the post, and yet you still have the effrontery to mock me. Do you not yet realize, Doctor, that, knowing much about your history, *I* chose Lily Cantrell to be your lover, that *I* engineered matters so that you would meet her in a flat that could not fail to remind you of the one in San Francisco, that *I* ordered her to act as if she loved you and then to lead you to me upon my telephoned signal that all was prepared? Her ancestress may well have loved you, for all I know, but *this* Lily Cantrell is no such dolt. She was intelligent enough to throw her lot in with mine from the first moment I contacted her, and she has followed my instructions to the letter ever since. *All* my instructions, Doctor Watson. Do you understand?"

Of course I understood—understood all too well. No longer could I deny what, on some level of my mind, I must have known from the start: that Lily had only seemed to love me and that she had, moreover, betrayed me to Moriarty. All my resistance wilted, and I sagged in my chair. Nor could I regain strength by telling myself that Moriarty must not see what effect his revelation had had upon me. My demoralization was simply too great.

Moriarty laughed shrilly. "See, Doctor," he cried, "see to what an extent you are under my control! Now I shall tell you what I intend, and then you will understand how the world, little though it realises the fact, will soon lie within my grasp."

His eyes blazed with fanatical purpose, sweat stood upon his forehead, and his limbs trembled. I looked up at him in amazement, this posturing, shrieking madman, and I could scarce believe, despite his appearance, that this was truly the same man who had masterminded the criminal world of London for years. Might this be some dreadful side effect of time travel, or possibly the result of the damage Sherlock Holmes had speculated the Time Machine had suffered? If either were the case, presumably Moriarty could not use the machine to escape again without suffering even further mental deterioration. And surely so mad a criminal did not pose a real threat to the world! My relief at this thought was a partial antidote to my despair at having lost Lily—sufficient antidote that I was emboldened to display some further resistance to Moriarty. "You must know," I told him, my voice firm once more, "that the world is a far more complex place than it was a hundred years ago, and that your murder of the Prime Minister caused only a minor and short-lived disruption, even in England. You are out of your time and beyond your depth, Professor. It would be easiest for you to surrender yourself now. I am certain Sherlock Holmes could find a nice, quiet place for your retirement—"

"Imbecile! Be silent!" He stalked out of the office into the factory proper, leaving me to reflect upon the signal lack of success of my attempt at applied psychology. However, it seemed that he had left the room merely to calm himself, for after a few minutes he returned, his aspect once more frighteningly quiet and dispassionate, his eyes radiating, not mad frenzy, but sane and evil power. If he were mentally unbalanced, then it must be a transitory phenomenon, not something which afflicted him full time; it might well be that between times he was as sane—and hence as dangerous—as ever.

He drew up another chair and sat down facing me. "Doctor Watson," he said in an even, amiable tone, "I would like you to demonstrate for me the analytical method you have made famous in your accounts of Sherlock Holmes' adventures. Can you deduce where we are?"

Under any other circumstances, I would have reacted with vast annoyance to such a question, since for all I knew we might be anywhere in the world, but the circumstances and the interrogator were such that I gave the matter my serious attention. "I have been aware for some time," I replied, "that the air is quite dry. From my own breathing and heartbeat, I am led to conclude that we are at a fairly high elevation above sea level. This implies a mountain range, but which one, I cannot, of course, tell."

Moriarty was obviously annoyed at my deduction, for he grimaced at me as might a child whose planned surprise has been spoiled. Quickly regaining his composure, he said mildly, "Anything else?"

"Ah, yes. Every now and again I have caught a faint, acrid whiff of what I believe to be air heavily saturated with salt. Combining all of these facts with the pattern of westward movement you have exhibited in the United States, I will guess that we are in the vicinity of Salt Lake City."

Moriarty leapt to his feet excitedly. "Indeed, an excellent guess! We are a few miles to the southwest of that city, on a mountainside overlooking the Great Salt Lake. Now look about you: Can you tell what this building is?"

"It is of course an abandoned factory, but beyond that, I must confess myself defeated."

Moriarty clapped his hands with delight. "Marvellous, Doctor: the perfect choice of words. This was until recently a plant for refining of salt extracted from the immense beds left behind by the ancestral sea as it evaporated to form the Great Salt Lake. Economic fluctuations caused this facility to be shut down, but all the equipment was left behind against the day when the plant might be reopened."

He seemed again to be growing overly excited and close to losing control of himself. However, he did not leave the room to calm himself; his desire to boast of his accomplishments was obviously so great that it precluded any attempt at self-control.

"Doctor," he said in a gleeful and mocking tone, "I'm sure you are familiar with the two disciplines, ballistics and nuclear engineering?"

This sudden and bewildering change of topic was sufficiently disorienting that I felt little anger at his open contempt for my intellectual abilities; rather, I was concerned at his interest in these topics. "I know what they are," I answered cautiously, "but little more."

"Let me rephrase my question, then," he said with even greater sarcasm. "May I assume that you know what cannons and atomic bombs are?"

A chill of fear ran through me. To hear Moriarty talk of these things made me feel, with no rational justification as yet, that the danger he posed to the world was even greater than either Holmes or I could have imagined. A great weariness descended upon me, a desire to have done with this tiresome escapade that had seemed so exciting at the start, but whether this weariness was due to Lily's betrayal, or the cumulative effects of my travels and exertions, or some failure of Holmes' elixir to effect a complete rejuvenation, I could not have said. "Give over, Professor," I sighed. "I am no mouse, nor are you a cat. Simply tell me what you are about and gloat to your heart's content."

He grew angry, and I could tell that he had wanted a greater show of resistance from me, more spirit, so that he might have the pleasure of crushing me despite my most vigorous protest. My emotional surrender to the situation, to his mastery over my fate, had deprived him of any such pleasure. He quickly removed the ropes that bound my legs to the chair, and he roughly pulled me to my feet and propelled me through the doorway of the office. Because I had been sitting in a rigid, unmoving position for so long, I had difficulty walking and I stumbled and fell against a large crate just outside the office. Moriarty grasped my shoulders, pulled me back to my feet, and, with a muttered curse, shoved me savagely forward.

After a long, circuitous, and thoroughly confusing journey through the gloomy factory, up metal staircases and around dusty machinery, we came at last to a place that was cleaned and lighted and held an immense cylinder, around which men were working. Here we halted.

"This," said Moriarty, his voice trembling with some profound emotion, "is a retort used in the refining process. It is built to withstand extraordinarily high internal temperatures and pressures. But where you might see no more than that, Doctor, I saw the raw materials for a cannon capable of projecting a large and heavy object for many miles with considerable accuracy. My men have completed the necessary modifications according to my instructions, and the retort has become a cannon. You will note the presence of a skylight in the roof of the building, above the retort." I looked up and saw a small window high above the cylinder. "One of the modifications," Moriarty continued, "was to tilt the cannon from the vertical, so that while it is still aimed so as to fire through the skylight, any projectile it fires will follow the parabolic arc I desire, rather than landing upon this building."

"And where," I asked, my curiosity aroused despite myself, "will that arc cause the projectile to land?"

"Aha, Doctor," he cried, "the matter still interests you! I will answer that question in a moment, but first, allow me to direct your attention to that large steel case just beyond the cannon."

I looked where he pointed and saw the case he meant. But in addition I saw, deep in conversation beside the case, Lily Cantrell. Moriarty was talking excitedly about the contents of the case, but I was oblivious to his words. Until now, I had been able to accept my loss of Lily—or so I had convinced myself. Now I knew that I had been deluding myself and that in fact my feelings toward Lily were as strong as ever, as was my need for her. Had I had any lingering doubts concerning the enduring strength of my own feelings, my racing pulse, shortness of breath, and emotional agony at seeing her again so unexpectedly would soon have disillusioned me. As though aware of my longing stare, she looked away from the workman with whom she had been talking and glanced in our direction. Even from that distance, I could see her start of surprise when she recognised me. For a long moment of suspended time, we looked at each other, and then she broke her contact and resumed her conversation with the overalled workman.

With an effort, I turned my attention again to what Moriarty was saying. I had missed only his boasting of his own knowledge of nuclear physics and his description of theoretical work he claimed to have done during the nineteenth century in anticipation, he said, of all that had been done by the greatest scientists of later generations. "Now that technology has at last caught up with my theoretical work," he continued, "I can use the devices built by others to create a weapon. Using material stolen during the last few weeks by my men and by certain others with whom I have formed contacts, I have assembled a fission bomb, what this century calls an atomic bomb. It is stored in that case— adequately surrounded by shielding material, I can assure you.

Only a small amount of work remains until the bomb is ready for use as a projectile in my cannon, and then all will be in readiness."

Feeling dazed by these revelations, I asked him, "In readiness for what?"

He ignored my question and said in a thoughtful tone, as though speculating aloud, "Perhaps I might yet have time to perfect a better detonating method, so that I can avoid the use of a timing mechanism. But time is short, and I must have dependability."

"For God's sake, man," I cried, "what Devil's work are you planning?"

He smiled with pleasure, and I realised that I had allowed myself to be goaded into just the reaction he had wanted, for it was for the amusement that this afforded him that he had shown me his cannon and told me of the bomb. "Doctor Watson," he said, adopting a tone as mild and amiable as might be that of one gentleman speaking with another in the smoking room of a London club, "the situation is quite simply this. Two days from now, the President of the United States will be arriving in Salt Lake City on what American politicians like so quaintly to call a fence-mending mission. His announced plans include a short speech to those assembled to greet him at the Salt Lake City airport, which is situated to the west of the city itself. Surely I have said enough."

"I don't see—" I began, puzzled, but then it struck me what this madman's plan was. "You will fire the bomb at the airport when he arrives!" I was stunned as much by the exotic audacity of the plan as by its evil.

"Indeed I shall." He stared lovingly at his cannon. "A bullet for the Prime Minister was a small and crude act, unworthy of Moriarty," he announced. "And England, as I found out too late, is now a very minor power. But this—aah! This is both worthy of my history and far more likely to bring me the power I desire!"

"But surely," I said in desperation, hoping to find some flaw in his design by the exposing of which I might change his mind and deter him, "surely such bombs are so powerful that the influence of this one will reach us here and destroy you along with the President."

He dismissed this objection with a wave of his hand. "Credit me with enough intelligence, Doctor, to have taken that into account. The bomb is both small enough and, in the current jargon, 'clean' enough so that only the airport will be destroyed. Most of the city will be untouched, and we shall certainly be quite safe here. From that you can conclude that timing is all. I will have a man stationed atop the mountain on the side of which this factory is located; he will have a telescope aimed at the airport so that he can see the President's aeroplane land and can signal me at the appropriate moment. For extra assurance, I will have both a wireless and a television set with me, tuned to stations in Salt Lake City which will be reporting on the President's arrival as it happens. As you can see, I have planned well."

"Your man on the mountaintop with the telescope: Will he not be in great danger of still having the telescope to his eye when the bomb detonates at the place he is observing, causing him to lose his eyesight?"

He shrugged. "He is aware of the risk. The times, as I am sure you know, Doctor, have changed since those days in London when I offered such complete protection to all who served me loyally. These are more self-serving days."

The greatest danger of all suddenly occurred to me. "Perhaps there is one thing you have not thought of, however."

He smiled indulgently. "I rather doubt it. Enlighten me, Doctor."

"First, let me repeat that murdering the President will probably do you no more good than did the assassination of the Prime Minister. Of greater moment, however, is the reaction of the American military forces to the mysterious explosion of a nuclear weapon within the country's borders, especially when that explosion results in the death of their Commander-in-Chief. Can you not see that a likely result will be a panicky assumption that one of the other great powers has attacked this country, and that the response of the military commanders, especially with the steadying influence of the President gone, will probably be to launch an all-out attack upon whatever enemy they decide is responsible? This would surely engulf the entire world in that awful nuclear holocaust it has been trying to avoid for decades. You will not gain a thing; instead, we will all, good and evil together, lose everything."

Moriarty shook his head. "Dear, dear! And you thought none of that had occurred to me. After all this time, Doctor Watson, you obviously still do not adequately respect my mental powers." His affected jocularity disappeared suddenly, replaced by a glare full of hatred on that grim, pinched face. "I want more than power over a handful of purse snatchers and blackmailers this time. I want control over everything, open power over all men in the world. If I cannot have that, if I cannot dominate the world which rejected me so many years ago, then I will be happy to see it destroyed. You spoke of a nuclear holocaust. I assure you that, if it comes to that, I will dance at the cremation!"

11

The Scheme Proceeds

FROM THEN ON, I was under the care of a workman, the same
one to whom Lily Cantrell had been talking when I had caught
sight of her in the room with the great cannon. Much of the
time during the next two days, I was kept in a large storeroom;
my scanty meals were brought to me there, and I was allowed
out of the room for two reasons only, one of which was the performance of necessary physical functions. The other was Moriarty's desire that I should be brought to see the cannon a couple
of times a day so that I might be aware of the project's progress
and he might gloat in my presence. Indeed, I was duly impressed
with the efficiency and organisation of his workforce, and once
again I reflected what great works of benefit to mankind Moriarty could have accomplished had his genius not become so
mysteriously warped toward evil during his young manhood.
Hour by hour, all approached the final state of readiness, and
Moriarty's insane joy as the fateful moment neared was frightening.

During those two days, I never saw Lily except once or twice,
at a distance, but I was of course frequently in the company of
the workman who was my guard. I should refer to him as a caretaker, for such Moriarty had explained he was. "This excellent
fellow," Professor Moriarty had said when placing me under the
man's guard, "was an employee of the company that owns this
factory. After I had already established myself here," he had continued, eager to demonstrate for me his influence over even the
meanest and most insignificant of his followers, "this man, Sam
Hudwell, arrived from Salt Lake City to inspect the facilities for
the owners. This was a duty he performed regularly, so that an
eye might be kept upon the supposedly vacant building. My men
surprised and captured him, and he quickly—and wisely—threw
in his lot with mine."

I tried repeatedly to strike up a conversation with Sam Hudwell, but I met with no success: He was the very embodiment of taciturnity, and, beyond that, his loyalty to his new employer seemed to be complete, unquestioning, and unshakable. He was tall and spare, a physical type I would have thought more typical of the nineteenth-century American labourer than the twentieth, and always dressed in blue denim overalls with the wide-brimmed cap so common among workmen of all sorts in the United States. Upon the front, this cap bore the emblem of a manufacturer of heavy machinery, consisting of a stylised leaping deer, and the caretaker wore the cap pulled forward and down so that his eyes were always hidden from me, and even that part of his face that was not fully obscured was shaded and unreadable.

One might almost have thought the caretaker knew only three phrases in English: "Yeah," "Uh-uh," and "Quiet, mister." I asked him if he knew what Moriarty planned? "Yeah." *All* of the details? "Yeah." Didn't the idea of helping to assassinate his President and endanger his country's safety disturb him? "Uh-uh." And when I persisted in my attempts at communication beyond the point Sam Hudwell seemed able to tolerate, it was "Quiet, mister!" My faint hope of subverting this true son of the Yankee soil and thus gaining an ally faded away, as all my attempts at communication with him were either ignored or brusquely repulsed.

Thus I was deprived of conversation. Without even any reading matter to hand (for, alas, that novel of mediaeval romance in which I had been so engrossed was lost to me), I had much time to think—about Moriarty, about myself and the predicament in which my own stupidity and carelessness had landed me, about Lily Cantrell (although those were thoughts I tried not to dwell on), and lastly about Sherlock Holmes and what he might be doing. So far, I had noticed no sign of him at the abandoned salt factory. Surely he would have contacted me had he been able. And if he had tried to contact, or perhaps rescue, me and been captured by Professor Moriarty's men, then Moriarty would have come to me immediately to gloat over his victory. I was therefore obliged to conclude that Sherlock Holmes had not entered the building and was perhaps quite unaware of Moriarty's and my location. With the time growing short in which a rescue of me and a foiling of Professor Moriarty's plan could be effected, I was overcome by despair.

Despairing or not, I could neither suppress nor ignore my professional curiosity concerning Professor Moriarty. From his manner and his words, it seemed to me that his desire to assassinate the President of the United States had little to do with his stated reason for the act. There were too many reasons to believe, as I had already pointed out to him, that the results he claimed to anticipate would in fact not flow from such a murder, any more than they had flowed from his murder of the Prime Minister. His brilliant mind should have been aware of the objections I had raised long before they had occurred to me, yet he had dismissed my words with an almost frantic anger. I had read some studies on the personalities of assassins of national leaders. Leaving out the very few cases where political issues were at the root of an assassination, these murderers have generally been of one sort: ineffectual, repeatedly defeated in their every major undertaking, unable to give or receive love fully, and with deep misgivings concerning their worth; projecting their inadequacies upon their society, they blame it for their failures and attack it in the person of some highly visible leader, usually a man, and usually a man who is admired in his nation for his manliness.

Although I had sometimes considered this picture overly facile and somewhat simplistic, and even though Professor Moriarty's personality did not conform to this picture in every particular, still I wondered now if the idea underlying that psychological analysis might not apply quite well to him. Granted that during his early years he had been awarded great honours for his scientific work, still the fact was that he had abandoned his enormously promising academic career—no one knew why—to pursue a life of crime. Even in that life, however, he had been unsuccessful in the end, for Sherlock Holmes had at last managed first to disrupt and then to destroy his organization. Could the explanation, then, be so simple—that Professor Moriarty's evident *idée fixe* concerning the assassination of presidents and prime ministers was no different from the sick needs that drove Oswald and Princip? Even if that were the case, however, there was much about Professor Moriarty that set him apart from other political assassins and made him even more dangerous than they. An act such as Princip's might lead to the destruction of a civilisation, as Princip had brought about the downfall of European civilisation, but what Moriarty had in mind might well lead to the destruction of mankind itself. And there was this in addition: Those other men had satisfied their sick needs with a murder or two, but while one might think that Moriarty's underlying need might also be so satisfied, in fact his recent history and his current plans showed clearly that it was a repetitive need, and each killing would only increase his need for another. His self-concept had become centred upon his need to murder national leaders, and I thought it likely that his self-delusion that he was planning these assassinations only as a means to power would only make matters worse, for, unable to admit to himself his real motivation, he would use his failure to attain greater power as a reason to plan yet more assassinations. Each inevitable failure to achieve the objectives he claimed to be pursuing would justify the next murder; the frightening cycle might continue for as long as he lived and was free to act.

Thus the time passed in gloomy introspection and frightening glimpses of Moriarty's terrible cannon—a short time, but it seemed an eternity. Hour by hour, the moment that might see the world's destruction by nuclear fire drew nearer. The evening before the President was due to arrive in Salt Lake City, I was brought to see the cannon once again. Even though I could not understand the details of the men's work, I could sense from their manner and the carefully controlled and ordered busyness of their movements that they were reaching the end of their task. The clutter of parts that had covered the floor when I was first shown the cannon had now disappeared, presumably already incorporated in the diabolical mechanisms Moriarty had devised. The skylight had been opened, and the brilliant stars of the western United States showed clearly above us. It seemed remarkable to me that, even a century later, Moriarty could command the same fanatical loyalty he had commanded in the London of the last century, for these men were apparently quite willing to follow this madman to either power or damnation, even though his path might lead through the wreckage of their world.

As if to emphasize their devotion, a group of Moriarty's workers, while I watched numbly and helplessly, opened the case he had earlier pointed out to me, and, with great care and using an arrangement of pulleys and ropes, drew from it a large, pointed cylinder. Was this innocuous object, I wondered, one of those fearsome devices that had for so many years terrified the world? The care the men were taking and their nervous glances at the object told me that it was indeed Moriarty's atomic projectile.

Had I still entertained any doubts as to the identity of the object—which, now that it had been drawn fully out of the case, I could see was indeed shaped like a cannon shell—Professor Moriarty's words would quickly have dispelled them. I had not noticed his approach, and so I was startled when he spoke from just behind me. "There it is, Doctor," he said, triumph audible in every word, "the object on which ride my fortunes. Is it not beautiful?"

I turned to face him. "To you, to whom death and evil are beautiful, perhaps so. But to me, Professor, this monstrous object is no more than the culmination, the epitome, of the bestial ugliness that has always been Moriarty!"

A flush of anger momentarily tinged his pallid cheeks. He was having obvious difficulty keeping himself under control. His whole body quivered with tension and the reptilian side-to-side motion of his pale, high-domed face became even more pronounced. "Is it so, Doctor?" he hissed. He paced angrily away from me toward the cannon, then turned and came back. It was as though through this nervous activity he hoped to free himself of irksome energies flaring within.

My situation and that of the world seemed so hopeless that, curiously enough, I no longer felt any interest in Moriarty or his doings; I might have been expected to be filled with trepidation over the planned events of the next morning, but in fact I was filled only with apathy. I was sure of defeat; I was certain Moriarty had doomed the world. Feeling that way, how could I con-

[75]

cern myself with the details of Moriarty's proceedings, with his posturing insanity? I turned away from this figure who, as Armageddon approached, brought about by him, seemed perversely less frightening, and I stared blankly into the distance.

Suddenly my eye was caught by a strange device projecting partially out of the shadows—a curious mechanism, for it was embellished in a manner that made it stand out from the plain, functional devices that surrounded it and caused me to think that it belonged more to the nineteenth than the twentieth century. It was a glittering, metallic framework, a squat, ugly machine for all that some effort had been taken to make it appealing to the eye, a thing of brass, ebony, ivory, and translucent, glimmering quartz. One of its railings was bent; the whole thing seemed somehow askew, as if the wonderful device had suffered injury at unfriendly hands. I puzzled over it for only a moment, before suddenly realizing what the machine was: It was the Time Machine itself, the fabulous creation of Wells' friend, the remarkable instrument that, because it had given Moriarty access to our time, lay at the root of the world's present predicament. With a muttered exclamation, I stepped toward the Time Machine.

A grip like a vise fastened upon my arm, and I was swung about to find myself staring into the furious eyes of Professor Moriarty. "Stay away from that!" he shouted. "Only *I* may approach that machine." He released me and stepped back, and, with a visible struggle, he became calm again. He spoke again, in an abruptly different tone and with a bewildering change of topic. "I have changed my mind. The President arrives in Salt Lake City tomorrow, and it is clear now that we will not see Sherlock Holmes here. Earlier today, I saw to it that word would reach your friend, should he try to contact certain underworld sources for information as to your whereabouts, that you were being held at the Salt Lake City airport. I am anticipating that he will arrive there tomorrow, just in time for the President's arrival."

My state of despair was such that the import of his words took a moment to strike me, but when they did, my knees grew suddenly weak. "But he will be there when the bomb goes off!" I gasped.

"How touching," he sneered. "Such concern for your friend's welfare. Do not worry, Doctor. You will have ample opportunity to warn him. You see, I have decided not to keep you here against your will any longer; instead, I shall deliver you to the airport tomorrow morning, so that you can see the effects of my handiwork at first hand—for a fraction of second, at any rate."

"Will nothing persuade you to give up this insanity?" I asked hoarsely.

He glared down at me. "Nothing could have stopped me before, Doctor, and now your ill-advised choice of words makes it inevitable that my mind will not be changed." He gestured to my caretaker. "Sam, take him back to the storeroom and lock him in for the night."

Soon I was back in my prison room, with the hours of night ahead of me—to sleep if I could, or to ponder the next morning with its searing, atomic death for John Watson and Sherlock Holmes.

12

The Scheme Is Ended

WHEN THE MORNING came at last, it brought with it my captor and two of his lackeys, one of them the caretaker, Sam Hudwell. Moriarty walked with the vigor of a far younger man, his step firm but light, his back straight, his eyes bright. I might almost have thought that he had found some elixir of youth like that which had kept Sherlock Holmes and me young, had I not known that it was in fact the imminence of his triumph that had temporarily given him back his youth. Was this the way he had looked, I wondered, in those pleasant days when he had been a blooming glory of the English mathematical world—before he went astray, stooped to evil, and became old and stooped in its service?

His own thoughts might have been running along a parallel track, even though their tenor was surely less uncomplimentary to his criminal career, for he motioned his men to remain at the door, and he came forward, leaned over my cot, and said in a low voice so that the waiting men might not hear, "Doctor Watson, here is something I want you to know and to have time to think about before you die. You and Sherlock Holmes have stayed young long after you should both have been dead of old age. Had I asked you for the secret, you would of course have refused to give it to me. Instead, I have been able to determine the whereabouts of your hideaway in Sussex, and after all this is over, I intend to go there and search the place until I find your machine, or potion, or whatever it is you have used." He straightened and gazed over my head into a future only he could see. "If I am to dominate this world, I will want eternity in which to enjoy it!"

I stared up at him in amazement and horror. His object had been to make my final defeat even more bitter to me, and he had succeeded, but now he did not stop to gloat over it; perhaps the knowledge that I would be agonising over his words during my final hours was enough for him. "Dress yourself," he snapped. "You will soon be leaving for the airport." To the two men, he said, "Watch him closely. Let him prepare himself like a proper Victorian gentleman, as I am sure he would wish. He has a half hour before he must leave us." He grinned ferally at an irony that seemed to appeal to him. "Let him eat a quick breakfast in that time." He laughed and stalked triumphantly from the room.

For some moments, I sat in a daze, unmoving. Insanely, poetic lines read long ago recurred to me: ". . . Death eddies near—/ Not here the appointed End, not here!" After all those peaceful years of fending off death, of thinking it would never come to me until the sun itself grew cold, was it to catch up with me at last, this very morning?

My reverie was broken by Sam Hudwell, speaking in a milder tone than I might have expected from him. "Better get a move on, Mister. You've only got half an hour."

It seemed silly to bother about my clothes, my appearance, or even breakfast with death only hours away, but in fact I was hungry and I was still, just as Moriarty had said so mockingly, a Victorian at heart, and therefore I would go to meet my death looking like a gentleman and with at least an outward show of courage. I washed and dressed myself rapidly, brushed my hair and combed my moustache, and then I was brought some food, which I ate as quickly as I could. And then, before the half hour was up, I was brought forth by Sam Hudwell and my other guard to one of the doors leading from the factory, where Professor Moriarty was waiting to taunt me for the last time. "Only minutes, Doctor!" he cried as soon as he saw me. "Fewer than a hundred minutes stand between me and the attainment of my object." He drew me aside. "And poor Sam Hudwell, of course, will share your fate, but forebear trying to subvert him, for you will find his loyalty unshakeable."

I looked around quickly, thinking I might spy an escape route, but there was none, only Moriarty's lackeys, surrounding me and watching alertly. Nor could I catch any sight of Lily, even though I looked eagerly—while telling myself that I was a fool for doing so, and that I was behaving like a beaten dog who slinks back, broken in spirit, for another beating. But, then again, did it matter, here at the end?

I was escorted out of the building by Sam Hudwell and my other guard. The other man watched closely until I was safely in the back seat of a car parked outside the building and Sam Hudwell was seated behind the wheel. It was the sort of vehicle I have always imagined police cars to be, with a screen to guard the driver from the occupant of the back seat and with no way for the passenger in the rear to open the doors by himself. Despite the bizarre and fateful nature of my situation, I found myself peculiarly fascinated by the outside world. I had, of course, been trapped inside for some time; but in addition, I had never seen any of this area, for I had been brought here semiconscious from the farm near Kansas City. I gazed about in wonder at the barren mountainside, glowing a rich, deep brown in the early light, at the silent lake stretching out vast below us, its wavelets just catching the light, at the waking city just visible on the slopes of the great mountain range to the east. How different all this was from England: the dry air, the brown, dusty barrenness, the great mountains, the immense, open, uncrowded scale of the scene. It was a magnificent morning, with the sun standing high already above the mountain range behind Salt Lake City—but then I remembered that this might well be the last sunrise our civilisation would see.

Whatever my thoughts, I was given little time to indulge in them, for I was quickly pushed into the car, with the door locked behind me, and moments after, Sam Hudwell had the vehicle in motion on the winding road down the mountainside. At the bottom, this road gave access to a broad, four-lane highway. This carried us for some miles beside the Great Salt Lake, in places along a raised causeway at the very edge of the lake, so that the lake lapped at the road on one side while on the other lay stretches of stagnant salt water. Had my earlier mood of fascination with this remarkable scenery remained with me, I would perhaps have used the drive as an opportunity to escape reality, to blind myself to the imminence of destruction, by staring in delight and wonder at the surroundings throughout the entire time. However, that mood had suddenly vanished as we left the road that led down the mountainside and turned onto the main highway to Salt Lake City. I was electrified by a sudden awareness of just how short the time was. This was surely my last chance to foil Moriarty's awful scheme; if there was anything at all I could do, then now was my last chance to do it.

I searched the back of the car quickly, almost frantically, looking for some means of exiting. This was irrational, of course, for, even had I discovered some way of getting out of the speeding car, I would most likely have gained little for my trouble save severe injuries or quite possibly death; however, so disordered was my mental state at that moment, that the danger simply did not occur to me. There was no way I could escape, short of breaking one of the windows, and for a moment I considered trying to do just that. But I reconsidered and decided to try yet another appeal to Sam Hudwell. Fortunately, I was separated from him only by a mesh screen, rather than solid glass, so that I could at least speak to him.

"Sam," I said loudly. He ignored me and kept driving stolidly. "Sam!" I repeated much louder. Still no response. "Sam!" I fairly shouted.

Evidently, he decided that he might as well answer me, if only to keep me from bellowing at him for the rest of the trip. "Yeah?"

"Sam, I don't know what Professor Moriarty told you, but I want you to listen to me. You're supposed to take me to the airport and keep me there for some time—I would suppose until the President's plane has landed. However, there is something else I'm sure he has not told you." I went on to detail Moriarty's plan to fire an atomic shell at the airport, pointing out that he, Sam, would be vaporized along with me and the President. As I spoke, though, I could sense the wall of disbelief building between us with every word of mine, a wall more substantial and unbreachable than any physical one could be. And even as I spoke, I began to have difficulty believing my tale myself. I looked out the window at the lake, the mountains, and, in the distance, a barely visible arm of that remarkable salt desert, all so vast and solid, eternal, beyond Man and his petty scheming, that what I was saying seemed silly, inconsequential at the least,

[81]

or perhaps even a fantasy concocted by my unconscious mind. A homemade atomic bomb, a President's assassination, a time-travelling master criminal who intended to live forever and to rule the world, the end of civilisation . . . How could I expect this simple caretaker to believe any of it? I gave up at last in despair and because I had said all I had to say and had begun to repeat myself.

Sam Hudwell replied not a word, but I thought I heard him chuckle once. I slumped back in gloom, lacking even the spirit or interest to look out of the windows any more. What did it matter? What did anything matter now? Thus I remained in silence and hopelessness for the remaining minutes of the trip.

At last we reached the airport. Sam Hudwell drove up a ramp to a parking lot which gave access to an observation deck. Now that the final moment was almost here, I was eager to be done with it, and I waited impatiently for Sam to get out and unlock my door, for that could only be done from the outside. Instead, however, he leaned forward and put his hands to his face. I could not see what he was doing, but I wondered if he were unwell, and so distraught was I that I forgot my profession and the oaths by which I was bound and cursed him under my breath for delaying matters.

Finally, he straightened and bounded from the car as if, far from being ill, he were as eager as I. I noticed that he had left behind his cap, without which I had never yet seen him, but he moved so fast that I could see little of him as he climbed from the car. He leaned against my door, so that little was visible through the glass but his stomach, and I felt a quiver of fear. Was this to be murder? Was he concealing a weapon? But in that case, why bother bringing me here? All of this flashed through my mind in the merest fraction of a second, before I heard the click of the door. I sighed with resignation, pushed the door open, and stepped out wearily to face the guardian of my fate.

"Good morning, Doctor," said Sam Hudwell, speaking with a voice cool and sardonic that was not his own but that I knew well.

"Holmes!"

"None other." His face, his manner, his stance, his voice, his accent—all were Holmes. During those few moments in the front seat before leaving the car, he had removed much more than his cap, and Sam Hudwell had vanished as if he had never been—as indeed, in truth, he had not really existed. "Really, Watson," he went on, affecting a lazy drawl, "I am more than a little disappointed in you. I had thought that the initials of my assumed name and your familiarity with my methods and habits of disguise would have supplied you with all the clues you'd need to identify me."

"Damn it all, man, stop blathering!" I snapped, surprising myself as much as him. "You can be as condescending as you wish afterwards, but for now, we must get away from here. Get back in, quickly."

He masked the offended look that had flashed across his face. Reaching down, he grasped my arm and pulled firmly so that I must step away from the automobile. "Come along, Watson," he said briskly. "We have nothing to fear, as you shall see for yourself soon enough." He stepped off toward the observation deck, stretching his long legs and striding along, and I scurried along after, trying to keep up with the world's greatest consulting detective—as it sometimes seemed I had been doing forever.

When we reached a certain point on the observation deck, overlooking a large, open cement area on which were marked curious short lines and arcs, and on which a crowd of people was already gathered before a stand bearing a multitude of microphones, Holmes said in a satisfied tone, "Ah! This should be just right."

No sooner had we stopped at the railing than a trio of anonymous-faced young men, all wearing identical suits, approached and looked us over carefully before moving on. "Holmes, who are they?" I whispered nervously.

"Clones," he murmured. "Guardian variety. So much has lost its individuality since the days of our youth, my friend. Now," he went on, still speaking quietly, "in the minutes that remain before the President lands and Moriarty fires his cannon, I will anticipate some of your questions.

"I'm afraid I was obliged to mislead you in Chicago. I arranged privately with Miss Cantrell that she give the appearance of following Moriarty's orders while she was in fact following my own. Remember that Moriarty had already told Lily of the old house outside Kansas City and even of the installation outside Salt Lake City before the call which she received . . . er, in your presence. The latter telephone call was intended both to mask her seeming duplicity and to serve as a signal to her that she was to bring you to Kansas City. Well before that, she had told me privately of the abandoned factory we left this morning, so that I was able to go there, calling myself Sam Hudwell, with what results you are now partially aware. In the meantime, you were obeying my command that you spend your time in the closest possible proximity to Lily Cantrell with admirable dedication and industry. Knowing your nature, I had little doubt that you would behave as you did—going after Professor Moriarty by yourself and consequently getting yourself captured."

"So I had no worthwhile part to play!" I said angrily.

"But you did, Watson. Your capture, quite in accordance with Moriarty's plans, kept him from suspecting that Lily had betrayed him to me. Convinced as he was that Sherlock Holmes was elsewhere, following a false trail, Moriarty never imagined that Sam Hudwell was anything other than what he represented himself to be. That was just the situation I wanted."

"And Lily was not following *his* orders when she pretended to fall in love with me," I said bitterly. "She was following *yours.*"

"Exactly. However, I am convinced she was not pretending."

"Since you insist on staying here until we're both killed by Moriarty's bomb, I suppose it is all quite academic."

"Hmm," he said noncommittally. "Ah, there, look." He pointed to an aeroplane taxiing along a runway toward the open place below us. "The final act is about to begin." Before I could say anything, he added quickly, "Contain yourself, Watson. One of your questions, at least, will soon answer itself." Then he turned his attention back to the approaching aeroplane with an air that told me quite plainly that he wished to speak no more.

As the aircraft drew near, there was a great stirring among the swelling crowd on the ground below us, as the reporters jockeyed for the most advantageous positions and the local dignitaries and politicians whose importance had earned them positions on the stand which the President would shortly mount adjusted their ties and smoothed their hair. The scene was drenched in bright sunlight, and even from a distance I could sense the air of expectancy and eagerness.

This was the latest in a series of passenger jets operated by the United States Air Force and devoted fully to Presidential service, and as such it bore painted upon its tail assembly the traditional large numeral *1*. It was a lovely machine, one of the very few supersonic passenger planes produced during America's recent, belated, and ill-fated attempt to enter the supersonic passenger jet market. A few of the craft had been produced by the nation's largest aeroplane manufacturer before the project had been abandoned for the second, and apparently last, time, and this particular craft had been given to the White House for Presidential use. Its beauty was inevitably derivative—the drooping nose and gracefully curved delta wing so reminiscent of the Concorde II in which Holmes and I had crossed the Atlantic—but nonetheless its clean and lovely lines caught my eye and fired my imagination: It seemed trapped down here on the ground, a wondrous metal bird obeying its human masters but yearning silently for the heavens.

The aircraft rolled slowly to the appointed spot near the microphones and stopped. A few minutes passed while a staircase mounted on a small vehicle was driven up and the door of the passenger cabin was opened; the crowd craned their necks eagerly. Involuntarily, I turned and looked to the west, the direction from which would come our destruction. The mountains of the desert were vague with distance, and I could not pick out the one on which Moriarty's headquarters were located. Holmes glanced at me and with a muttered exclamation leaped forward and clapped his hand over my eyes. "Hold still!" he ordered. "Keep your eyes closed." After such a stretch of years, the habit of unquestioning obedience to his commands was so ingrained, that I stood motionless, eyes squeezed shut beneath his hand.

Suddenly there was a flash of light so intense that I could see it faintly even through Holmes' hand and my own eyelids. I pushed his hand away and opened my eyes to an astonishing sight. Out in the desert a great column of dust was rising. As it rose, the top spread out like an umbrella, but at the edges it curled under until it met the stalk and then curled further under until it was rising with the stalk. I knew it immediately, of course: It was the dreaded mushroom cloud of a nuclear explosion. "Great heavens!" I shouted. "The shell didn't reach us!"

Holmes, however, was leaning over the balcony with a look of fascination. "Observe the ant heap," he commented, directing my attention to the scene below us. There was utter confusion down there. The cabin door of Air Force One had been slammed shut and the great aircraft was already beginning to move, ready to whisk the President away from this startling and mysterious danger. The reporters had scattered in all directions, seeking shelter. The local dignitaries had abandoned their dignity and had joined them. They had all been sheltered by the airport terminal buildings from direct viewing of the initial glare, but they had seen it reflected from the building tops, and they had soon been able to see and recognise the top of the mushroom cloud. Perhaps Holmes had not chosen the most apt simile in likening them to ants, but the difference in their behaviour after the blast as opposed to before was certainly worthy of remark.

I was not, however, inclined to an attitude of indifferent or perhaps cynical superiority, as was Holmes. It struck me as terrible that, had the people below us not been shielded from the nuclear glare, then many of them, not forewarned as I had been, would have been blinded, and that there must have been many unfortunate souls in the vicinity of Salt Lake City who had by chance been looking in the direction of the blast at the instant of the explosion and had thus been blinded, perhaps for life. It was at least some small comfort to me to recall Professor Moriarty's words concerning the bomb's "cleanness," for that implied that, if the shell had fallen far enough out in the desert, and if the winds were not unfavourable, then the city would be spared serious harm from radioactive fallout.

At last, Sherlock Holmes looked to the west at the rising, rolling cloud and responded to my words. "Not only did the professor's shell not reach us," he explained coolly, "in fact it did not even leave his cannon. I took the opportunity, during my recent employment in that factory, of making certain modifications to

Professor Moriarty's timing device." He stood silently for a moment, then added, "Instead of vanity, for him all is vapour."

"Lily," I groaned. "She is gone, too."

"You *still* have no faith in me," he said drily. "You know my views on women and marriage, but if you *will* persist in all of that, then turn yourself around and look."

I turned about and beheld Lily herself, gazing at me with a look full both of love and uncertainty. "He told me to come here early this morning and wait, John," she said hesitantly. "He told me what he planned to do to the timer. Now that you know I didn't really betray you—"

"Say no more!" I interrupted, clasping her to me. "From now on, we will never be parted, absolutely never. We must dash back to Sussex and seal the matter with a celebratory bottle of wine." She looked quite bewildered, but I ignored that and turned to Sherlock Holmes. "You have no objections, I presume?"

"None," he said in a tone of resignation, but he wore a faint smile that could have been one either of affection or of condescending amusement.

"Then all is perfect!" I exulted. "We can concentrate at last on our own happiness, for we have finally seen the last of Professor Moriarty!"

Holmes stared at the distant, still-rising mushroom cloud, Moriarty's spectacular and ominous funeral pyre, for a few moments. "I wonder," he muttered.

Interlude

AT THAT most terrible instant, Moriarty had just managed to turn on the crippled Time Machine. For the first time since his departure from the Prime Minister's office, when the machine had suffered such major damage, power flowed through the device and crackled from its brass fittings. As the countdown droned toward zero behind him, Moriarty felt the first stirrings of temporal shift as the time field expanded outward and swept over him, and he exulted.

From behind him, expanding far more rapidly than the time field, came the Hell-blast of heat, pressure, and charged particles as the fission device blew up within the cannon. He had not even time to realise that Holmes had defeated him after all, no time even to feel pain as the plasma enveloped his body. The Time Machine's temporal field and the atomic bomb's blast crossed each other precisely where Moriarty stood, and Professor Moriarty, the Time Machine, the cannon, his men, the factory, and most of the mountain vanished together.

13

Shocking Events in the Orient

WHEN I BEGAN this narrative, I mentioned that sixty-five years had passed since my last previous recording of the exploits of Mr. Sherlock Holmes. That hiatus ended in 1992, when I spent a relaxed and delightful autumn in Sussex in the company of my new wife and my very old friend, writing down the events of the preceding year. These formed the episode you have just read, ending with my reunion with Lily at the Salt Lake City airport.

Having finished that narrative, I looked forward to having it published, if Holmes would agree to the exposing of his longevity secret before all the world. After that, I would be able to spend a peaceful eternity with my beloved Lily in our unchanging little refuge. Sherlock Holmes, however, for reasons he did not make clear, refused to permit the publishing of the story, saying only that I should wait, for he believed it to be as yet incomplete. As a result, my manuscript was to languish for many a decade in a desk drawer, while in the larger world beyond the confines of the farm the reading public was inundated by a seemingly endless stream of Sherlock Holmes pastiches poured forth by my many would-be literary successors. I could scarcely have imagined that Holmes was right in his surmise and that 175 years would pass before I could write the last chapter. Now at last I can present it to a public to whom, alas, written entertainment is largely an historical curiosity. (Indeed, am I not, myself, little more?)

Lily brought some changes to our farm that proved to be beneficial. A product of late-twentieth-century America, she was far from content with the Hewisham *Daily Mirror* for her news and Holmes' extensive library of bee books and crime notebooks for her entertainment. She even spurned my collection of historical romances, authored by our one-time neighbor—dead, alas, these sixty-odd years. Thus it was that our old farmhouse sprouted the bizarre headdress of a television antenna and our library was nightly invaded by cowboys, murderers, detectives, betrayed women, comedians, and calm BBC news announcers. The world was very much with us, and I for one rather enjoyed it. And I suspected that Holmes, despite his scowls, enjoyed it, too.

Thus it came about on a muggy midsummer day early in the new century that all four of us were gathered before the television screen watching a special broadcast of the latest episode in the odyssey of Xian Phitsanulok. And thus it was, too, that Holmes saw something of which he would have known nothing had he been limited to the Hewisham *Daily Mirror* for his information.

Phitsanulok was, of course, the great Southeast Asian leader who seemed likely to unite the desperate peoples of that sad region in peace, prosperity, and democracy. This mystery man had emerged from the peasantry along the Thai-Cambodian frontier to claim the leadership of all of Southeast Asia. Visionary, charismatic, a man of immense physical and spiritual presence, he swayed crowds with ease, and with equal ease swept aside archaic social and political systems and ancient feuds and hatreds. With all the power that gave him over his tens of millions of followers, he was nonetheless a firm believer in constitutional democratic government, and the world looked on in fascinated approval as that long-suffering region moved energetically forward toward the glowing future promised by Xian Phitsanulok. But unknown to him, the dark forces Phitsanulok had fought all his adult life were preparing to reassert their immemorial right to rule Asia.

Laos had just agreed to join Phitsanulok's Pan-Asian Union, and the great man himself had come to Vientiane to accept what I can only call the Laotian government's submission. The camera panned across the group of senior ministers waiting nervously for the advent of the man who had been called the Asian Bolívar and the Asian Garibaldi. As the short, rotund, fat-cheeked liberator (a most unheroic figure, to be sure!) pushed his grinning way through the cheering, weeping throngs jamming the streets of Vientiane, a knot of men forced their way until they stood immediately before him. In unison, they raised their right hands, disclosing pistols, and fired again and again.

The crowd tore them limb from limb, of course, but Phitsanulok was dead by the time his body reached the ground. In the pandemonium, Phitsanulok's corpse, mistaken for some moments for that of one of his assailants, was unfortunately dismembered as well. Within minutes, though, the police, demonstrating that they had not lost the skills learned during more than a generation of Communist rule, were able to quell the crowd and retrieve the several pieces of the liberator's body.

This whole ghastly episode had in fact taken place earlier in the day. Having heard the news earlier, we were now watching the grisly scene being reenacted for us in full color and three dimensions on an evening news broadcast. During this replay of the final moments of Phitsanulok's life, which the BBC was obligingly presenting in slow motion, Lily averted her eyes, while I muttered some sententious words on the sad loss to the world of such a man and the probable consequences of his death. Sherlock Holmes, however, sat with his gaze fixed on the screen in what I could only consider an unhealthy fascination, his forehead wrinkled in a slight frown. Outré as the crime undoubtedly was, I considered, there was surely no element of mystery about it to pique his interest.

He leaped to his feet suddenly with an exclamation and stood staring even more intently at the screen. To my repeated questions, he responded only with an impatient wave of his hand, signalling me to silence. When the horror had finally run its course and the screen was filled with the fashionably handsome face of an English announcer (the previous year, they had all been ruggedly ugly) explaining to us what we had just seen, Holmes broke at last from his pose of extreme concentration and stepped to the television set to enter a command. This was a new model, capable of storing roughly 10,000 hours of viewing in its nonvolatile solid-state memory, and Holmes had taken to recording news broadcasts in it as a virtual replacement for his eternal notebooks filled with newspaper clippings.

He ran through the entire assassination again very slowly. "Come, Holmes," I protested, "surely this is unnecessary. Consider Lily's feelings, even if you persist in ignoring mine." I would have added something about the sensibilities of our house-keeper, but that I had noticed that Mrs. Hudson's interest had been diverted by the discovery of some fresh dust on the mantelpiece.

But Holmes' attention was fully occupied by the replay of the murder. "There!" he exclaimed triumphantly. "It has happened, at last." Perhaps, I speculated, this meant he had been anticipating the assassination of Xian Phitsanulok and was now, in his curiously unemotional way, celebrating the fulfillment of his prediction. Holmes reset the television and gestured to me. "Watson, come here. Look at this."

Reluctantly, I came forward to look. Before me, Xian Phitsanulok drifted again to the ground, blood spreading across his shirt front and covering his face. "Holmes, why am I forced to watch this again?"

"Not Phitsanulok," he said impatiently. "Look at the front of the crowd, just behind the assassins." His long, bony forefinger tapped the screen. "Watch that spot."

And then I, too, saw it. A human figure faded into existence for a fraction of a second, and then faded away again. "Good heavens," I whispered, "what was it? A ghost?"

Holmes grunted. "In a manner of speaking, perhaps. Wait a moment." He manipulated the console, found the instant he wanted, and froze it on the screen. "Look again, Watson."

On the screen, Phitsanulok hung suspended in midair, his grin become a grimace. But this time I had no attention to spare for the martyred liberator. Instead I stared astonished at the phantom figure now frozen for my inspection. It was slightly blurred, as if a fault in the camera's lens had caused only that spot to be out of focus in contrast to the sharply defined figures in the rest of the scene. Nonetheless, I could make out the bewildered expression on the pale face, and I could see that the man was tall and thin, with hunched shoulders, and a head that protruded forward on his slender neck. A ghost, yes! *My God*, I wondered, *will he never die!* "How can it be?" I asked.

Before Holmes could reply to my question, I heard a scream of terror from behind me and a thump, and I spun around to see

Lily senseless on the floor. She had stepped forward herself, drawn at last by our manner despite her horror at the murder held static on the screen, and she too had instantly recognised the phantom figure.

Holmes helped Mrs. Hudson and me get Lily into our bedroom. As I was drawing the covers over her, she awoke and, flinging her arms about me, buried her face against my chest and burst into frantic sobs.

Holmes averted his face, to give us something like privacy, and said thoughtfully, "As for how it can be, or what it means, I have only suspicions, and no explanations as yet. An interesting speculation occurred to me many years ago, and the time has come to investigate the idea further. I must go to London immediately." So saying, he turned and strode from the room as though he meant to set out for the metropolis on the instant on foot.

It was two days before he returned. Lily had recovered quickly, and I had spent the time giving her all my attention and trying to keep her cheerful. She was oppressed, she said, by a conviction that some disaster for the two of us was destined to flow from the apparition we had seen. And for my part, I found it increasingly difficult to recapture the sense of isolation and timelessness I had enjoyed on the farm for all those decades before Lily. Perhaps, I speculated, it was our present electronic contact with the outside world—our being plugged in, as it were, to the vast net of etheric vibrations linking the cities and nations of the world—that was responsible for making that world a constant and sometimes jarring presence in the very rooms of the farmhouse.

Holmes returned unannounced, as had so often been his custom a hundred years earlier. I entered the library one afternoon to find him fiddling with the television. "What," I said, "no sooner home than already seeking mindless entertainment?"

The face he turned to me, however, was so pale and drawn that my flippancy died instantly. "Watson," he began, "I fear we are faced with— No, never mind." He waved his hand. "You shall see for yourself." I saw now that he held a small, coppery disk.

"I was able to borrow this from the BBC archives through My-croft's intervention. It's a direct rerecording of the original videotape, with not even the smallest fraction of a second lost. I was most particular about that. There, now." He had inserted the disk in the slot in the console designed for that purpose and started it playing. "In a moment, it will be stored in our set's memory." His voice dropped to a low murmur. "And how many more will there be, I wonder?"

His manner and his expression, no less than his enigmatic words, filled me with foreboding. Lily had joined us silently in the meanwhile, and I drew her close to my side, my arm about her waist, in an instinctive reaching out for the comfort of phys-ical contact, and perhaps also because her fear of the last two days had infected me with a terror that something awful was fated to come between us.

A soft beeping from the console announced that all was ready, and as Holmes played his fingers over the buttons, a scene from a nightmare sprang to life on the screen. Two men, virtual sil-houettes against the brilliant background, emerged from the side of a large vehicle on the right of the screen and threw something toward the left. They stepped back and then they, or perhaps others, reemerged and ran across the open space, firing rifles as they went. All was blurred, vague, yet horrifying—for I knew all too well what this historic sequence was. The camera tilted cra-zily upward, but we were not to be spared seeing the murder of a great Near Eastern leader. The entire scene was replayed, this time from another angle. Obviously there had been taping of the event by cameramen other than those whose work had become part of the public historical record. From this view, we saw the men throw their grenades at the reviewing stand and then rush forward toward the stand, gliding balletically in the slow-motion reenactment. They reached the stand, and then they stood there, firing steadily and at will into the panic-stricken crowd of gov-ernment officials and foreign guests. Chairs flew in all direc-tions. While the three of us watched in horror, as though it were all happening at that moment, the assassins, completely unop-posed, shifted their positions, moving along the perimeter of the stand to finish their bloody work. And then I saw it, what I had been waiting for unconsciously since Sherlock Holmes had started the recording playing on our screen.

For a fraction of a second, a figure appeared at the far end of the low barrier surrounding the reviewing stand. He stood at the barrier, head projecting forward as he stared at the grisly scene, drinking in the death of a great man. The bewilderment his pale face had worn during the assassination of Phitsanulok gave way even as I watched to dawning understanding, to growing delight, to vampirish eagerness.

Lily gripped my hand fiercely. This time, she didn't faint, but I almost wished to do so myself—to escape into unconsciousness in the hope that I could then awake to find this waking nightmare over.

The figure on the screen vanished again, and all three of us released the breaths we had been holding. "How can it be?" I asked again.

Holmes shrugged and began to pace in his long-legged way about the room in a display of nervous energy. "How am I to say? Time is a phenomenon little understood even by modern men of science. I spent part of yesterday in Cambridge with Hawking. I took him into my confidence, but even he could only hazard a guess. Perhaps it was some bizarre side effect of the nuclear explosion, mediated conceivably by the very presence of the Time Machine. Or perhaps the arch-devil had even managed to put the machine in working order again, and what we have seen was the result of an interaction between the blast and the field produced by the Time Machine."

"But, Holmes," I protested, "surely it is equally likely that what we have seen on our television is nothing more than the results of Moriarty's early experiments with the Time Machine!"

"Oh, it must be that," Lily said in a relieved tone. "That's all it was."

"Perhaps. However, there is another factor to be considered. It might be coincidence, but I very much doubt it, and Hawking is inclined to agree with me. If you will check the dates and times carefully, as I have of course already done, you will discover that the time interval from the appearance of the phantom during the assassination of Anwar Sadat in Egypt to the explosion of the fission device in the Utah desert is precisely equal to that from the explosion to the murder of Xian Phitsanulok in Laos two days ago. To me, this suggests a definite connexion—and something ominous."

What he could mean was quite unclear to me. "Then you have a theory to explain this. Tell me, what is it?"

Holmes shook his head. "No, no, Watson. The facts are inadequate as yet, and therefore, as I have had to explain to you too often in the past, any hypothesis would be quite premature. It appears I will have to do a considerable amount of historical research to gather those facts."

I thought I detected in his hooded eyes a gleam of anticipation.

Interlude

THE SEARING HEAT and terrible light blinked out the instant they had begun, remaining but the faintest memory. For that instant, though, compression had hit him an agonising blow all over his body, and a flood of high-energy particles had buried themselves in the skin and flesh and muscles of his back. The factory and the Time Machine and the other surroundings of the mountainside in Utah all vanished.

He became aware of vast noise and heat and damp, and of the presence of a crowd pressing around him. Bewildered, he watched a short, chubby Oriental, grinning hugely, walk into a rain of bullets that snuffed out his life. This transient observer of the tragedy seemed to be living for long, timeless moments, as if time moved more slowly for him than for the assassinated states-man and the Laotian crowd, so that the scene was almost static, so nearly devoid of motion that it took forever for the murder to run its course. The awareness of a fierce burning pain in his back grew slowly, ignored in his confusion.

The blow of compression hit him again, along with a sudden increase of pain, and again the scene changed abruptly. Again, there were heat and noise. He found himself standing before a shoulder-high barricade. Beyond the barricade, chairs and bodies tumbled in chaos, while near him scattered assassins poured bullets over the barricade. Time raced for him but not for them.

By the time the compression and the flare of pain came again to wrench him from the place, his brilliant mind had already deduced the nature of his state. He had already begun—either despite the pain or because of it—to anticipate his next visit hungrily.

14

Sherlock Holmes Hypothesises

WHERE ANOTHER MAN might have gone to one of the great libraries in London or one of the Universities to do his research, Sherlock Holmes valued his continued privacy too much: He had the mountain of books delivered to him. Day after day, packages and boxes of books and videotape arrived at the farm. What had always seemed a spacious house rapidly grew cramped, and Mrs. Hudson was in despair.

In vain I remonstrated with him that we could subscribe to one of the many electronic information services then already available. Technology, I pointed out, had made all of the old methods of research obsolete. Through our television set and a small computer attachment, available in any large town for a negligible sum, he could have available at his fingertips all the great libraries and newspapers of the world. He was adamantly against the idea.

"Have you never felt, Watson, as you held a book in your hand, how it transmitted ideas and intellectual stimulation to you through the medium of touch? You read a well-researched treatise, you pause to mull over what you have read, and inspiration comes to you through your very hands!"

"Travelling through your arms to your brain, no doubt. That's all very well, Holmes, but—"

"No, Watson. I am firm in this. I must have something I can touch, not words on a screen."

Observing his growing happiness over the next few days, I came to understand more clearly the deeper reasons for his attitude. For ten years now, ever since the events subsequent to the assassination of Mrs. Chalmers, he had buried himself on the farm, by his standards sunk in idleness. Once, long ago, he had told me that his mind, when not occupied with a task worthy of its strength and training, was like a powerful engine running at high speed with no load attached, racing and tearing itself apart. Clearly, he had at last a crime or crimes sufficiently outré to excite his interest, the investigation of which would require the sort of amassing and cross-correlating of facts and propounding of complex hypotheses in which he delighted. This alone was one reason for his growing cheerfulness. Another, though, was that this recapturing of past industry was only complete in his mind when the methods used to do the work were the old ones. One could scarcely imagine Sherlock Holmes doing his researches seated before a video display terminal, using statistical methods to correlate his data and storing his hypotheses on disk!

And yet in time he did adopt modern methods. Perhaps in the end it was winter that won him over. Many weeks passed in which he strolled happily over the downs or sat in a chair outside the house, producing vast clouds of tobacco smoke and poring through one of the many books he had ordered, but little that I could see came of all of this in the way of conclusions. Winter set in late in 2001, but it bade fair to be a hard, cold one; Holmes' days of strolling around the countryside seemed likely to be limited.

Finally a new collection of boxes arrived, and Holmes spent some hours alone, locked in the library, from whence issued many loud thumps and curses. When I was at last able to enter, later that evening, I found him seated before a small, glowing screen taped to the wall, typing industriously on a lightweight keyboard held in his lap.

"Well, well," I said heartily, "so the twentieth century has at last invaded the work of the consulting detective!"

For a moment, he seemed determined to ignore me. Then he turned from his terminal and swung around to glare at me. "The subject is closed, Watson," he snapped. He wagged a long, bony forefinger in my face. "If you insist on discussing it, I will be obliged to ask you to leave the farm!" Only then did I remind myself that he had never taken well to sarcasm. Nonetheless, his anger and his words both astonished me, and I stared at him dumbly, mouth agape. An awkward silence ensued for some moments, which Holmes at last broke. "Forgive me, Watson," he said gently. "What I have uncovered has unnerved me. Give me a week more, and then I will tell both you and Lily of my findings, such as they are."

For me, that week dragged, but Lily spent the time happily tending the bees. Indeed, this was a duty she had early taken over from Holmes, displaying an enthusiasm for the task that surprised me and stood in opportune contrast to Sherlock Holmes' own declining interest in the insects. As long as the supply of rejuvenating mead was steady and abundant, Holmes was content to let her exercise her newfound delight in apiculture. For her part, Lily told me often that a good part of her happiness with this duty was due to the knowledge that she was thus ensuring that the two of us would have a virtual eternity of youthful joy together. "Until the sun goes nova," as she put it—an image which struck me as more frightening than poetic. Her efforts had assumed even more importance in the light of my continued failure, despite decades of analysis and testing, to isolate from our honey wine the substance responsible for its remarkable powers.

When, a week later, Lily and I joined Holmes in the library at his request, we found him pacing nervously about the room. A fire crackled cheerfully in the grate. A storm had swept in from the Channel; the wind whistled around the house and roared across the top of the chimney, and now and again hail rattled against the window. Ever since her arrival at the farm, Lily had pressed for the installation of central heating, and she had even managed to bring Mrs. Hudson over to her side. Holmes and I had, however, stood firm against any such innovation. And indeed, I thought now, what could be finer than such weather, such a room, such a fire, and in the middle of all an animated Sherlock Holmes expounding his theory to explain away the latest wave of ghastly crimes? It brought back to me the best of the old days.

"You both know," Holmes began, "that for some months past I have been absorbed in historical research. You probably have not guessed of what that research consisted. Briefly, I have been studying assassinations." He paused to observe our reactions.

My own was bewilderment. Lily said, "Just because of what we saw on TV? Come on, that doesn't make any sense!" She would have said more, but Holmes cut in.

"My dear Lily, surely I need hardly remind you, of all people, who that was we saw so fleetingly on our screen?"

Lily paled and remained silent. I said, "So you have an explanation, then?"

He shook his head. "I have the essentials of a pattern, and an hypothesis, but it may take a decade or even a century more to either prove or disprove it." He paused and stared unseeing into the writhing flames, then spoke again. "Certain things struck me about the two assassinations at which the phantom figure appeared. One, of course, was the time span. As I have already pointed out to you, the interval from the assassination of Anwar Sadat to the atomic explosion in Utah was precisely the same as that from the explosion to the recent murder of Xian Phitsanulok. By itself, that would have seemed little more than a curious coincidence, but surely of no significance. But now consider the expression on the phantom's face on those two occasions. I think you both noticed how bewildered he seemed to be during Phitsanulok's assassination, and then how much more enlightened, even eager, during Sadat's. That gives us an obvious progression. It forces us to assume that Professor Moriarty somehow escaped death in Utah, escaped by travelling forward ten years in time, to appear for an instant at the moment of Phitsanulok's murder, and then backward precisely that amount to the murder of Sadat."

"An oscillation," I exclaimed. "Rather like a spring, or perhaps a pendulum."

"But *they* get smaller each time," Lily objected.

"Precisely," Holmes said. "Obviously, different natural laws than the conservation of energy are at work here, although it also is possible that Moriarty is still drawing energy in some way from the atomic explosion."

These bizarre concepts, coming one upon the other so rapidly, made my brain reel. I groped for a chair and fell heavily into it. "My God!"

Holmes smiled slightly. "We may safely leave Him out of it.

The existence of a Moriarty I take to be conclusive evidence of the nonexistence of a God. But to continue. You will recall, Watson, that ten years ago, when you were Moriarty's captive, you theorized about his *idée fixe*—his need to plot and carry out the assassinations of powerful leaders. I would add to that another element: His preferred target was a leader who seemed likely to usher in a new and better age for his people. Or hers," he added sombrely, obviously remembering Mrs. Chalmers. "And possibly for the world, as well."

"But Holmes," I said in exasperation, "where is all this leading?"

Lily had apparently understood better than I. "Like Sadat and Phitsanulok."

Holmes nodded. "How can we forget the ruinous war that devastated the Near East in the aftermath of Sadat's death? And the results for Asia of Phitsanulok's assassination could well be far worse."

"Surely you aren't saying that Moriarty somehow planned those assassinations!" I protested.

"No, no." His thin cheeks glowing and his eyes shining, Holmes paced excitedly about the room, fairly bounding from the floor. "What I *do* say is this. You, Watson, conceived of Moriarty's fixed idea as a ruling passion, governing his behaviour, causing him to order his whole life, all his schemes, about his desire to commit a certain type of murder. Let us now carry that a step further and conceive of this monomania, this fixation, as exerting a real force, temporally if not spatially. Careering through time as a result of the interaction of the nuclear explosion and the operation of the Time Machine—careering forward, Watson—Moriarty passes the point in time where Phitsanulok dies. His fixation *draws him to the spot!* And then this very eruption into the world of normal time reflects the temporal energies stored in him, so to speak, and he is flung back again, into the past—"

"Drawn to Sadat's assassination by the same fascination," I interrupted. "In which case, Holmes, the equality of time intervals you had noticed *is* merely a coincidence after all."

"Quite possibly. And that remarkable coincidence has perhaps resulted in his oscillating back and forth forever between those two points."

"The poor man!" Lily said impulsively.

"Indeed. It is a fate one would not wish even on such a fiend as Professor Moriarty! There is, however, another possibility, which I find far more distressing. Let us suppose that the correspondence of time intervals is not entirely a coincidence. Suppose that the coincidence lay rather in the intervals being only *approximately* equal—that is, in the absence of Moriarty. Surely that is the most one could anticipate in the case of two unrelated historical events, both of which required long planning by the murderers. In that case, one can easily believe that the precise timing of Sadat's assassination was *forced* by the temporal nearness of Moriarty, rebounding from the time of Phitsanulok's murder."

"What an astonishing chain of supposition!" I said. "And quite metaphysical, too. This scarcely sounds like the man who so often cautioned me against hypothesising too readily or too extravagantly."

Holmes cast on me a sour look. "I am also the man who has often had to remind you that once you have eliminated the impossible, whatever remains, *however improbable*, must be the truth." Suddenly he laughed. "In fact, however, neither precept applies in this case, since I have other data of which you are unaware. Consider, for instance, Mercader Ramon."

"What?" I said, and simultaneously Lily said, "Who?"

"The assassin of Leon Trotsky. Apprehended moments after the crime, he told his captors, 'It's them. A man. I don't know who he is. He made me do it.' He also said, 'They are keeping my mother a prisoner.' That, however, proved to be untrue. Eight years later, the saintly Gandhi was murdered. I have uncovered a contemporary police document in which a witness was quoted as having watched a tall, slender Englishman accompanying the assassin toward the place where the Mahatma was killed. For obvious political reasons, the report was suppressed at the time.

"Consider the many great leaders of history, struck down before their best work could be consummated. About how many of those deaths does mystery not yet linger! Mrs. Chalmers, of course, in 1991. Xian Phitsanulok in 2001. Anwar Sadat in 1981. Martin Luther King in 1968. John Kennedy in 1963. King Abdullah of Jordan in 1951. Gandhi in 1948 and Trotsky in 1940. Pyotr Stolypin, the great reformist Russian premier, in 1911. And one of our own again, Prime Minister Spencer Perceval, murdered in the very lobby of the House of Commons by John Bellingham in 1812."

I shook my head. "My dear Holmes, if death by assassination, eminence of the victim, and a degree of mystery are to be the touchstones, then surely almost any such murder qualifies. Abraham Lincoln, certainly, or Hendrik Verwoerd, or Robert Kennedy, or William of Orange, or—or—Chancellor Dolfuss. Or . . ." I racked my brains frantically.

"Enough, Watson." He held up his hand. "You have adequately demonstrated that steel-trap memory which is the delight and amazement of all your friends."

Abashed, I subsided. Lily, however, sprang to my defence with eyes blazing. "That's enough of that! Old friend or not—"

Holmes retreated in confusion. "Quite right, quite right," he said hastily. "You defend your man. Quite right. Watson, please forgive me."

I waved a magnanimous hand. Lily quieted and Holmes continued.

"The cases I mentioned are only those concerning which my data have a bearing on our investigation. Ramon, for instance. Questioned further, he described his mystery man as English, tall and slender, with a pale face and a high, bulging forehead and deeply sunken eyes. He insisted he had felt as if hypnotized by the Englishman's strange way of oscillating his head slightly from side to side."

"Jesus!" Lily said. I was unable to speak.

"Professor Moriarty, of course," Holmes nodded. "The description of the Englishman seen accompanying Gandhi's killer is again that of our old enemy. As for the other assassinations, you may read the notes I have made on them. However, here is something you will find of interest." He stepped across to the small table he had set up to hold his papers in this investigation, now quite covered with books, photographs, and scraps of paper.

He dug around in the unruly pile for a few seconds, and then finally withdrew something that he passed to us.

It was a still, an extracted moment, from a famous segment of film. The ghastly moment was frozen for us. In the background, the blurred crowd, still unaware that anything untoward has happened. In the foreground, the even more blurred limousine, the vertical white bar of a streetlamp incongruously interposed. But unfortunately it is not enough to hide the unfocussed image of the President jerking forward, the top of his head exploding. A fog of particles hovers above him. In a few moments, it will rain down upon the watching crowd, an awful rain of blood and bone and flesh and brain. Moments more, and the cavalcade will roar away at high speed, headed for a major Dallas hospital. But it will be far, far too late.

My stomach knotted as I stared at it. The photograph evoked the film from which it had been taken, and that in turn elicited memories of my mingled horror and despair in 1963. My eyes blurred with tears.

Lily had not even been born in 1963. She was thus able to see the important detail in the photograph with vision unmisted by emotion. She took it from me and stared at it intently. "Yes. He's there, isn't he? I can see him, I think."

"Ah, well done, indeed!" Sherlock Holmes said. "I've used the computer to enhance that shot, to focus the spot better. That and the frames that follow it. Here." He handed her a small stack of photographs.

I looked over her shoulder as she perused them. Thankfully, the attempt to define more precisely one particular spot in the crowd had distorted the rest of the scene even more, so that I was spared what would otherwise have been an even clearer view of Kennedy's public and ignoble death. That one spot, however, stood out with remarkable clarity. A tall man stood there, watching the President's death with a smile and with eagerness clear in every line of his body. Need I describe him for you? It was, of course, Professor James Moriarty.

He was visible in every frame, moving from left to right as the camera panned in the opposite direction to follow the limousine.

"You will note," Sherlock Holmes said coolly, "that the Professor shows no diminution, or fading, from one frame to the next. Clearly his stay in 1963 was much longer than in either 1981 or 2001. Extrapolating from these pictures and from what I have measured on the recordings we viewed earlier, I would estimate his stay in Dallas to have been perhaps as long as two minutes."

"Does that mean," I asked, frightened by the thought, "that the length of his stay increases with the—the *distance* from 1991?"

"Watson, your mind improves with age! Another hundred years or so, and you'll be quite—" At this moment, however, he glanced at Lily and quickly changed the subject. "Yes, it does seem to mean that, although I have not gleaned sufficient data to deduce the precise relationship. We can presume, however, if the pattern holds, that Moriarty will appear for up to two minutes in 2019. We have only eighteen years to wait for that."

He paused as if to give us time to digest that idea, and then he said, "This increase in time is a crucial matter. The Englishman who visited India in 1948 was seen with the assassin of Gandhi for a period of about five minutes. We can thus expect that to happen again in 2034, or thirty-three years from now. A mere eight years earlier, Mercader Ramon's mysterious persecutor spent enough time with the young man to talk him into the murder of Trotsky. Even given Moriarty's supposed ability to mesmerize those of lesser intellect—as who is not, next to Moriarty!—and assuming a Stalinist persuasion on Ramon's part that could have predisposed him to the assassination, we still have to assume Moriarty to have spent quite a few minutes with him, especially so if he was able to concoct a ruse that convinced the young man his mother was being held hostage. Can we say less than five minutes? Surely more. What, then, will the Professor accomplish in 2042?"

"But why should we assume he will have any effect?"

"Because his rôle has changed. Observe how, in what to him must seem only a matter of less than half an hour, he has progressed from bewildered observer of assassination to instigator. The increase in time, of course, is what makes that possible."

Lily said thoughtfully. "You said something about a Prime Minister murdered in the House of Commons."

"Yes. Spencer Perceval, assassinated in 1812."

"Well then, according to the pattern, Moriarty must have been there for a long time."

"Indeed. Perhaps many hours, or days, or perhaps even weeks. And that will be repeated in 2170."

I forced a laugh. "We have some time to prepare, at least!" Both of them appeared to ignore me.

"Also," Lily said, "Perceval would be the first of the cases you mentioned that Moriarty would already have known about. It was recent history when Moriarty was a kid. And he'd also know about any assassinations before Perceval's, when he'd be around for even longer. So it seems to me he'd have left lots of evidence of himself in earlier times. Enough for historians to have noticed it already."

Holmes beamed at her. "Precisely so. Watson chose wisely, after all! The curious thing is that I turn up no trace at all of Moriarty before 1812, rather than the even greater evidence you deduced. Perhaps the records are too scanty from so far back. Or it may be that I have misinterpreted my data, and in fact, after some point, the period of his stay diminishes. Or perhaps . . ."

"Perhaps?" Lily prompted.

"Or perhaps I simply need more data. Quite literally, time will tell. As your husband remarked a moment ago, time is a commodity of which we have a fair amount to deal with."

"And is that all?" I said in amazement. "After all you've said, are we to sit back and collect data while that monster threatens civilisation?"

"Watson, we must move along a day at a time, precisely because Nature constrains us to do only that: to travel forward through time at the rate of one day per day, while our enemy leapfrogs. And if I am right about the murder of Martin Luther King, then Moriarty's next leap will bring him to us in thirteen years. His visit will last for more than one second and less than two minutes."

I'm not sure whether it was the thought of that visit or Sherlock Holmes' perfectly cold, unemotional, analytical way of announcing it that chilled me so.

15

Much Experimentation, an Explanation, and a Vacation

THE ASIAN WAR did not come about. And indeed, I was sure it was no coincidence that Sherlock Holmes was gone from his farm for some months toward the end of 2001 and early in 2002, during which time the increasingly ugly situation resulting from the Phitsanulok assassination suddenly and mysteriously eased. It was clear to me that Holmes must have gone to Asia on a secret mission, either for one of the governments of that region or else on the behalf of the British government, no doubt at the behest of his brother, Mycroft, and that while there he had worked so successfully that he had averted what might otherwise have become the germ of a world war. Upon his return, he verified my suspicions and provided me with the details of his adventure, which remain filed away among my other notes, under the title *The Loathesome Mandarin and the Trained Penguin.*

Left alone (for Mrs. Hudson had taken advantage of her master's absence to indulge in one of her rare holidays), Lily and I pottered about the place cheerfully, dithering in the greenhouse and with the bees, quite like an old, retired couple. And indeed, I suddenly realized, while Lily was still in her late thirties, I was almost 150! Physically, of course, we were both in our midtwenties, but objective observation of my own manner and mannerisms renewed my old fear that, while the mead might keep the body young indefinitely, quite possibly it did not prevent the brain from aging. Alarmed at the thought, that winter I flung myself afresh into the study of the miraculous wine, desperate to uncover its secret. And strange to say, for the first time in decades I believed I was making some headway.

The only blot on what would otherwise have been a very happy time was Lily's harsh attitude toward Sherlock Holmes. Since coming to the farm, her feelings toward him had undergone a significant change. While she had earlier admired him—had, indeed, held him in awe—it would be fair to say that she now held him to be a boor and a lout, his oafishness only barely disguised by his veneer of culture. "He loves fine cuisine and fine music and fine art," she said hotly, "but the way he treats you—!"

I talked much to her of my long friendship with the man, my admiration for him, which had stood the test of a century and a quarter, and most of all of what I perceived as his hidden unhappiness and insecurity. "He's effectively been barred for decades from following the vocation for which he's best suited and for which he trained himself so assiduously."

We were in the greenhouse at the time. Lily stopped her vigorous spading of a vegetable bed. "You mean because he wanted to protect his privacy?"

I sighed. "I wish it were only that. No, he's been left behind. He was once at the very forefront of criminology, not only because of his deductive methods but also because of his pioneering application of the very latest discoveries of science to the pursuit of the guilty. For decades, though, he has felt left behind by the progress of science, unable at times even to understand the technology now being used by Scotland Yard or the Sûreté! Remember his reaction to my suggestion that he use new methods to fight Moriarty—and his overreaction to my twitting of him when he did so.

"And perhaps worst of all, consider the futility of his knowledge of tobacco blends and bicycle tyre prints and London soils and the effects of various professions on the shape and callosities of the hand, and so on. He solved crimes with that vast knowledge, that encyclopaedia contained entirely in his head; he wrote monographs on those subjects. With mass production of tobacco and tyres and with every man an office worker, what good does it all do him now? And as for types of soil . . . Well, where today in London or any other major city is soil left exposed, rather than being paved over? Don't you see that I can hardly resent his occasional . . . well, churlishness?"

"I guess," Lily said grudgingly. Suddenly she threw her spade down. "Oh, you know what it is, John. We've been cooped up here for years. I haven't been really alone with you since that time in Chicago, ten years ago."

"That *was* a wonderful time," I said wistfully.

"Nowadays, when Sherlock isn't around, Mrs. Hudson is, and *vice versa*. By the way, does she even have a first name?"

"If so, I've never heard it," I confessed. "You know, dear, neither Holmes nor Mrs. Hudson is here now."

She grinned, as charming a sight when she did so as ever. "Uh-huh. Come on, Stuffy. We can dig in the dirt any old time."

I knew full well that Lily and I both needed a long holiday together, well away from the farm, and I promised both myself and her that we would go away on one very soon. I simply could not leave my work on the mead in the middle, though, not with my studies finally showing some indication of progress. Lily could not understand my fanaticism, but then, Lily had never known old age. And so nearly thirteen changeless years slipped by.

When the breakthrough came at last, it seemed anticlimactic. Almost a century of experiment and calculation, and yet my main reaction, when I had proved to my own satisfaction that our lives could now be prolonged indefinitely with a mixture of ingredients available at any good florist's, was pity for our bees. After decades of toil in our behalf, the life's work of untold generations of bees going to satisfy our selfish need to live forever, the little fellows were now superfluous.

Sherlock Holmes' own interest in the insects had waned long ago, continuing only as a desire that they should stay healthy enough to produce the life-giving honey. Mrs. Hudson from the first had been irrationally frightened of them. I had always found the buzzing, industrious workers, with their mindless and selfless devotion to the hive, more than a little sinister. And now that I had at last found out their secret, thus freeing us to roam the world for as long as we wished, Lily would no longer need her work with them to help her forget her frustrations. While life would now open up again for us, all life would soon end for our miniscule, tireless servants.

*

On a fine, clear spring day in 2014, Lily and I loaded our new luggage into an equally new automobile to begin our drive up to London, the first stage of our long-delayed, long-awaited holiday. Holmes was there to shake my hand, and Mrs. Hudson was there, with brimming eyes, to clasp Lily to her and even, demonstrating to what an extent she had left the nineteenth century behind, to embrace me.

"Well, Watson," Holmes said cheerfully, "I have programmed the car for you. When you reach the airport, release it from manual control and it will return here. You haven't told me where you're going."

"Where no plane or car can go."

"Where no—Dear me, a mystery. Outré and bizarre. And in what direction do you go?"

"In no compass direction."

"What? Impossible!"

"Come, Holmes. You know my methods. Apply them."

He laughed delightedly. "Then I suppose I must apply your surgical scalpel, in the guise of Ockham's Razor, and shave away the impossible. Hmm, no compass direction . . . That leaves only up and down. Since I know well your aversion for caves, mines, and the ocean floor, the latter is eliminated. Up, then. Not Helium City: Aeroplanes land there. By Jove, not the Libration Satellite?"

I confess I felt a twinge of annoyance at the ease with which he had solved my riddle. "You show promise, Holmes. Yes, Lily and I have leased a cabin in the wilds."

"The only wilds left, I understand. A good choice. An excellent choice! I've half a mind to go with you." Unseen by Holmes, a look of horror crossed Lily's face at those words. "No, that's impossible. I fear I must disappoint you. I have too much work scheduled for myself on Earth. Mundane duties, as it were."

And then Lily dragged me into the car, lest he should change his mind, and we were off with a flurry and a bustle, roaring past the silent, empty hives and onto the northward road.

Interlude

SOMETHING NEW. This time, he felt the pull even before he arrived. The previous times, he had deduced the existence of the attractive force after the fact: He had been intellectually aware that the deadly attraction must exist, was the explanation of his strange condition. But this time, he *felt* it. It was a development, a progression, he welcomed.

His eagerness for this newest episode suppressed almost all awareness of the fearsome compression and the awful pain in his back.

He was out-of-doors again, just as before, but the air was milder. Although he sensed the nearness of a crowd, he seemed to be in a clearing in a forest. He was aware too that night—or something much akin to it—was approaching. It was all quite idyllic, but he had no thought for that. His attention was drawn instead to two men, standing beneath a tree a few feet away and talking in low tones. He felt that pull again and went forward to join them. He felt strangely light on his feet.

16

The Turning Wheel

AT THE START, our holiday was a pastoral idyll. There were very few others vacationing in the area, and we could pretend we had the two thousand-odd square miles of wilderness to ourselves. Rarely, while tramping along the trails, we'd meet other couples or individuals or small groups, but not often enough to intrude on our sense of solitude or to mar our happy feeling of being utterly removed from Earth and from civilisation and—to put it plainly—from Sherlock Holmes.

It was easy at times to imagine we had been transported back a thousand years to that woodland England, heavily forested and sparsely populated, in which our one-time neighbor in Sussex, the old writer of historical romances, would have preferred to live. Walking along a forest path, I would half expect to round a curve and find myself face-to-face with a jolly archer in Lincoln Green leaning indolently against his trysting tree. Once that feeling compelled me to say suddenly to Lily, "Robin Hood in Barnesdale stood. Think we'll meet him here?" Her response, however, was limited to a dutiful smile. The illusion of the primeval forest would have been complete had it not been for the evenly spaced windows, each hundreds of miles long and many miles across, that formed the "roof" of the satellite and let in shafts of brilliant sunlight that moved grandly across the concave landscape. That and a gravity slightly lower than Earth's and a welcome absence of insects and vermin.

In better economic times, this was a popular vacation spot, and had it not been for the worldwide depression, just then at its worst point, our wilderness hideaway would no doubt have been as infested by people as rural Sussex itself had become. As it was, it was only due to Lily's discovery of an impending political event on the Satellite which interested her that we were drawn back into the hurly-burly of human affairs.

I should explain first that not all of the Libration Satellite was wilderness. Perhaps a quarter of its vast area was so reserved, for tourism had become so vital a source of revenue for the man-made world. The largest single user of land, however, was agriculture, the products of which were in high demand on the Mother World. There were also numerous industries and, of course, many scientific establishments. As the study and exploration of the moon and Mars very slowly progressed, the Libration Satellite drew increasing profit from serving as a way station. And so its growing, prosperous, industrious population lived not only in scattered small villages, but even in one town that almost deserved the title "city."

In a stadium in that city, a political rally was now to be held. I have no idea how Lily had heard of it, but she was eager to attend and wished me to accompany her. I was little interested in the doings of the Outward Movement, as it was usually called, but rather than be separated from her for even a matter of hours, I decided to go.

This Outward Movement had sprung up on Earth only two years earlier, coincident with the first successful manned landing on Mars. As I understood it, the tenets of the Movement's founders were that Earth was hopelessly corrupted and decadent and that even the Libration Satellite and the moon were too close to it to escape its evil influence. Thus the only real hope for mankind was to start afresh on some distant world, where a new society could be built along cleaner, healthier lines. This automatically meant Mars, the farthest planet men had reached which could conceivably someday become a home to humans, and apparently, if I understood the Movement's literature, the new life to be built on Mars was to be a Spartan, grim, dedicated, purposeful, boring, and unpleasant sort of existence.

One would not have thought that any of this would appeal to the soft, decadent peoples of Earth. Perhaps, though, we were in the same state as the Romans of late Imperial times: desperate for any new religion, any new-seeming answer to our troubles, no matter how bizarre or outlandish. The residents of the Libration Satellite, however, certainly did resent the Outward Movement, for if it were somehow to succeed, it would threaten much

of the satellite's livelihood. At the same time, there were among
the Librationists many of an adventurous nature who had found
that the move to the satellite resulted more in claustrophobia
than excitement. To them the Outward Movement appealed
mightily. And, too, there were those who felt that the Libration
Satellite epitomised rather than stood above or against that very
decadence against which the prophets of the Outward Movement fulminated, and to these librationists also there seemed
much good sense in the idea of a fresh start far from the influence of Earth.

To the majority of Librationists, though, members of the
Movement, the so-called Outwarders, were more than just a
nuisance they were willing to put up with for the sake of tourist
dollars. Rather, the Outward Movement was a direct threat to
the satellite's economy. Should a major colonisation drive get
underway on Mars, bypassing the expanding Earth-moon route
and with it the Libration Satellite stopover, where would these
dwellers between Earth and moon be then?

It was this tension between two naturally mutually inimical
groups of space explorers that fascinated Lily. "It's a lot like the
beehives I used to take care of, this place," she said. "I don't
mean it's superorganised or stratified. But it does kind of look
like a hive, doesn't it? And I think that since it first began, it's
gotten a lot more serious and sober and . . ."

"Money-grubbing?"

She chuckled. "That's the word. Materialistic, anyway. It's as
if the Librationists spend all their time storing up their honey
for winter, even though they know there aren't any seasons up
here and never will be. Haven't you noticed that you never meet
any of the natives out here enjoying the wilderness? It's always
tourists, like us."

"By George, I *hadn't* noticed it, but you're quite right! Well,
then, what rôle do the Outward Movement people play in this
metaphor? Surely they're worker bees too, but even more so."

"To you and me, maybe, but I don't think the locals see them
that way. You ought to listen to some of the local newscasts.
Back on Earth, they'd be sued for some of the things they say
about the Outwarders. Let's see, now." She frowned momentar-

ily in thought, and then her forehead cleared. "Wasps, of course! Invading wasps, here to steal the product of the Librationist bees' labor. The Outwarders want to benefit from the groundwork these people have laid, but without having to pay any dues themselves."

Now we were speeding over the landscape in our rented flyer. The expanses of forest, clearings, and rivers gave way to ordered stretches of cultivated land and increasingly to small towns. I said to her, "Isn't it odd that the Outward Movement chose the Satellite for this rally? Of all places! Their famous orator will be faced with a hostile audience. Enemies, one might almost call them."

Lily, who was flying the vehicle, kept her eyes riveted on the controls. At first she seemed not to have heard me. Then suddenly the import of my words struck her. "That's right! If the Librationists could get rid of Junior Rex, the whole Outward Movement could collapse overnight. That makes him quite a target, doesn't it?"

The thought cast a dark shadow over my holiday mood. Junior Rex, reportedly a native of the East Texas Gulf Coast, that area so heavily influenced during the preceding half century by the American manned space program, had emerged not only as the Outward Movement's most widely known spokesman, but by far as its most influential, as well. He was reputed to be an orator of hypnotic ability; his speechmaking powers were credited by many with being the primary cause of his movement's growth and appeal. Because of that very growth, in turn, he had achieved a position of significant political power and influence. Were we to see once again a change imposed on Man's history by a handful of men? Once again, would an important actor be removed from the world stage before he had played out his part? I didn't speak these gloomy thoughts aloud, however. Instead, I said reassuringly, "Of course, nothing violent could happen in such a small, closed society as this."

Wilderness invaded—permeated—even the one city of the Libration Satellite. The stadium, in fact, was little more than a natural—man-made natural!—bowl in a park, with terraces cut into the sides of the bowl to form bleachers. Most of the crowd had already gathered and was waiting with some impatience for the appearance of Junior Rex, who was already late by a few minutes. Stragglers were still ambling across the open meadow toward the stadium. The sunlight was still bright, but far away across the upward curving landscape one could see an inky shadow sweeping toward us. On the floor of the stadium, lights had already been lit in anticipation of the coming few hours of darkness.

At times it seemed to me that it was not only my brain the mead had not fully rejuvenated, but my bladder as well. Or perhaps the blame should be laid at the door of Mrs. Hudson, whose licorice-colored tea I had been drinking daily for a century and a half. Whatever the cause, the effect was that within minutes of our finding seats, and before Junior Rex, who had just appeared on the platform in the middle of the stadium floor, could even begin his speech, I was forced to leave in search of the nearest public convenience.

If one was provided, I missed it. I found myself instead in one of the many small wooded areas that abutted the stadium. My need was becoming most urgent, however, and the light was already dimming noticably. I feared that if I wandered about searching for the proper building, I might well lose myself and leave Lily alone through much or all of Rex's speech. I visualised Lily's cold anger if that were to happen. I suppressed my hesitations and chose the only course left after the impossible had been eliminated: viz, I chose a likely tree and undid my fly.

At that instant, I became aware of low voices nearby and approaching my position. Hastily I passed my finger over my trousers again to close my fly and then, trying to appear to be a mere casual stroller, I walked in the direction of the voices.

Two men emerged from the trees and the gathering gloom. They were walking toward me, but at first they didn't notice me. They conversed in low tones and an urgent manner, and they kept casting glances over their shoulders. Then they saw me. I said "Hello!" in a cheerful, hail-fellow-well-met sort of way, but instead of replying, they exchanged a quick glance of alarm with each other and then hurried past me. It was still light enough that I could see that their faces were pale and frightened, but wore expressions of determination.

An instinct told me that I should follow those men, that they intended evil and I might prevent it. But my physical need was more powerful than the urgings of intuition, and besides, I feared what their glances behind them and their furtive, conspiratorial manner might mean. Was there someone ahead of me lying in-jured, someone in immediate need of my professional atten-dance? If so, the coming man-made night, due to last for a mat-ter of hours, made it all the more urgent that I find the victim soon. I hurried along in the twilight, threading my way between the trees, my overfull bladder momentarily forgotten. Quite sud-denly, I found myself in a clearing.

And face-to-face with Professor Moriarty.

For an instant, he was as stunned as I. We stared at each other, and for the first time, I was struck by his nineteenth-century clothes. How out of place he was! Perhaps for the first time I truly believed in his temporal oscillations and knew fully that this was indeed the same man I had defied so unsuccessfully in Utah in 1991. He transfixed me with his sunken eyes, his head oscillating slightly from side to side in that repugnantly familiar reptilian manner.

Then Moriarty's face contorted and he hissed, "You! You *still* survive!" He flung himself at me, his face that of a madman. At the very instant of impact, while I was still staggering backward, unmanned by terror and curiously unable to defend myself against the bony hands clutching at my throat, a spasm crossed his face and he faltered. I felt an intolerable heat and was forced to screw my eyes shut against a brilliant light. Both were gone almost as soon as they had come, leaving me to doubt whether either had even been real. When I opened my eyes, Moriarty had vanished as well.

Yells and screams erupted from behind me. Even as I turned and raced back toward the stadium and Lily, I knew what had happened. And I knew, too, why I should have followed the two men. Because of my failure to do so, I knew with a knowledge beyond all reason or logic that they had succeeded. It was the first of August, 2014.

17

Graphs and Goals

WE RETURNED to Earth on the ship carrying Junior Rex's body home for burial. My facial burns had healed overnight.

To Earth, but not to the farm—at least, not to stay. "For all those decades," I told Lily, "I had a goal, something to aim at."

"Analysing the mead."

"Yes. Even though I'd get discouraged and put the work aside for years at a time, it was always there before me. I always knew I'd return to it eventually. Now, though, I no longer have that to do." I rubbed my hand over the small plastic box in which I kept our supply of the pills I had prepared as our substitute for the mead. "One a day keeps the Grim Reaper away."

Lily laughed. "And now you're bored."

"Not yet. But after a few weeks back on the farm, I certainly should be. Eternity is a long time to do nothing but watch the Channel grow ever more crowded with ever larger ships."

"And I can tell you I don't want you getting cranky, like your friend. Giving *him* the benefit of the doubt as to causes, that is."

"Hmm." It was a subject we had both learned to avoid. "I've thought of writing. Historical romances, like that old gentleman in Sussex I told you of."

"But you know you've never had anything published other than your true stories about Sherlock Holmes, and you've often told me yourself that *they* only got published because he was famous. Also, dear, you're much too stuffy and old-fashioned for a modern audience."

I sighed. "The duty of a wife: to keep her husband's feet on the ground."

"Christ! We haven't even reached Earth yet, and already you're starting to talk like him!" Her eyes were flashing. I tried to take her in my arms to pacify her, but she pushed me away. "I also don't like to hear you being sorry for yourself. There *is* something for you to do. Men like you are needed back there." She pointed over her shoulder with her thumb.

"The cabin next door? They need a 162-year-old-man?"

"No, you idiot!" She punched my shoulder in exasperation. "The Libration Satellite. They need doctors. And eventually so will Mars, and any other new colonies in space."

"Good heavens! Emigrate, you mean? Leave England permanently?"

She snorted. "I'm sure you could find tea and Scotch even on the Libration Satellite. They're almost civilised, in case you didn't notice. Doesn't the idea excite you?"

I had to admit that it did. "It would be a worthwhile thing to do, wouldn't it? Even a noble one. But, you know, I stopped practising medicine over ninety years ago, and I stopped reading journals not long after. The advances in that time—! I'd have to start all over again, get an education, as if I were some young chap just entering college."

"Oh, sure. But you know you could do it and qualify to practise. After all, you've already done it once. You wouldn't have to be tops in your class, either, John. The Libration Satellite's probably desperate for anyone with an M.D. who'll move there. And don't underestimate yourself, Doctor." She grinned. "You've still got great hands."

I was pleased, certainly. Moreover, the idea of such a fresh start appealed to me more and more as I thought about it. "Lily, what's *your* interest in space?"

She shrugged. "It's the future of mankind," she said simply.

Sherlock Holmes reacted less to word of my new direction than I had expected. "To be frank, Watson, I had somewhat expected some such decision on your part. As for me, the problem of Moriarty will provide sufficient focus for my energies for some time to come, but I've long been aware of your restlessness. And Lily's, certainly. Even when you were old, your impulses were quite youthful, and now that they are matched by your physical state, Sussex is no fit place for you. And it's appropriate, too," he said, waxing philosophical. "Englishmen have always been quick to settle new territories, from which they can look back toward Home with nostalgic fondness and not the slightest desire to return.

"By the way, have you considered how you will handle the mechanics of all this? Birth certificate, school records, and so on: all those nuisances colleges generally require?"

I confessed I hadn't. "I suppose it would be possible to stay here and study electronically, hook the computer in to the college's, and take the examinations when I felt ready. However . . ."

"Precisely." He nodded. "I'm sure Lily would prefer it if both of you began your fresh start wholeheartedly and as soon as possible. I shall speak to Mycroft about it, if you wish. He could probably arrange everything for you."

"Would you, Holmes? By Jove, that's very kind of you!"

He waved his hand. "A bagatelle. Now, Watson, I have something of interest to show you." He led the way to the computer in the library.

The device had grown by the accretion of components. Many of the books had been removed from the shelves to make room for the additional equipment. This told me most eloquently how salutary for Sherlock Holmes had been the focusing of his attention on Moriarty to which he had earlier referred. Clearly he had thrown himself wholeheartedly into the most modern of methods, even to the extent of virtually abandoning the old. Even the small screen of early days, which by its size had symbolised for me the tentative nature of Holmes' experiment with the use of a computer, had been replaced by one far larger—perhaps five or six feet on a side—and more imposing. Indeed, it dominated the room I could scarcely still call a library; there was something about that screen that struck me as bold, aggressive, self-assertive.

Holmes sat down at his desk and typed rapidly on the keyboard now occupying the place of honor in the center. "This," he said while typing, "is a graph of the data I described to Lily and you some years ago." A numbered grid appeared on the screen. Then dots, with small circles around them, appeared on the grid, one after another, forming an upward curving progression from the lower left-hand corner toward the upper middle of the grid. Along the bottom, or X-axis, of the grid appeared the legend TIME INTERVAL IN YEARS FROM 1991, while along the left-hand side, the Y-axis, the computer wrote the label DURATION OF STAY, MINUTES. A smooth, curving line grew from the lower left-hand corner and shot through the points. In the meantime, Lily and Mrs. Hudson had come quietly into the room, and both were now watching the screen with the same fascination as I.

Holmes turned toward me, noticed that his audience had increased from one to three, and smiled in pleasure. "These points represent the data I discussed with you some time ago: my estimates of the time periods spent by Moriarty at the end points of his oscillatory jumps. Watson, your encounter with him on the Libration Satellite was also taken into account. Now we have three direct observations of him. Combining those with the careful guesses resulting from my historical research, we have this graph." At that moment, the computer added, across the very middle of the screen, the title THE OSCILLATORY TEMPORAL ADVENTURES OF THE FRIGHTFUL PROFESSOR MORIARTY.

Lily and I gaped. Mrs. Hudson giggled. Sherlock Holmes spun around to see what was the cause of our reactions. "A momentary whimsy," he muttered. He typed an instruction, and the aforementioned title disappeared. "You will notice how the time Moriarty spends in each time increases with the temporal distance from 1991. This, of course, we deduced long ago."

"A dramatic increase, I should say," I added, noticing how sharply the curve trended upward.

Mrs. Hudson shook her head and murmured, "Dear, dear." Lily, her face pale, said nothing.

"Guessing that the relationship might be exponential," said Holmes, "I tried this." Again he typed. The screen went blank for an instant, and then the grid was replaced by a new one. The axes were labelled as before, but this time the Y-axis was clearly logarithmic. The curve drawn through the lines had become a straight line from lower-left-hand to upper-right-hand corner; the circled points were all either close to the line or, in the case of those at the left, directly on it.

"So it *is* exponential," I exclaimed.

"Perhaps so," Holmes said. "One must bear in mind, however, that I have a direct measurement for only one of these points." He pointed to the leftmost one on the graph, the one labelled as being ten years from 1991. "This is the point representing both Sadat's assassination and that of Phitsanulok. The others are derived from partial observation, as in the cases of John Kennedy's murder and your recent encounter on the satellite, Watson, or from deductions based on historical documents, as with the assassination of Gandhi, or simply extrapolation." He pointed now to the rightmost and highest point of the graph. "Spencer Perceval," he said quietly. "Like Mrs. Chalmers, a prime minister. Eighteen-twelve, which is to say, 2170. If the underlying physical relationship *is* exponential, after all, and this straight line is even approximately correct, then the duration of Moriarty's, er, visit in 2170 will be about three days."

"Three days!" I repeated, horrified. To Moriarty, three days might as well be forever. The amount of evil such a man could accomplish in so much time was inconceivable.

Holmes nodded. "You understand now, perhaps, Watson, why I say that Professor Moriarty is sufficient preoccupation for me. I need no emigration into space, no new career. His deeds threaten civilisation itself. In all the world, only I can stop him."

"But surely there is no way to stop him," I said pessimistically. "Even if your graph is correct," I gestured toward the screen, "it tells you only when Moriarty will appear and for how long, but not where. As we now know, it need not even be on Earth. Holmes, at any one time, there are *too many* great men."

"Ah, yes. An accurate analysis." A look of great sadness appeared on his face, mingled with frustration.

Lily said quickly, and with a degree of sympathy in her voice that surprised me, "I'm sure you'll think of something, Sherlock. You did in Utah in 1991."

He smiled at her gratitude. "Mohammed went to the mountain, that time, didn't he? And in disguise, moreover. Well, well. We shall see what we shall see. But now," he said, abruptly changing the subject, "tell me more about this Outward Movement. I find it quite intriguing. You know how isolated from politics I've been out here, while working on what must surely

[123]

be the longest case any detective has ever been involved with! Lily, didn't you say you thought the Outward Movement would collapse without the oratory of Junior Rex?"

"Why, it could for sure," she said, "unless someone else shows up to take his place in the movement."

The two of them delved into a deep and long discussion of the politics of the Outward Movement in particular and space exploration in general. I had long known that Lily's interest in the subject was intense, so that her willingness to discuss it at length was understandable. Holmes, however, had always been so singleminded in his pursuit of criminals and his study of crime that I found his present intense interest in the Outward Movement puzzling in the extreme. This, after all, was the man who had once told me that he cared little whether the earth went around the sun or vice versa, unless the fact could somehow be of use to him in his investigative work! And yet here he was speaking profoundly on a most closely related subject.

Puzzling as it was, however, I could only applaud this broadening of his interests, especially if the result proved to be that his obsession with Moriarty was put aside for even a short while. I knew all too well that once Lily and I had moved away from the farm, Sherlock Holmes would sink back into his old ways.

Interlude

FROM NOW ON, the pull grew stronger with each oscillation. And increasingly he felt—knew—the larger, more general pattern in mankind's activities to which he was responding.

They thought it was expansion, but he knew better. He knew it was really escape they longed for: consciously, escape from the restrictions and turbulence of the Mother World; unconsciously, escape from him.

He laughed soundlessly in the grey nothingness of between-time. Despite the agony of his back, the compression attacking every square inch of his skin, and the awful, blinding light he could not see but knew was chasing him, Moriarty laughed. Escape from him? No! That they could never do!

18

Death in Venice and Elsewhere

IN 2018, I completed my medical studies. Lily's prediction that it would be easy for me because it was my second time had not proved entirely correct. After all, so much had changed since the days of my young manhood, that I was, as *I* had predicted, in much the same case as any other new university student. My intellectual powers, however, I was pleasantly surprised to see, had seemingly increased, and I sailed through the qualifying examinations with one of the highest marks the board had ever seen. Nonetheless, when recruiters from the Libration Satellite approached me (as they did each new M.D.), I jumped at their offer. My short vacation on the satellite had, I suppose, opened my eyes, and I had spent the next four years fretting at growing pollution, decreasing room, and the ever more oppressive sense that, for Earth, there was no future. I knew that, when the time came to leave, we would both do so with a mighty sense of relief.

Lily and I spent the last months of 2018 at the farm—as guests on vacation, this time, not residents. I took advantage of our stay to show Sherlock Holmes how to produce the rejuvenating pills, so that I would not be obliged to ship a constant supply of them back to Earth for him. He picked up the technique quickly, of course, as one might expect, but he was preoccupied with another matter. Not Moriarty, this time; rather, a development he chose to treat as an epic tragedy.

A new political party, the Renascence Party, had recently come to power in England, promising to restore the nation's empire. To my mind, such movements, common in many countries, were simply more proof (if any were needed) that Earth was decadent. The fad for Renascence would pass, I was sure, but its very success, stunning in its suddenness, was indicative of a turning away from the future and a retreat into a semi-mythical past. The whole matter was of philosophical interest to me, but certainly no immediate practical concern. Holmes, however, had latched onto the broadcast statement of the previous evening by the new Prime Minister to the effect that true Renascence necessitated the elimination of certain evil habits that had for long sapped the strength of Englishmen.

"No more fine, cobwebby old bottles, Watson," Holmes mourned. "Think of that." He clutched at my arm. "And worst of all, no more shag!" For tobacco, too, had been outlawed by these twenty-first-century Cromwellians. He seemed on the verge of tears. The disturbing thought crossed my mind that he was behaving as if senile.

"Oh, well, Holmes," I said soothingly, "remember what happened in the States when they instituted Prohibition. Criminal gangs had a field day with it. With prohibition of tobacco and dance music added to it, Britain will no doubt experience a stunning upsurge in all types of crime. *You* will have a field day!"

"That's true," he said, brightening immediately. "Although I'll be without my Boswell, this time around. Ah, well. Still and all, Watson, shag tobacco I must have. My brain cannot function properly without it. If they persist in this idiocy, I may be forced to move elsewhere."

"How does Mycroft get along with his new masters?"

"Mycroft has left the government."

"What? Good heavens! I didn't think that possible!"

"Nor did Mycroft. In time, no doubt these Renascence nitwits will ban fatty foods, too, and then where will the poor fellow be?" He smiled mysteriously. "I convinced him to shift his vast intellect and his vast bulk together to a more fruitful, more important, and longer-term enterprise."

"More so than the welfare of England?"

My offended patriotism must have been evident in my tone, despite my attempts to mask it, for he chuckled and said, "Times change, my old friend, and we must change with them. And besides, an emigrant like you is a fine one to talk so!"

And no matter how doggedly I questioned him, I could get from him no more information about Mycroft Holmes' new career or about this vital new enterprise to which Sherlock Holmes had referred.

Early in 2019, we left the farm for what, unknown to us, would prove to be the last time and moved permanently to the Libration Satellite. "To the hive, my queen," I said to Lily.

"Listen to you—the last drone of summer!"

Shortly after our move, Johnny Wu was murdered in Venice.

He had gone to California to dedicate the new American headquarters of the Outward Movement, of which he had been the titular head for the past year or so. Other leaders had indeed arisen to take the place of Junior Rex, and other orators, of whom Wu was one of the best. The Movement had matured rapidly from a philosophy, a true movement, recruiting largely those who already agreed with it, to something far more organised and purposeful. Now it gathered funds, built buildings, and even trained would-be Mars colonists. I believed I saw evidence of surer organisation and direction in its inner recesses. The spacefaring governments no longer ignored it or accorded it only amused tolerance. More and more, they treated it as a potential equal. They spoke to it. Most often, it was Johnny Wu to whom they spoke.

I have no idea how fully his death was reported on Earth. On our new home, it was the day's top news story. Cameras had been present, as it seemed they always were in the twenty-first century when something gruesome happened. Mindful of the date, I watched carefully when the episode was replayed on the evening news.

Wu stood on the steps of the movement's austere white building. The polished, twenty-foot-high brass doors behind him reflected the Pacific Ocean, the beach, and the backs of Johnny Wu and his interpreter. Wu spoke quietly, thoughtfully, as though unconscious of the crowd and the cameras. It was the interpreter's voice, amplified, that boomed across the beach front. ". . . glorious moment . . . next step in Man's evolution . . . cleaner, purer . . ." I scarcely noticed the words; all my attention was on the visual details.

A woman burst from the crowd and leaped toward Johnny Wu.

He stopped talking and stared at her in confusion; his interpreter boomed on, unaware of what was happening. Sunlight flashed for an instant on something in the woman's hand, and then Wu was staggering away, hands to his neck. Blood spattered on the pure white steps and then flooded over them as Wu collapsed and slid down them, body limp, the severed arteries and veins of his neck throbbing out his life.

Time stood still for an instant, and then Lily shouted, "There!" and leaped for the television controls.

She froze the picture and then zoomed it in toward the brass doors. The rest of the picture fled from view beyond the edges of the screen as she manipulated the controls. The scene reflected in the great brass doors of the Outward Movement building expanded. Distorted, the reflected strip of beach grew. The picture shifted, centered on a pier jutting out to sea. The dark object on it, almost lost against the brilliant blue of the Pacific, became a man, facing toward us.

The nineteenth-century clothes were more out of place and time this time than ever before, but frightening and ominous rather than laughable. The forward-jutting head, high, bulging forehead, and sunken eyes expanded until they filled the screen. Moriarty's face, ten feet across, dominated the room, staring through us and grinning with maniacal eagerness. Lily and I backed away until we stood pressed against the opposite wall, clinging together like two small children made mindless by fear.

From the kitchen, the coffee pot chimed, breaking the spell. I sprang across the room and slapped my palm against the OFF button, and Moriarty flicked from existence, replaced by a perfectly domestic wall hung with pictures.

"Would you like some coffee?" Lily said shakily.

"With considerable Scotch in it." I activated the communications console and directed it to contact the farm in Sussex for me.

Because of the expense of such calls, I hadn't spoken to Holmes since our move to the satellite. Now I gave no thought to the money. However, the voice that answered my call was that of neither Sherlock Holmes nor Mrs. Hudson. It was a cultured, urban voice, hardly native to South Sussex, which identified itself as the farm's new owner. No, it had no idea where Mr. Holmes had gone: The farm was already vacated when the voice had bought it a week before. Clearly, the voice didn't care what had become of the previous owner. It hoped that was all, because it had work to do. Would it be willing to switch on the visual link? It most certainly would not! The connection was broken abruptly.

This was an utterly unforeseen development, and one which disturbed me profoundly. I sipped the coffee-flavored Scotch Lily had prepared for me and pondered the matter. Somehow, I knew that the voice had *not* been one of Holmes' disguises. Something, some intuitive sense perhaps, told me that he had indeed, as he had hinted before my departure he might do, left the farm forever. For the third time in our lengthy acquaintance, I had to face the possibility that I might never see my old friend again.

By way of compensation, it was true, this time I was not an old and dying man, but rather a physically youthful one with eternity ahead of him. And this time I was not alone: I had Lily to share eternity with. I tried to put Sherlock Holmes' disappearance from my mind. He had disappeared before—once, indeed, to all appearances dead and lost in the fearsome Reichenbach Falls—and had always shown up again.

And about a week later, he did just that. Not in person, perhaps, but still it was a reassuring reappearance.

I was using the computer in our home, updating the file of one of my patients, when the display of symptoms I had been staring at intensely suddenly blanked out and in its place a message began to scroll upward on my screen. MY DEAR WATSON, it began, PLEASE FORGIVE ME FOR CONTACTING YOU IN THIS UNORTHODOX MANNER. I HOPE THE DISPLAY YOU MUST HAVE JUST LOST WAS NOT SOMETHING THAT CANNOT BE RECREATED.

"Good God!" I shouted.

Lily came running in to see what the problem was, read the words moving up the screen, and collapsed on a nearby sofa laughing helplessly.

AS YOU DOUBTLESS KNOW BY NOW, the message continued, I HAVE REMOVED MYSELF FROM SUSSEX. EVENTS COMPEL ME ONCE AGAIN TO ORDER MY LIFE OTHERWISE THAN THE QUIET, SOLITARY

RETIREMENT OF MY COUNTRY SQUIRE ANCESTORS FOR WHICH I HAVE ALWAYS LONGED. I CANNOT TELL YOU WHERE I AM. MESSAGES ROUTED TO VERNET, HOWEVER, VIA THE COMPUTER AT ST. SWITH- INS' YOU ACCESSED THIS MORNING WILL FIND THEIR WAY TO ME. WHEN I NEED TO CONTACT YOU, I WILL USE THE METHOD I AM USING NOW. CONVEY MY BEST WISHES TO LILY. The words stayed on the screen for a second or two; then it went blank, to light up again with my earlier medical display.

"Another man would have used the telephone or written a letter, but Holmes must always be original," I grumbled to Lily, but secretly I was filled with pleasure at this demonstration that he was alive and so much his old self.

There were other deaths on Earth, other assassinations, in the years that followed. But the dates were wrong, and the doings of the Mother World seemed ever less important to me, so that I ignored those murders. And indeed, that was easy to do on the Libration Satellite, where what occurred on Earth received less journalistic attention every day.

Twelve years after our arrival on the Libration Satellite, how- ever, Sir John Morgenthaler and an entire shipload of innocent scientists and tourists on their way from the satellite to the moon died when a carefully timed series of explosions blew open all the hatches of their ship. Later investigation would show that the computer in charge of sealing off the separate parts of the ship in just such an emergency had been competently sabotaged.

On the very heels of this tragedy, I received another commu- nication from Sherlock Holmes, but in a most surprising form.

19

"And I Only Am Escaped Etc."

THERE WERE fourteen doctors in the city at that time, and every one of us was waiting at the landing dock when the *Exeter*, become a ship of the dead, was brought back to the Libration Satellite. The piloting was accomplished by the only living being remaining onboard—the ship's main computer—obeying instructions transmitted from the satellite. By the time *Exeter* docked, the passengers and crew had been exposed to the utter cold and utter dryness of space for better than ten hours, so I knew as well as anyone how far beyond help they must all be. I foresaw that my real duty in the disaster would be to sign death certificates.

Spacesuited workmen bustled about outside the satellite, securing *Exeter* to the dock and repressurising her. As soon as it was safe to board, my fellow physicians and I spread out to search the cabins, recreation rooms, dining halls, and work places in hopes of finding life but in certain knowledge that we would find only death.

The end had at least been quick and painless for most of them. Almost without exception, the bodies I found wore peaceful expressions, and many of them sat slumped in chairs, as if they had but that moment settled down for a doze. For most, there had been no warning, no cause for alarm, perhaps nothing more than a momentary shortness of breath. . . .

On each body, I placed a red tag bearing my name. The attendants who followed would take care of collecting these now officially dead corpses and filling out the necessary forms with everything but my signature. In the meanwhile, I could continue the search.

I kept hoping above all that I'd find Sir John alive. I was not the one who finally found him, but he was found, and he *was* dead. It appeared he had been taking an afternoon nap in his cabin. From his position, it was judged that he had awakened at the fatal instant, had tried to leave his bed, and had fallen halfway. He was found hanging half out of bed, his hands trailing on the floor. With him had died the major hope for peace between nations and for an amicable settlement of the Mars question.

I passed from the passenger area of the ship to the offices where the captain and his command staff lay dead in various attitudes, caught in positions ranging from the pitiful to the compromising, and so on to the *Exeter*'s true work area. That is to say, I was now where the crew spent most of its time, keeping the ship in smooth performance of its shuttle duty while the captain and other officers paraded in their uniforms for the passengers' benefit.

I walked through the ship's great central chamber, where the pile gave off its unceasing heat somewhere deep within the bulbous metal vessel in the room's center. At intervals I found a body sprawled on the floor, and I would stop to give it a *pro forma* examination and affix a red tag. Bizarrely, the sounds of mechanical life clicked away busily all around me: *Exeter* was alive and well; only her human cargo was dead.

Beyond the reactor room, I found I could go only up, via a narrow, circular metal staircase. I did so, my clanging footsteps echoing unsettlingly through the long room I had just left. I emerged in a corner of the galley where the crew's meals had been prepared. After this, if I remembered the ship's layout correctly, my path led back toward the tube to the dock; I had effectively used up all chances of finding survivors. I stood there unhappily staring about at the bodies of the chef and his helpers scattered about the room. And heard a weak cry for help.

It was so faint that for a moment I wasn't sure I'd really heard it: Perhaps my urgent wish to hear such a call had caused me to imagine it. Then I heard it again. "Locker!"

"Locker?" I muttered. I could make no sense of this, for, conditioned by intensive boyhood study of sea stories in which lockers on shipboard were always of the sort on which sixteen men and a bottle of rum were to be found, I looked around for a seaman's chest and could see none. Then I noticed a cabinet, perhaps eight feet high by five across, with its door ajar, opened inwards, and my mental image shifted sharply. A food locker, of course. Even as that realisation came to me, I heard the call again, and this time I was sure it came from the food locker.

He was lying just inside the door, a grizzled old veteran of space. As I loosened his collar and placed my finger against the pulse beating in his neck, I recognised him as the space sailor who had come to see me only a week earlier. I had found his physical health then to be remarkable for a man of his age, and I had told him so. He had not seemed pleased, as I remembered well. Indeed, he had scowled and cursed at me and muttered something about the value of illness when a man wanted to re-tire early.

I found him remarkably healthy this time, too, and consider-ably friendlier. He was partly covered by a pile of packages la-belled DEHYDRATED HAM that had slid from a shelf above him, and he was able to speak and move only weakly. Judging him to be without serious injury, however, I first pushed the packages off him and then helped him to his feet and over to a chair. The poor fellow was quite unable to carry his own weight and leaned heavily on me for support. Fortunately, he was no taller than I. Considering what he had been through and his general weak-ness, the skinny hand with which he grasped my arm to support himself was quite remarkably strong.

"There, old fellow," I said soothingly, easing him onto the chair. I fetched him a glass of water from a nearby sink and watched him drink it down greedily. At his plea, I refilled the glass for him twice, and he swallowed those two glassfuls just as quickly and asked for still more. I refused, however, feeling that his system must be allowed to return to normal at a proper, controlled rate. His voice was noticably stronger already in re-sponse to the water he had drunk. I leaned over and examined his ears, despite his grumbled objections, for signs of eardrum damage resulting from the decompression. "Do you know," I told him, "you're the first living thing I've found on this ship."

"Likely the last, too," he grunted. "I only am escaped alone to tell thee, I betcha. Know that line? *Moby-Dick*. Yessir. Crummy book. Crummy doctor."

I jerked upright. "What! How dare you?"

He chuckled. "If doctor ye be, Doctor Watson."

At last it dawned on me. "Holmes!"

"None other." He stood and stretched luxuriously, saying in his normal voice, "Ah, what a relief! I've been keeping myself at your height for weeks, and it's delightful to regain my lost inches."

I sought the chair he had just left, needing badly to sit. "But, Holmes, I don't understand. What are you doing here? How did you survive?"

He sighed. "I'm here because I thought this was the surest way I could protect Sir John Morgenthaler, whom I had deduced to be a target for assassination. And I survived because I failed and the assassins outsmarted me. There's your answer."

"Thank you, Holmes. I know less now than before I asked. I will say, though, that the blanket under which I found you was a singularly appropriate one."

He shook his long forefinger in my face. "Avoid asperity, Watson. It is unseemly in you. Remember that despite the risk of exposure, I came to you in disguise just to reassure myself that you and Lily were still well." He waited until I had muttered an appropriately humble request for forgiveness and then continued.

"I managed to stay close to Morgenthaler for months, in one disguise or another. And indeed, I foiled more than one plot against him. When he boarded *Exeter*, however, I was sure he would be safe—except, possibly, during the stopover here at the Libration Satellite. Once that had passed uneventfully, I became so confident that I fear I grew careless. As you know, it was on that final leg of the trip that the killers struck." He sighed again. "And as a low-ranking pilesman, I was perhaps as isolated from Morgenthaler as I could possibly be." He paced restlessly about the galley, stepping unconsciously over the bodies of the chef and his helpers.

He stopped suddenly and said, "And then I overheard two of my coworkers discussing the murder plot. Theirs was a suicide mission. They were fanatics who were determined to give their own lives to make sure that Morgenthaler would lose his. Can you imagine such hatred, Watson? Such determination that good will not be done?"

"Morgenthaler may yet be alive. He may have survived, just as you did."

Holmes shook his head. "No, Watson. A coincidence of that magnitude would require both that God exist and that He be good, whereas all about us we see stark evidence contradicting both hypotheses." He struck his fist into his palm. "Those two I overheard—I almost managed to stop them. I was following them. They passed through the galley, and I was close behind them."

"They were unaware of your presence?"

He snorted. "Good heavens, Watson! Of course! I was ambling through this room, to all appearances merely a sailor off duty in search of a way to kill time. And then . . ."

"And then?" I prompted.

"And then," his voice fell to a whisper, "I saw *him*. My old, my ancient enemy. Moriarty. He was standing here, as if waiting for me. Oh, he had no idea who I was, of course, but he realized what my mission was. I stopped in astonishment when we met, right there." He pointed to a corner of the room. "And while I was still frozen with amazement, he struck me with something. I awoke in the food locker at the instant of the explosion. The decompression slammed the door shut, saving my life. Those lockers are made airtight, you see, to protect the dehydrated foods stored in them from any possible moisture. No doubt Moriarty feared that if he stopped to kill me, he would alert the galley crew, busy only a matter of feet away. Simpler to drag me a short distance to the locker, all under cover of equipment and furniture in the room, and leave me there, confident that I would die with everyone else on board. Fortunately for me, this one time his brilliance missed a vital detail, namely the way the locker would preserve my life."

"The air within and the vacuum without created a pressure difference that kept the door sealed?"

"Exactly. When the explosion awoke me and I could not open the door of the locker, I realised that the plot whose details I had overheard had been carried out. I knew that I was trapped within the locker until help should arrive—should it do so at all. I knew, too, that the amount of air trapped within the locker with me would be insufficient for more than a matter of hours. As you no doubt remember, I was fortunate enough to spend part of the years 1891 to 1893 in Tibet, during that time when I wished to mislead the followers of Professor Moriarty into believing that I had died with him in the Reichenbach Falls, and while there I learned certain techniques of autonomic nervous system control from the Tibetan masters. They stood me in good stead in this contretemps, I can assure you! And as for food . . ." He grimaced. "I dare to hope that I will never taste ham again, either dehydrated or fresh!" Suddenly Holmes shivered. "Even so, I was convinced at times that not even the powers of those pills of yours would enable me to survive. I think I have not been so close to death since the time I was trapped in the old house in Throgmorton Road by the reprehensible Jack Hengist."

I nodded. "I remember it well. So, Holmes, what now? You have been concerning yourself with Professor Moriarty for a century and a half now, and all you've accomplished by it is to nearly get yourself killed three times, at least. Why not give it all up at last and settle down here on the Libration Satellite with us? There's crime here, too, you know. You could be quite happy here, surely."

Holmes sneered. "Crime on the Libration Satellite! No doubt the high point of the year for the local constabulary is the failure of some Farmer Jones to meet his assigned wheat quota."

"Well," I admitted, "possibly more emphasis is placed on such matters than is really warranted. Nonetheless, we do have our share of rape, murder, and embezzlement."

"Pah! Even Scotland Yard can handle such crimes! But you should know by now that I'm a fish that requires more exotic bait. And that's truer now, after all those decades of ennui, than it was in the past.

"But enough of this, Watson. Since I *have* failed to preserve Morgenthaler's life, there can be no doubt now that the split between the Martians and Earth will continue to widen."

"Martians" was the name by which the members of the one-time Outward Movement had by now become known. They had a couple of colonies struggling to survive on Mars, with more planned, and already, it was said, most of them no longer regarded themselves as Earthmen. "It matters little enough to me, Holmes. Lily is as fascinated by such political matters as ever, but I'm thoroughly absorbed in my life here, and I have neither the time nor the interest to follow the doings of starving settlers in the Martian desert."

He smiled. "What a colorful phrase! I see there is still a frustrated novelist buried in you. However, you make a mistake, Watson, a serious error. With their Spartan philosophy as a basis, their present hardships will only make the Martians leaner and purer."

"Come, come. That's simply the rhetoric we've been hearing from those people for decades."

"Admittedly. But now at last the conditions are ripe for it to become reality. Consider how far they've come since their beginnings. They'll go much, much farther."

"Perhaps so, with the right leadership and a generous supply of luck. However, this is neither the time nor the place for such a discussion. I've told you the Martians are of little interest to me in any circumstances, let alone these." I waved my arm in a gesture meant to include the ship and all the dead aboard it.

He shrugged. "Just as well, then. It's time for me to resume my rôle of humble crewman and to make my way out of here unseen."

I knew better than to question his motives for continued secrecy: Had he wanted me to know them, he would have told me without being asked. "No doubt I can help you with that," I reassured him. "But after that, Holmes? Then where to? Or do you plan to disappear into obscurity for another twelve or twelve thousand years?"

He seemed to grow shorter before my eyes as he shrank back into his rôle. "This time, I'll tell you where." His face and voice had changed back, too, the former seeming to wrinkle visibly, the nose and chin growing toward each other, while the latter became rasping, high-pitched, querulous, and hostile. "Mars, young fella, that's where! Yessir, Mars." Switching abruptly back to his normal voice, he added, "Remember Mohammed and the

[138]

mountain, my dear fellow, and do you and Lily consider seriously the idea of moving to Mars as well. Doctors are certainly in demand there."

"An echo of the past! Well, come along. The demand on this doctor just now is to get you off this ship unremarked."

20

Martians

SHERLOCK HOLMES vanished from the Libration Satellite shortly after I managed to get him unseen off the *Exeter*, his disappearance as unannounced as his coming.

His visit disturbed me surprisingly. It was more than just the echo of old times, breaking through the thin barrier of years that separated me from the grand old days. It was rather my complacency that was shattered. I tried to explain my reaction to Lily after I had described my encounter with Holmes.

"I'm not sure just what it is. Purpose. I don't really have any purpose. Holmes, now, he's every bit as energetic and vigorous as ever, and it's not just because of his physical youthfulness. It's more that he still has that goal, as he has had since 1991— to stop Moriarty. And of course, you have your history of Man's expansion into space. But what about me?"

"Your work, of course," she said quickly. "You're an important man here, needed and loved."

"Hmm. But not for myself. Any other doctor, just halfway competent, would be just as important and therefore just as needed and loved." I held up a hand to forestall her protest. "However, that's not the real problem, the heart of it. There's simply no overall *purpose* to what I do here—have been doing for twelve years. I cure physical wounds, certainly, and even on rare occasions spiritual ones. But so could any other doctor, and many who aren't even M.D.s. And what comes of it all in the end? The recovered patients go off to make more money, perhaps, or to become more efficiently functioning cogs in the Libration Satellite machine. What's the point of any of it?"

"What about your contribution to Man's thrust into space?"

"Hah! What thrusting are any of these self-satisfied Librationists doing? Other than into each other, that is."

"Not that there's been enough of that around here lately," Lily said pointedly.

I ignored *that* thrust and said, "They *should* be on the cutting edge of exploration, or should at least view themselves in that light. They're leaders in the greatest adventure of all, and yet you'd think they were all businessmen or city administrators on Earth. Where would your own homeland be now had it been only that sort of colonist who emigrated from England?"

"Well, in fact, John, it was."

"What? Nonsense! They were empire builders, every one."

"No." She stood up and roamed about the room as she formulated her ideas. I observed her with as much interest and admiration as if we had just met. Yet how she had changed since those ancient days! Not that she had aged, of course: Rather, it was her inner intensity, her self-confidence, and her spiritual and intellectual toughness and adventuresomeness that struck me— and, yes, aroused me. "That's all a common misconception," she said, "one we Americans are particularly fond of. Oh, no doubt the early explorers and settlers were often adventurers and empire builders. But not all of them, and later on, when the huge numbers of English emigrants started pouring over to the East Coast, and to all the other colonies all over the world, it wasn't hardship and adventure and building the Empire that attracted them. It was ease and comfort and the good life. Much like the later Eastern European immigrants who thought the streets in America would be paved with gold. Those willing to face hard times, adversity—they stayed at home. It was the weaklings who left, emigrated. They were lured by land-developer hype, of course. You're a European, John. Haven't you ever been struck by how lazy Americans are in their personal lives, how they always look for the easy way and the facile explanation?"

I was horrified by all of this. "How can you say such things about your own country? According to your theory, Britons should be the same as Americans. After all, everyone but the Ethiopian is descended from an immigrant."

She grinned. "True enough. Of course, the various waves of invaders frequently washed up in England—Scotland, in the case of your ancestors—because they knew they'd be destroyed by other invaders if they stayed where they were. Except for such bully-boys as the Vikings and the Normans, of course. Oh, by the way, pursuant to all of this, did you know that Eric the Red was only able to con his fellow doughty Vikings into settling in Greenland by lying outrageously about the place? First he came up with that utter lie of a name for the island, and then he convinced them they'd escape winter and eat meat and fruit without having to work for it if they bought his worthless plots of land from him. So much for your heroic world-conquerors! Comfort-loving slugs, all of them."

"I don't like the implication."

"I'm sure you don't," she purred.

"Not only are you trying to destroy all my boyhood illusions and heroes, you're also undermining my belief in my own reasons for immigrating here."

"I certainly didn't mean to do that! No, on second thought, maybe I did. You know how complacent I found the locals a generation ago. They've gotten a lot worse. I've about finished my historical research here now, and I'm sick of the place. In another sixty or so years, you realise, we'd both have to die anyway."

"Yes, I know." Appear to die, she meant of course. With the increase in lifespan for residents of such favored environments as the Libration Satellite, people of the age Lily and I both pretended to be—early forties—still looked perfectly youthful. In another decade or two, however, we'd both be obliged to start adding wrinkles cosmetically. As the years passed, we'd have to feign all the other outward physical signs of advanced age. And eventually, as Lily had said, we'd have to counterfeit our deaths. "Sixty more years on the Libration Satellite, Lily! Fancy that!"

"I *don't* fancy that," Lily said emphatically. "I suppose we could go back to England."

"Not until the Renascence is over and the country regains its senses."

"And its whisky and its tobacco?"

"Precisely. You know, with Morgenthaler dead, the Renascence Party might get its war, after all. I doubt they'll manage to recreate the Empire, but Earth could be an unpleasant place until it's all over. And no Paradise even then."

"Well, that seems to leave only one place. I'd planned it as my next volume, anyway."

I sighed. "John Hamish Watson, M.D. Stands for Martian Doctor."

Lily chuckled. "Arguing with you has always been a matter of getting you to realise that you've already made up your mind anyway."

"Hmph."

I discovered that the Mars colonies had an efficient and well-run immigration service, with offices in all of Earth's major cities and even one small one on the Libration Satellite itself. If that pleased me, the Martians' initial reaction to my inquiries did not. To my utmost astonishment, they flatly rejected the idea of the two of us moving to their world.

"But, look here," I said angrily to the impassive, aloof young man behind the desk, "I know you must need doctors, and surely there's a place on Mars for so accomplished an historical scholar as my wife!"

He sneered openly. "History doesn't interest us, Doctor MacWatt." (I had obtained my diploma under the name Hamish MacWatt, and was so known on the Satellite.) "Let Earth have the past: The future is ours."

"Yes, yes, that's all very well," I said impatiently, for I have always deplored the habit of slipping into overblown rhetoric. "But—"

"No, Hamish." I stopped talking in astonishment at his effrontery. "Your wife would be welcome anyway as a bearer of future Martians—"

"Good God!"

"—and because of your profession, which *is* high on our priority list. But you have to realise something about us. Not many people do. We're not just planting colonies up there, simply settling another world. We're *building* a *new* world, a new way of life, forging the next link in the evolutionary chain."

"That's quite delightful, I'm sure. However, I'm no Neanderthal. Pure Sapiens, I assure you, and I have a university diploma to prove it."

He shook his head. "I'm sure you and your wife are quite intelligent, Hamish—at least, by Earth's standards. It's entirely possible that you both satisfy the I.Q. requirements for immigration. But the problem, you see, is that you're both too old."

"What! Too old!" Beyond that bellowed outburst, I was speechless—rendered so as much by the irony of the situation as by his impertinence.

He nodded. "Exactly." He laced his fingers together and, leaning back comfortably in his executive chair, turned professorial. "You see, Hamish, life is very hard on Mars. Physically demanding, even for someone in a profession like yours. Everyone has to pitch in with the physical work of building the new way, you see, and it's wearing. Along with that, there's the problem of adjusting to the air and gravity, and the hard effects of both. That's why we had to set thirty years of age as the absolute upper limit for new settlers, no matter how professionally qualified they may be. That way, the new citizen can give Mars at least twenty years of hard work before wearing out and becoming a burden on the State. People just don't last as long up there as in a place like this. The older you are when you come there, the more the work and the gravity and air wear you down. You, for instance, could give us ten years at the most, probably far less, and then Mars would have to support *you* for who knows how long. And your wife, of course, is past safe childbearing age; any children she might have on Mars could well become charges on the State from infancy."

I strove mightily for a crushing reply, but, unable to think of one, I was forced to derive what small satisfaction I could from casting a furious glare at him, turning on my heel, and striding out.

Recounting the episode later to Lily, I said angrily, "Old! I was tempted to challenge that young twerp in any contest he cared to specify."

"Aah, he'd probably have chosen a foot race to the summit of Olympus Mons, without respirators."

"Are all the charming, gracious, likable people, all the non-fanatics, to be found only on the decadent Mother World, do you suppose?"

"Not on Mars, it appears."

"What are we to do now?"

"Yes. That's the real question, isn't it?" Suddenly, Lily looked tired and sad, and uncharacteristically defeated. "I suppose all we can do is what we talked about before: pretend to grow old. That'll give us a few more decades before we have to make any real decision. Maybe by then Earth will have calmed down or grown up or something."

"Perhaps. Oh, well, look on the bright side." I gestured toward the stack of boxes, now over four feet in height, holding the manuscript of Lily's multivolume work. "It will be that many more years before we have to move all of that."

"On the other hand, think how much more of it there'll be in fifty or sixty years."

But we were not to be required to face that problem. Only two days later, I received a communication from the obnoxious young man at the Martian immigration office. I was surprised; he was embarrassed.

His face filled the wall as Moriarty's had years earlier, but for the first time in years, that incident did not recur to me when I responded to the communication console's chime. Instead, I said harshly, "And just what do *you* want?"

With his face blown up so huge, I could see every drop of perspiration on it, and there were many. "Uh, Doctor MacWatt," he mumbled, and I was glad to see that he no longer presumed to call me Hamish, "I have some good news for you, if you and your wife are still interested in emigrating to Mars."

I said stiffly, "I will at least listen to you," but my heart was singing within me. Lily was shut away in her study, sifting through mounds of old bills from the Satellite's parliament. I typed a quick instruction on the terminal before me, certain that she wouldn't object when her data vanished, to be replaced by the face I was seeing and the words that went with it.

What little of his self-confidence was left evaporated entirely at my reply. He tried to mask the fact with a laugh, but it emerged as a nervous whinny, and he gave up. "I've just received some orders from New Way City, sir. Very surprising."

"From where?" I interrupted.

"New Way City. Uh, that's now the official name of the largest of the colonies. The others are now called Hopetown and—"

"Spare me." I grimaced. Was I really so sure I wanted to move to this place?

"Yes, well, you see, sir, I'd transmitted a copy of your application, which is standard procedure, and just this morning I received a priority message ordering me to approve the application immediately and to welcome you both as honored new citizens of Mars."

I was quite stunned. "Why was that done, I wonder? And by whom?"

"Oh, the orders are signed," he said quickly, suddenly eager to ingratiate himself with me after this evidence of the high regard in which Lily and I were apparently held on Mars. "I know it's all proper, because of the channels it came through, but I don't recognise the signature. Siger Sherrinford. Isn't that a weird name?"

"Nonsense," I said coldly. "It's a new name, a purer name, well suited to the cleaner, purer world up there."

The young oaf looked depressed as he signed off. No doubt his own name was John Smith, or something else along those lines, and he was wondering whether it might not be politically wise to change it.

Lily burst into the room, laughing uncontrollably. "Siger Sherrinford!" was all she could get out. "My God! Siger Sherrinford!"

Interlude

MORIARTY PONDERED in the grey of intertime.

Watson's survival had surprised him that last time. He had earlier concluded that his plans for Watson's and Holmes' destruction had miscarried, that his great enemy had freed the insignificant doctor from the caretaker, Sam Hudwell, and that the two of them had then managed to sneak back into the factory. (How? he asked himself. With the help of Lily Cantrell, perhaps? Had she been able to beguile even him, then, after all? To what extent, he wondered, had he been outsmarted by inferior intellects?) Once there, they had sabotaged the cannon, perishing with the factory, believing, no doubt, that their sacrifice bought the assurance of Moriarty's destruction.

Did Watson, then, escape the blast in the same way as I? Is he dogging my steps through time, trapped in the same ineluctable oscillation? So Moriarty had reasoned some six minutes ago plus the interminable, unmeasurable time spent between time, after encountering Watson in the forest.

And yet he had seen the flaw in that argument himself. Watson's clothes at that most recent encounter had not been the same as those he had been wearing at the Great Salt Lake in 1991; indeed, Watson's clothes were now much the same as the bizarre coverings of those two men in the forest. The unavoidable conclusion was that Watson had arrived at the temporal interval coincident with Moriarty's visit by surviving the 1991 nuclear explosion and living through the intervening period. *That damnable elixir of Holmes' still preserves him!*

If Watson, why not Holmes himself? A terrible thought, but wasn't there something familiar about that crewman he had felled on the ship? *Was it he?* Moriarty cursed himself for not realizing it at the time and killing his ancient enemy. With Holmes' ability to survive, how could Moriarty feel any assurance that the detective had perished with the *Exeter*?

"Sam Hudwell!" In intertime, the shout was silent. *Why couldn't I see it then?* How Holmes must have been laughing at Moriarty's inability to penetrate that particular disguise! Moriarty shrieked and shrieked without sound: "Holmes! *Holmes!* HOLMES!"

Compression, burning, that pull again, fiercer than ever. Another chance at his enemy. And again the awareness of the blast somewhere just behind him, bordering on sentience, seeking him through the ages.

21

Down in the Valley

UNFORTUNATELY, the contract with the Libration Satellite under which they had paid for our move from Earth and had established my practice for me at virtually no cost to me, specified a full fifteen years of service on my part to the satellite's population. At the time we received that enthusiastic invitation to move to Mars, I still owed the satellite another year and a half of service. Thus it was that we were obliged to delay our move to Mars until 2034. At times I could fall into the almost mechanical routine that had typified my first twelve years on the satellite, and then the time would fly. At others, I would look anxiously at the calendar every few minutes and calculate how many days, hours, minutes, and seconds were left before our departure, and on those occasions, true to the adage about a watched pot, the time crept by with maddening slowness.

At last the day arrived and we embarked for Mars on a Martian ship, the *New Hope* (of course!). There were few regrets and even fewer tears. We had made few friends on the Libration Satellite. This was not because either of us was by nature unsociable or misanthropic (quite the contrary, in fact), but rather because of our hesitation about forming the sort of friendships which could lead to inadvisable frankness about our ages and histories.

During our fifteen years on the Libration Satellite, we had both been as dedicated to work at the expense of play as any other Librationist. Not once during the fifteen years had we found time to escape to that wilderness that had once drawn us to the satellite in the first place. Ironically, then, the long, suspended-time outward fall toward Mars aboard a Spartan sardine can was our first truly intimate and carefree vacation together in fifteen years. The environment was harsh, man-made, unnatural, and one would therefore have thought ultimately unromantic, but for us the time aboard the *New Hope* was an idyll.

Which ended abruptly when the orbital shuttle landed us on Mars.

The spaceport terminal was oddly crowded. We saw many doleful faces and police uniforms, neither of which we could explain. We stopped a passing local (distinguishable from non-Martians by his air of righteous superiority) and asked him for an explanation. He was unwilling to speak with us until we explained that we were new immigrants, offically credited new additions to the super race, at which his stiffness and disdain disappeared and he became almost amiable.

"Someone just got murdered right here in the spaceport," he told us. "Man named, um, Hrachia Dashnakian."

"The Armenian nationalist!" Lily exclaimed. As the Turko-Russian Empire crumbled, Dashnakian had seized the opportunity to try to recreate his ancient nation. "But what was he doing here?"

"Something about wanting the colonies to allow a mass emigration of his people to Mars." The Martian snorted. "Couldn't have happened anyway, of course. Immigration must be handled on an individual basis. But what's really awful is that he got assassinated here, on Mars! That's a real black eye for us." He walked off shaking his head. After a few paces, he stopped, turned back toward us to say, "Oh, say, welcome to Mars, folks!" and then continued on his way.

In a low voice, Lily said to me, "Black eye for Mars! It's a real tragedy for the Armenian people. It may mean the end of their nationalist movement, and eventually the end of them."

The date, I thought. I wasn't sure, and I would have to check my suspicion by looking in a history book for the precise date of Mahatma Gandhi's death and then computing its mirror point, but I feared I would discover that Hrachia Dashnakian's death would prove to have an extra significance: Namely, that Professor James Moriarty was once again involved.

What a welcome this was to our new home! We left the spaceport in a state of deep depression.

*

The spaceport, in common with the three towns and many scattered smaller settlements of the so-called New Way colonies, was located on the floor of Valles Marineris, or Mariner Valley. This was the remarkable geological feature, reminiscent of the Grand Canyon of the Colorado River of North America but utterly dwarfing it, whose existence had been revealed to mankind by a pilotless space vehicle sent out to orbit Mars during the seventies of the preceding century. The mighty valley, over 3,000 miles long, sixty miles across, and in places five miles deep, was apparently created by tectonic activity, the slow pulling apart of two of the planetary crust's majestic plate structures. The valley's size was then exaggerated when the heat released by this geological activity melted the permafrost underlying the surface, causing slumping and erosion.

Both types of activity were still underway when Man arrived in the flesh. As a result, the valley floor held considerable reserves of underground water, and an atmosphere of almost breathable density and composition hung trapped between the valley walls. Assiduous planting, agriculture, and sinking of wells to underground gas deposits were rapidly bringing closer the day when the struggling colonies of New Way would be a continuous settled strip as long and as wide as the valley itself, and when the air in the valley would approximate in density that of the settled mountainous regions of Earth. Life on the harsh plains beyond the valley would be a far longer time in coming, certainly, but the more I learned of the determination of the citizens of the colonies, the less I doubted that it would come in the end.

For the present, however, Mariner Valley was quite enough. (Drawing on my classical education of two centuries earlier, I loved to point out to offended Martians that *Valles Marineris* could also be translated "Marinated Valley.") My job was that of a circuit doctor, as one might say. I spent my time travelling the length and breadth of the valley floor by whatever means were available—often on foot, but more usually by catching rides on vehicles of various kinds on their way from one small settlement or farm to another—and treating illnessess along the way. Lily, of course, had the perfect excuse to accompany me: My patients were *the* primary source for colonial history, and my travels along the valley floor would in themselves provide her with a meaty chapter or two.

Both of us had loved the Grand Canyon on Earth. We had vacationed there during a spring holiday in the midst of my second schooldays, when I was earning a medical degree for the second time. We had delighted in the winding canyon and its multitudinous tributaries, its varied wildlife, much of it found nowhere else on Earth, the layers of rock making up its walls and forming a geological history of the world, so that one travels backward in time as one descends into the canyon, the bracing dry heat, and the river rushing madly through the middle of it all. Throughout our three days there, a violent spring snowstorm covered the plateau a mile above us with deep snow and bitter cold, and yet, except for the greyness of the sky above us and wireless bulletins, we were utterly remote and cut off from it. It made our microcosm all the more a world apart.

Mariner Valley was all of this a hundred times over—all but the river running down the middle. The life found nowhere else on the planet, the fascinating scenery, the intriguing tributary canyons, the unique climate: We had all of these. And as for hostile weather on the surrounding plateau, well, we had, beyond the valley, a climate in which unprotected humans simply could not survive at all. And that climate included, at regular intervals, the most fearsome dust storms known to Man.

For the moment, it was true, one had to sleep either in a sealed and oxygenated bedroom or under an arrangement much like the old hospital oxygen tent, and during the waking hours one had to wear a respirator when performing any strenuous activity. However, I had been assured repeatedly that this would change soon. The tectonic activity that had contributed so largely to the existence and shape of the valley also meant that magma was not far below the surface. Wells had been sunk successfully at regular intervals along the valley completely through the thin crust and into the molten rock beneath. These wells supplied the colonies' energy and a steady supply of the water needed for agriculture. The plants were also supplied with carbon dioxide from gas wells in the valley and returned oxygen. In addition, chemical columns broke down gases from the gas deposits and the magma to produce oxygen directly. Yearly, the increase in atmospheric density within the valley was noticeable. Hopes ran high that well before the end of the century, the valley floor would be comfortably habitable, without mechanical aids or protection—at least, to those born on Mars.

The end of the century, when we moved to Mars, was only sixty-six years away. We could scarcely tell our new neighbors this, but Lily and I would live to enjoy the Earthlike atmosphere. In fact, we had already discovered that the elixir first discovered by those long-dead Sussex bees not only prolonged our lives indefinitely, but also conferred on our bodies a wonderful adaptability. As the tissues were constantly and tirelessly renewed, they were renewed in accordance with new conditions. Thus, far from being worn down by Martian conditions, we were soon as well adapted to them as if we had been born in Valles Marineris and had spent our lives there.

Politics in the valley might be curious indeed by Earth standards, dogma too all-pervading, and too many of the residents given to speaking like Old Testament prophets combined with New Testament apostles, but the physical environment, Mariner Valley itself, was to Lily and me a fairyland.

22

The Curious Appearance of
Siger Sherrinford, et al.

EVER SINCE our arrival, I had been badgering the officials in New Way City to put me in touch with the mysterious Siger Sherrinford. Not that he was mysterious to either Lily or me, of course: We were both quite convinced he must be Sherlock Holmes. For two years, I received only replies ranging from the bland and uncooperative to the outright rude. My official base of operations was in Hopetown, a full thousand miles away from the capital city, and so far my circuit had not taken me in that direction (there *were* other doctors on Mars, also assigned to circuit duty), so that I had been unable thus far to make the attempt to see him in person. Finally, damning the growing inflexibility of Martian government, I took matters into my own hands.

First, to completely mislead anyone who might be keeping occasional track of our whereabouts (although it would have been quite ineffective against a serious attempt at surveillance), Lily and I vacated our apartment in Hopetown and purchased a charming cabin in an isolated side canyon outside Newmanton. Although this put me at the farther end of the valley from the capital and thus at the extreme end of my circuit, it might reasonably appear to be an appealing location to a couple unhappy with the growing population density of the center of the valley, around Hopetown. Indeed, this was not entirely subterfuge, for Newmanton was at the most recently settled end of the valley, a full twenty-seven hundred miles from New Way City and almost fifteen hundred from Hopetown, and it had a rough-and-ready pioneering spirit to it that appealed to both of us. The straitlaced sobriety of the older areas had not yet afflicted New-manton and its environs.

Lily stayed at home this time, in our new cottage, and I set out, ostensibly on my circuit. Indeed, I did perform my medical duties quite conscientiously as I travelled up the valley until I was well past Hopetown. As usual, I set innumerable broken limbs and digits, extracted teeth and implanted substitutes, and delivered babies by the score. (I often considered performing a study—although I never did so—to try to determine whether it was the lighter gravity, the thinner air, something in the dust of the cyclical storms, or simply the longer days and therefore longer nights of Mars that had led to this remarkable fecundity.) At that point I departed from my assigned route and, instead of heading back again toward Hopetown and eventually home, I continued up the valley.

What few people there were in the valley who were not part of the one-time Outward Movement, now called the New Way, were those manning research stations belonging to various Earth governments; how much longer they would be allowed to remain was an open and often discussed question. To everyone else, "the government" meant a small group of office buildings in New Way City, and it was there that I was bound.

Transportation was not much of a problem precisely because this end of the valley was relatively so heavily settled. There was an abundance of traffic along the dirt roads of the valley and a virtual stream of official vehicles carrying men or supplies from town to farm to mine to gas well, and so on. I was given a ride for the last two hundred miles by two taciturn, bearded young men wearing the ubiquitous shirts, shorts, and sandals of Mars. They were both water engineers, on their way to perform scheduled maintenance and upgrading at a pumping station north of New Way City, and beyond telling me this, they told me nothing about themselves. Nor did they ask me for information about myself, a Martian habit for which I was most grateful, since what I was doing was no doubt illegal under some law or other.

The capital city of Mars consisted of five streets parallel to the local valley axis and three perpendicular to it (the standard coordinate system for the colonies) and poles stuck in the ground to show where future streets would lie. It was all very severe and regular and presumably representative of some future, boring stage in Man's evolution. The small buildings along those streets—mean buildings for mean streets—were ramshackle and motley, and inevitably stark and unadorned. Those housing the government were no different from any of the others, except for the simply lettered signs which proclaimed them as Government Building 1, Government Building 2, and so on. I had to admit there was something refreshing about that.

There was no indication of what offices were housed in which building. On the assumption that Government Building 1 would be too conspicuous for "Siger Sherrinford," while his pride would not allow him to inhabit a building with a number lower than two, I turned in at the second doorway.

To the asexual young woman manning the reception desk, I said crisply, "Siger Sherrinford, please."

Her jaw fell to her severely restrained breasts and then snapped shut again. "I'm sorry, sir, but there's no one here by that name."

Her initial reaction, however, had told me otherwise. I leaned forward over her desk and scanned the labels on the buttons of her console. I saw neither the name nor the initials I was seeking, and for an unsettling moment I wondered whether I had made a mistake after all. One button only was blank, and, at a guess, I leaned over and pressed it. "Watson here," I said firmly, ignoring the receptionist's ineffectual and frantic shoves.

From the console a voice spoke in tones of startlement. "Watson! My God!" A sigh. "All right. Send him in." Perhaps it was simply electronic distortion, but it certainly didn't sound like Sherlock Holmes' voice.

A moment later, a slender, harassed-looking young man came hurrying along the hallway behind her desk toward us. The receptionist, still glaring at me, said sourly, "Here comes his seckaterry. He'll show you the way."

I nodded cheerfully to her and followed the nervous young fellow back down the corridor. We passed a row of identical doors on either side, all closed. At the last one on the right, he turned, pushed the door open, and then stood aside for me to enter. I strode in, right hand outstretched, and saying loudly, "Holmes!"

With my other hand, I had slammed the door behind me, shutting the secretary outside.

Then I stopped in confusion, for the tall, thin, sour-faced man facing me across a small, cluttered desk was definitely not Sherlock Holmes. His face resembled my old friend's, however, and was definitely a familiar one. "Holmes?" I let my hand drop. Was this Sherlock Holmes in disguise, then?

"Oh, for Heaven's sake," he said testily, "do stop bellowing my name."

I stepped forward and examined his face more closely, and then it came to me. "Mycroft! Good Lord, is it you?"

"Did you expect Moriarty, you ass? Of course it's me."

I shook my head. "Mars has undermined both your diet and your grammar, Mycroft. I would not have believed either possible."

"I," he said hastily. "It is I. But that's unimportant. Language and food are equally unimportant, when set against building the New Way."

"Ah! Yes, indeed. In short, you have become a dedicated man."

"I was always a dedicated man," Mycroft said, "intellectually dedicated to small and limited goals, and physically dedicated to sloth and sensual pleasures. However, when Sherlock gave me his elixir, with its promise of an eternity of life and youth, I decided I had to dedicate myself to something more substantial."

"You were already quite substantial," I interposed.

He set his jaw and said, "I felt I should dedicate my abilities to the service of something higher. Years later, when Sherlock drew my attention to the Outward Movement, I knew that I had found what I had been seeking for so long."

"So," I said, "*yours* was the organising hand I used to believe I detected in the Outward Movement."

He nodded, his face alight with pride.

"I remember your brother once saying, 'It would not be too much to say that Mycroft *is* the British government.' And now would it be too much to say that you *are* the government of Mars?"

Mycroft blushed, shrugged his shoulders in a modest disclaimer, waved his hand. "No, no. A mere laborer in the vine-yards, that is all. A minor actor in the great drama of Man's social and moral evolution."

"Whose final act I await with undiminished interest," I assured him.

Upon entering the room, I had put the young secretary utterly from my mind. Now, however, the door behind me suddenly swung open and the young man himself entered. From his mouth there issued a long-familiar voice. "As usual, Watson, Mycroft understates the importance of his rôle. I can assure you that he is far more than a mere spear-carrier in this opera called *Ares*."

"Holmes!"

The secretary vanished, instantly transformed into the ever-youthful figure of the world's oldest consulting detective. We shook hands heartily, smiling at each other with pleasure. "Still addicted to the dramatic entrance," I said.

Sherlock Holmes nodded. "And the dramatic gesture. Behold." He pressed a button on his brother's desk. Immediately, the wall behind Mycroft was transformed into a grid of vertical and horizontal lines, the vertical ones evenly spaced but the spaces between the horizontal ones diminishing and then increasing again in cyclical fashion as one went upward. From lower-left corner to upper-right ran a straight, thick red line, slicing across the green lines of the grid. Points along the red line were circled and labelled in black.

"Good heavens," I muttered as recognition came. It was an enlarged version of the graph Holmes had drawn for Lily, Mrs. Hudson, and me on the farm more than twenty years earlier.

"You recognize it. Good," Holmes said approvingly, as though I were a schoolboy and he the master. "I've been able to add a few more points since Sussex, of course."

Leaning closer, I could see what he meant. The circled points I had noticed earlier were labelled, to the left of each, with the names of leaders assassinated before 1991, while the first five points were also labelled on the right—but these were the names of victims since 1991, at the mirror points in time. Thus the lowest point of the graph bore to the left the name Sadat, to the right the name Phitsanulok; the next lowest point was identified as King to the left and Rex to the right; and so on through Kennedy/Wu, Abdullah/Morgenthaler, and Gandhi/Dashnakian.

As Sherlock Holmes moved toward the chart, his brother Mycroft move aside, clearly deferring to him. "We are now here," Holmes said crisply, placing his bony index finger on the diagonal red line at a point slightly beyond Gandhi/Dashnakian.

"And in, um, six years," I said, "we'll have Trotsky slash whom?"

"And," Mycroft added, his tone one of deep pessimism, "where?"

"Yes," I agreed quickly, "that's the old problem, isn't it? And it's still as insoluble as ever. Think of the surface area of Earth and the number of political leaders there, and then add to that the Libration Satellite and Mariner Valley." I shook my head. "It's utterly impossible, Holmes."

He laughed at me. "Still trying to practise your psychoanalysis on me, Watson? I thought you had learned a good hundred and fifty years ago that I have no subconscious! No, no, I assure you that my obsession with Moriarty is not an unhealthy one, but rather a logical result of my estimation of the danger he represents.

"Moreover," he continued, "the pursuit is not so impossible as at first sight it might appear to be. Not at all, Watson. Consider first the clear trend of Moriarty's *idée fixe:* Indisputably, it is in our direction, toward Mars. I refer to his increasing attraction to men of power who are somehow connected with the doings of these three colonies. And secondly I ask you consider once again Mohammed and his mountain."

While I waited impatiently for him to elucidate this cryptic remark, he perversely grew silent instead and drew from his pocket an object I had not seen in decades and had not expected to see ever again. It was his old huge briar, darker than ever with age and the accumulation of tobacco exudations, and with it he had brought forth a pouch which could only contain that shag which had sustained him through so many a lonely hour.

"Tobacco, Holmes?" I exclaimed. "Surely that is not part of the New Way. Surely Man's next great evolutionary leap entails—nay, necessitates—that he leave such vices behind."

He chuckled. "One must choose one's dogmas only as they are appropriate and useful, Watson. You're right enough about the official Martian view of tobacco, though. It's certainly not a normal import. However, what Siger Sherrinford asks for, Siger Sherrinford always gets." He loaded and lit his pipe in a smug and self-satisfied way and soon began to emit the huge clouds of hot smoke I remembered so well from Baker Street, ignoring in the meantime the stiff back and disapproving scowls of Siger Sherrinford.

Had tobacco changed or had I? I who had once happily smoked any tobacco product available in England now could scarce keep from recoiling in horror from the smell and acridity of the fumes. Whichever was the case, my distaste for Holmes' smoking led me to end my visit shortly thereafter.

As I journeyed slowly homeward, I asked myself why, after all, I had bothered to come.

For, despite his easy ways, his relaxed and almost teasing manner so reminiscent of the Sherlock Holmes of old, I was aware of a subtle but impenetrable barrier separating us. It may have been simply his preoccupation with Moriarty, distracting him from other matters. It could have been that, but I sensed instead that there was something new to him, as if his character had, for the first time in a century, developed some important new dimension or depth, and for reasons of his own he wished to keep this hidden from me.

And as for Siger Sherrinford, alias Mycroft Holmes, I could scarcely say I had found his company pleasant. As Mycroft, in earlier days, he had been rather intimidating simply because of his mighty intellect, but I had found him nonetheless a convivial host and an amiable, if determinedly sedentary, companion. Now, as Siger Sherrinford, he had become as stiff and starched and humorless a fanatic as one could dread finding in the colonies.

Thereafter, however, Sherlock Holmes not infrequently visited Lily and me. He seemed to know when we would be at home in our small cottage outside Newmanton. Clearly he had sources of information concerning our movements, for we were not at home often, and certainly there was little in the way of routine or schedule to our movements.

He would show up disguised as one Martian type or another—transport driver, farmer, magma tender, and so on—and gladly revert to himself once safely inside and out of view of prying eyes. After dark, after the short twilight occasioned by our low latitude and the depth of Mariner Valley, and before the numbing chill of a valley night set in, driving us inside to pressurised warmth, he would light up his pipe and chat with us, pausing occasionally to blow into the air of Mars vast clouds of particles and gases that that long-suffering planet had never before known. Despite our joint distaste for his smoking, Lily and I felt flattered indeed that after so much time, after such a gulf both temporal and physical in our relationship, Sherlock Holmes still felt so relaxed, so at his ease, and so safe in our home. Occasionally on those visits he would bring with him a gift of sinful indulgence whose virtual absence from the New Way colonies made it priceless to me: a bottle of Scotch whisky. On those occasions, Holmes would puff on his pipe and Lily and I would sip Scotch gratefully; those evening were idylls.

And yet even on those most relaxed and congenial evenings, I could still sense the barrier separating Sherlock Holmes from me. He would be full of questions about my work and Lily's and would listen with every appearance of fascination to our replies, urging us to continue whenever the flow of words ebbed, but he would never be as communicative himself in return. Pressed about his own doings on Mars, his stock reply was, "I? Why, building a mountain, of course."

23

Concerning Martian Vegetables

IN THIS FASHION, busy and yet generally peaceful and uneventful in comparison with the excess of events taking place on the Mother World, almost four decades passed.

A new colony was begun in Claritas Fossae. What we all called Mariner Valley is actually a huge system of canyons and rifts, some of them connected to each other by nature and others by the hand of Man. The result is a vast area of essentially continuous valley floor, making the spreading of human settlement down the valley relatively easy. Claritas Fossae represented our first serious attempt at settling a valley not physically connected with the one we had already tamed. Claritas Fossae is geologically yet another extension of the system, but from the human point of view it is a separate valley, running north and south, perpendicular to Mariner Valley, and at its closest point to the old colonies separated by about 200 miles of open Martian plains.

The techniques learned in making Mariner Valley habitable were applied to Claritas Fossae with satisfying results. Unfortunately, the stirring up of ancient dust, combined with the addition of moisture and an atmosphere, brought to virulent life a microscopic Martian organism which must have lain undisturbed for ages. Astronomers had long suspected that Mars goes through brief, violent, well separated periods of heavy liquid water flows—floods—on its surface, otherwise so frighteningly arid. Perhaps the existence of the organism was proof of such episodes in the past. What was undeniable was its reawakening to vicious life with the arrival of Man in Claritas Fossae and the consequent severe illness of most in the new colony.

It was a seriously debilitating illness, complete with the fever, nausea, and diarrhoea symptomatic of the body's attempt to rid itself of an invader. That it was fatal to fewer than one in ten of those who caught it was perhaps a tribute to the wisdom of the stringent selection criteria for new colonists decreed by the Martian government. Offended as I had once been by those criteria, I was now forced to admit that they had proved their worth strikingly.

Lily and I proved quite immune to the disease, as did Sherlock Holmes. I could only conclude happily that this was yet another side effect of our youth-preserving chemical.

My immunity made it possible for me to work with the victims in search of a cure. It was largely through my efforts that the organism was isolated and a specific cure and a vaccine developed. However, I had learned long before to shun publicity, and so it was that I encouraged those working under me to publish our results in an Earth-based journal under their own names. Personal aggrandisement, I realised, no longer meant anything to me. So long as I had Lily and worthwhile work, and an eternity to devote to both, I felt I would be content.

With the disease under control, the settlement of Claritas Fossae proceeded apace. Because of the rôle I had played in making Claritas Fossae safe for human evolution, I was asked to suggest a name for the new colony. Thus it is that I can take credit for one of Mars' cities not being called New Evolutionary Hope for Mankind, or some such thing, but rather bearing the good, solid English name of Hewisham.

My circuit now expanded to include Hewisham and the smaller settlements spreading down Claritas Fossae. This necessitated many hours at a time in a sealed vehicle, trundling along High Road 1, the highway across the bleak plains from New Way City to Hewisham. Despite its grand name, it was in fact nothing more than a cleared and marked trail.

The successes with Claritas Fossae were repeated with other valleys, and with craters, and so the number of settlements kept spreading. The number of doctors on Mars, however, did not increase at a matching rate, and so I spent a steadily increasing number of hours travelling along the spreading network of highways crossing the plains. Thus my life became ever fuller and my leisure time and the time I could spend with Lily ever less.

*

[163]

The year 2042 arrived, the mirror year for the murder of Leon Trotsky. The murder we had awaited with such dread occurred, but it was on Earth, and it had nothing to do with Mars. Nor did it even fit the parameters long ago enunciated by Sherlock Holmes for the involvement of Moriarty. I must admit I exulted.

"A minor Japanese member of Parliament!" I said gleefully. "Hah!"

"Diet," Sherlock Holmes said placidly between puffs on his pipe and sips of whisky, for it was during one of his visits, and the three of us were on the verandah I had recently built on to our cottage, enjoying the air that daily grew more benign.

"I beg your pardon?"

"Diet," he repeated. "It's properly called the Diet, not the Parliament."

"They may call it what they wish," I snapped, "but it's copied from ours, and therefore it's a parliament." He chuckled, but I rushed on to forestall his burdening us with his favored old saw about my being the one unchanging point in a changing world. "The *point* is, Holmes, the point *is* that Kambayashi was a very minor figure, even in Japan and certainly on the world stage, and that his political philosophy, as I understand it, was to achieve parliamentary longevity by drawing as little attention to himself as he could and by making no enemies."

"He made one, at least," Holmes observed mildly.

"Damn it all, Holmes, that's quite irrelevant. You can't avoid losing this argument that way! So Kambayashi voted indiscreetly on some issue in someone's view. That doesn't alter the fact that he was of little importance in the world or his own country and that he satisfied none of the requirements you hypothesised long ago for Professor Moriarty's *idée fixe*."

"Actually, Watson, *you* hypothesised them, if I remember correctly, in Utah in 1991."

"Irrelevant again! Just as Kambayashi was irrelevant, insignificant, trivial! What d'you say to that?"

"*I* say," Lily cut in, "that he was probably very important to his family, and I wish you wouldn't ignore that fact."

I waved a hand. "Oh, of course. I'm fully sympathetic to Mrs. Kambayashi and all the little Kambayashis."

[164]

"John! How cruel and unfeeling!"

"Why, Lily," Holmes interposed, "surely you noticed long ago how cruel and unfeeling a brute you're married to? He only pretends to appreciate fine music and fine wine and fine tobacco and fine women, but in fact," Holmes shook his head, "in fact he is devoid of all the softer emotions." Calmly alternating sips and puffs, he stared thoughtfully into the deepening darkness. Lily and I exchanged a startled look, and there was a long and awkward pause in the conversation.

Holmes broke the silence at last. "The fact is, of course, that you are perfectly correct about Kambayashi, Watson."

"Aha!"

He held up his hand. "About Kambayashi," he repeated. "Once again, you have leapt to a conclusion without being in possession of the relevant data, and thus your conclusion is false, as conclusions prematurely reached so often are."

I foresaw already that I would end by admitting defeat, but to cover my dismay I blustered. "Data! What data? You're bluffing, Holmes."

"Tsk, Watson. I never bluff. Kambayashi's assassination on the right date was a mere coincidence, and if you had checked the figures carefully, you would have discovered that the *time* of his murder missed the proper point by several hours."

"But I *did* consider the time of day, and—" Then I cursed, for I realised that in my haste to exult over Holmes I had used the time given in the news report of Kambayashi's death. However, since the report broadcast on Mars had originated with the BBC in London, the time had been Greenwich time, not Tokyo time.

Holmes grinned. "I deduce that you were off by nine hours, the difference between London and Tokyo. A further coincidence, I grant you, that the time in London when Kambayashi died was correct to within a few minutes of the precise mirror point, but a coincidence nonetheless and one that should not have misled you. Moreover, at *precisely* the right time, an attempt was made here on Mars on the life of Siger Sherrinford."

"Good God!"

Lily gasped. "Your brother! He's—"

"Oh, no, no," Holmes said quickly. "I should have said 'an

unsuccessful attempt.' Mycroft is perfectly unharmed, his giant intellect clicking along with its usual mechanical efficiency." He added coolly, "This is the first failure at a mirror point we are aware of."

"But no one knows of Mycroft's importance outside the innermost circles of government," I protested.

"Indeed," he nodded. "But it's the old story, you see. Moriarty knows nothing of contemporary politics here or on Earth, of course. How could he? He has no need to know. It is the *aura of power*, the importance of the victim, the concentration of authority in one man, which draws him, and no doubt quite without Moriarty's conscious intervention. Mycroft's rôle was itself the attractant. And by the way, as far as Mycroft and I can determine, this attempt was made *by Moriarty himself*, rather than by assassins of our own time with whom fate and the laws governing time oscillation had associated him."

A chill ran down my spine. Lily said in a frightened voice, "This is something new. Now he's actively doing it all himself."

"Yes, Lily," Holmes said gently. "And I very much fear we will see even more of such activity by him in the future." His mood abruptly lightening, he said, "So you see, Watson, I am more unable than ever to follow the advice you were so obviously about to give me earlier: that I overcome my own *idée fixe*, Moriarty, and turn to more wholesome pursuits. The problem of Professor Moriarty remains as urgent as ever it was."

"It would seem so," I said sombrely.

"Yes. So I have much to do during the coming decades." And then he uttered that enigmatic phrase that had already become his stock answer to any questions of mine concerning his activities: "I have a mountain to build."

The years passed and life grew busier, more and more cluttered with detail and duty, and my old complaints began anew.

"I'm vegetating here, Lily! Turning into a genuine Martian vegetable. I fix cuts and set broken bones and deliver babies . . ."

"And find cures for major epidemics and force sensible place names on these stuffed shirts and help open up vast new tracts for human settlement."

"Well, yes," I admitted, quite pleased. "That, too. But what does it all really mean? Where is it all leading?"

"Why should it lead anywhere? John, there's no further to go. Mars is it for now. Of course, we could go back to Earth. . . ."

I shuddered at the thought. The Renascence wars had ended at last a few years earlier, leaving Britain, Europe, and North America shattered and the rest of the world reeling. The Renascence Party had been swept from power in the United Kingdom in the aftermath (more because it had failed than because the public had rejected its ideals), but it had left the world an ugly legacy. Equivalent nationalistic movements had sprung up everywhere, each promising voters a return to some imagined past glory. Clearly, Earth was in for decades of war and unrest. The Libration Satellite, meanwhile, had withdrawn into a smug, self-contained prosperity, and the political and economic chaos on the Mother World had made any new colonisation movement, whether on the moon of Earth or on those of Saturn or Jupiter, unthinkable for perhaps the rest of the century. Only on Mars was there the combination of peace, prosperity, and a vigorous, outward-looking population. Indeed, if there was to be further colonisation in the solar system before the start of the twenty-second century, it was clear to me that the new settlers would call themselves Martians and not Earthmen. No, for all its many faults, Mars was definitely the place for us. "No," I sighed, "no, of course not. But . . . Oh, I don't know."

"Ah, but I *do* know," Lily said, returning from the kitchen with two steaming mugs of cocoa *cum* whisky. "It's the old, old problem, darling. No, actually it's absolutely new in the history of the human species. You are suffering, my dear, from the inevitable depression of the immortal who realises that he doesn't know what he's going to do with the next few billion years. We were brought up to think in terms of much shorter lifespans. In your case, grow up, become a doctor, practise for forty or fifty years, grow old, retire, and die. Not terribly purposeful, maybe, but at least it's straightforward and well defined."

"Yes, you're right! That's it. Male menopause, but far worse. What *am* I going to do for the next few billion years? Or even the next few million? Or thousand?"

"Oh, let's give it a couple of centuries, and *then* we'll decide.

Maybe we'll have interstellar travel by then. Think of the scope *that* would open up! In the meantime, you say you're a Martian veggie. So settle down and put down a tap root."

I burst out laughing. "What botanical nonsense!"

Lily shrugged. "So next time around marry a computer. Anyway, it wasn't my brain that attracted you in the first place, was it?"

"No," I admitted, eyeing her. "Not primarily."

"Good. Because it wasn't *your* brain that I wanted to get my hands on, either. And a good thing, too."

We retired for the night, leaving our cocoa to grow cold.

And so matters rolled along.

By the 2060s, Earth was more a shambles than ever, with first one nation or alliance or race trying to assert dominance and then another, and with none of those attempts succeeding.

Mars, meanwhile, went from strength to strength. It was increasingly prospereous and productive, exporting food, raw materials, and manufactured goods to Earth and even to the Libration Satellite. Its population reached the ten million mark, spread out in settlements in many valleys and craters. Already in places and at certain times of the year, one could travel the dusty high plains between settlements without special oxygenating equipment. The future looked ever more interesting, and I was becoming almost reconciled to my vegetable existence, since the Martian soil promised more diversion than most vegetables have any right to expect.

If there was a cloud on the horizon, it was the evolution of the original Outward Movement fanaticism into an extreme Martian nationalism and Spartan devotion to duty and planet that reminded me disturbingly of the fascism of 130 years earlier and of the Renascence movement of much more recent times. Even the phrase "place in the sun" reappeared, used with the implication that it would soon be the turn of Mars to rule all the haunts of Man. This was most frequently evident in the rabble-rousing speeches of Meesian, the apparent leader of this element, whose resemblance in terms of influence and effect to Adolf Hitler was frightening.

[168]

Perhaps, I suggested to Lily, Holmes and his brother, Mycroft, were in a position to channel Martian energies in more wholesome directions. Certainly they should try to muzzle Meesian. However, whenever I suggested this to Sherlock Holmes, he would only reply with an enigmatic smile.

24

Rache

PERHAPS EXTREMISM of any kind inevitably elicits a movement at the other end of the spectrum. Be that as it may, it was certainly the case that, during the late sixties, a Martian named Philo Tremusson, a third-generation son of the New Way, began agitating for something quite the opposite of both nationalism and fascism.

Tremusson stood in opposition to Meesian in virtually every way, calling repeatedly for loyalty to the human species rather than a nation or a planet or a race or a movement. "The Mother World," Tremusson proclaimed, "calls out to us in her agony. We are her children, grown rich and technologically advanced. How can we ignore her pleas?" Martians, he said, should cease to call themselves that, should instead call themselves simply human beings, and should use their great wealth and high technology and abundant extra food to help the suffering multitudes of Earth.

To my surprise, not all Martians reacted to his message with antagonism. Certainly the majority did, and there were too many who were willing to accede to Meesian's fulminations that Tremusson was a filthy traitor who should be exiled forthwith to the Earth he apparently loved so much. Yet a substantial number of the patients I visited in Mariner Valley and Claritas Fossae and elsewhere and people I encountered socially said in private that Tremusson's appeals touched something within them, while Meesian they considered a lout, an oaf, a boor, and a danger to Mars.

I reported this to Holmes, journeying to his office in the capital solely for the purpose, since I didn't think it would be wise to say anything about it on the public communications net. "And so you see," I concluded, "the seeds are there. It should be rela-

tively simple for you and Mycroft to shut Meesian up and pro-
mote Tremusson and his message."

Sherlock Holmes was relaxing in a deep armchair as I spoke,
almost lying on his back. This had become, in latter days, his
favored substitute for the sofa he had so loved to lie on a century
and a half or more earlier. When I had finished, he snorted. "Tremusson is a mole, undermining my mountain slowly but surely.
Whereas Meesian . . . Well, Watson, let me say simply that I do
not find Meesian's words uncongenial."

I sprang to my feet. "What? That latter-day Hitler? This is an
unexpected shock, Holmes, and a most unpleasant one! I would
not have expected sympathy for fascist nationalism from the man
who foiled von Bork."

He held up a hand, smiling gently. "The times have changed,
Watson, and so have the circumstances. My fight with the Count
von und zu Grafenstein was more due to patriotism than to any
philosophical disagreement. Had I been born a German instead
of an Englishman—why, who knows, it might well have been
Herr von Holmstein spying on England in 1914, rather than Herr
von Bork."

"Tsha! Disgusting! Let me tell you, then, that I intend to make
contact with this Tremusson and do what I can to help him."

Holmes shrugged. "Do so if you wish. Do as you feel you must.
You will find the offices of his fledgling political party only a
few blocks down the street from here. I must warn you, however, that in my estimation you would be making a mistake. To
paraphrase what I told you after we had defeated von Bork, there
is a wind coming, a cold and bitter wind, and many of us may
wither before its blast. I think the future of this world lies with
Meesian, not Philo Tremusson."

"Perhaps so, Holmes, but *my* future lies with what is right
and proper."

He threw back his head and laughed. "It always has, Watson!
Well, well, we shall see what we shall see. Perhaps we'll meet
on the hustings."

It would have required more than the derision of my old friend
to sway me from my determination. I did join Tremusson's new
group, called simply enough the Union Party, and so did Lily.

She made it clear, however, that her own feelings were mixed.

"Maybe it's evolution, John. Natural selection, survival of the fittest. Maybe we *should* let Earth stagnate or even die. The worthwhile people will emigrate out here, if they're able to. As for Earth as a whole—well, maybe it doesn't deserve to survive any more. Out *here* is the future, as I told you a long time ago."

"Now who's cruel and unfeeling?"

"Oh, gosh. Oh, gee. Oh, wow. All right, you win. I'll join up. Where's the dotted line?"

"I didn't expect sarcasm in my own home," I said bitterly.

Despite Lily's undisguised half-heartedness and frequently expressed cynicism about this new enthusiasm of mine, I now included political campaigning for the Union Party and its goals with my medical work, even when Lily happened to be travelling along with me. Because of my many trips, the vast area I covered, and the esteem in which I was held in the remote settlements, I believe I was a most effective spokesman. Until now, elections on Mars had been little more than an occasional ratification of the leadership's policies: After all, there had never yet been any large-scale disagreement with or opposition to those policies, and certainly nothing resembling a political party. The next election, I felt sure, would be a different matter. What a pity it was a full six years off, in 2073.

In response to our growing influence, Meesian announced the formation of his own party and its intention to run candidates for all major offices in 2073. "The Mars First Party," Lily said with a giggle. "Straightforward and aboveboard, anyway, isn't it? The MFP. Wasn't that a toothpaste or something when I was a kid?"

"They ought to call it the MUAP," I said with heavy sarcasm, "the Mars *Über Alles Partei.*"

Sarcasm, though, couldn't change the fact that public opinion polls showed the MFP holding a fairly secure margin over the UP. That lead could only be eliminated, I knew, by the hard and unceasing work of such UP stalwarts as John Watson.

Ever since that long-ago time on the Libration Satellite when Lily had said something about a foot race up Olympus Mons without respirators, the idea of climbing the highest and widest volcano accessible to Man had intrigued me. Six hundred and forty kilometres across at its base and twenty kilometres high, with a crater roughly seventy-five kilometres wide—all of this, and only 1,000 kilometres away from New Way City. To one who had loved the Alps and the Rockies, this was truly irresistible. Even so, it had taken more than thirty years for us to get around to it, but we finally did.

We joined an intrepid little group from Hewisham and spent two weeks struggling up the flanks of the mighty volcano. (And only Mars' light gravity made even that possible!) The view across the surface of Mars in one direction, and in the other into the vast and frightening crater, made the long effort worthwhile.

I was so impressed that that evening, with all of us safe inside our large, pressurised tent and ready for sleep, I made an impromptu speech boosting the policies of the Union Party. Considering the time and the place and our common physical exhaustion, and except for two hecklers who insisted they would much rather be allowed to sleep, it was rather well received.

So well received, in fact, that during our slow, tedious descent of the mountain, I confided my latest enthusiasm to my wife and helpmeet. "By George, Lily, I begin to wonder if I shouldn't run for office myself! Philo seems so content to stay behind the scenes, that perhaps even the top position isn't beyond my grasp. Planetary Administrator, eh? What d'you say to that?"

She twisted her respirator away from her mouth. "Actually, I would've preferred going to sleep to listening to a speech, too."

We both replaced our respirators and continued the descent in silence.

The idea stayed with me, however. Tremusson seemed just as taken with it. As I had told Lily, he was a retiring sort, dedicated wholly to his philosophy of union with Earth and its peoples, but uncomfortable when making speeches. It was a pity, too, for his appearance was a good one for a politician. He was middle-aged, with a full head of dark hair, a well-defined, clean-cut face, and a clear, determined gaze. It was a face to inspire confidence and belief, and in my opinion he had a voice to match. When I told him as much and encouraged him to make more speeches, he grimaced.

"No, Hamish, I just hate being on camera or in front of a crowd.

It's . . . I feel like I'm naked. You know what happens to me when I try to make a public speech. I drop my eyes to the floor and I turn red and I stutter. An inspiring figure!"

"But contrast that with Meesian," I urged. "He's never seen at all. His speeches are made by flunkies. You know, the popular opinion is that at the least he must be horribly ugly. Anyway, by appearing in public, you would emphasise the difference."

He shivered at the thought. "Suddenly," he said, "I feel this deep sympathy for Meesian. Tell you what, I'll write the speeches and the UP will pay for the time, and then you deliver them."

"In short," I explained to Holmes later, "he's happy to have someone so handsome, well spoken, and capable as Hamish MacWatt as the party's public figurehead."

Holmes' reaction was an amused smile. "A rare bird, this MacWatt," he agreed. "Wherever did you dig him up?"

Lily went along only reluctantly with my emergence as a political candidate. "If it'll help you through menopause, I shouldn't complain, right?"

"I had wished for a heartier enthusiasm."

A look of guilt crossed her face. "I'll try to whip some up."

On the basis of this shaky truce, this uneasy, implicit arrangement, we let the subject drop. Later, though, as a peacemaking gesture, Lily began to work for a few hours a month as a volunteer at Union Party headquarters in New Way City.

And now I have arrived at that episode, the recording of which I have dreaded ever since I began writing the latter half of this chronicle, for to recount it is to relive it.

In 2071, I was in the middle of a visit to a small research station far from home, bringing the lonely scientists a touch of contact with their own homes, healing their fortunately minor hurts, and doing a bit of political campaigning on the side. While I was dressing an electrical burn on the arm of a young technician, I noticed that the book he was reading to distract himself from my ministrations was a thick work on Russian history. "Did you bring that along in case I had to operate?" I asked him. "So there'd be no need for an anesthetic?"

"Oh, no, Doctor. It's fascinating stuff. It makes you realise how even back then, people were like us."

"Back when?"

"1911, the part I'm reading right now."

"Just like us in 1911? Young man, I refuse to believe that. What was happening in Russia in 1911?" And why, I asked myself, did that year strike a faint chord in memory?

The young technician chuckled. "Oh, about a zillion bombs were set off by anarchists. And assassinations. Hell, they even got a prime minister."

"Who was that?"

"Um . . ." He checked quickly in the book. "Stolypin. Pyotr Stolypin. Hell of a name."

I had stopped stopped working on his arm as memory returned. "The date?" I whispered.

"Huh? What date?"

"Stolypin's assassination, man! What was the date?"

"Oh, uh, September 14, 1911. He was a good man, too."

And now it was the 18th of February, 2071. Some overpowering intuition told me not to pause to make calculations but to return to New Way City instantly. Hurriedly I began to throw my instruments and supplies into my bag.

"Doc? What're you doing?"

It was my young patient, whose existence had utterly fled my mind. "What? Oh. I must get back to New Way City immediately."

"But you're not finished here yet. And anyway, they say the dust storms are starting up already. Earlier than expected this time around."

I didn't spare the time to answer but instead grabbed my almost-full bag and rushed from the room. I had a sealed vehicle; why should I hesitate for a mere dust storm? I had been through the dust-storm cycle twice already during my thirty-seven years on Mars and had found them nothing to be concerned about: The sky had darkened and fine particles had filtered down into the valley, but that had been all.

As I climbed into my sealed, ten-wheeled car, ignoring the base personnel gathered about and urging me to wait the storm out with them, the horizon was already growing indistinct. I had not gone far out on the plains before the horizon disappeared completely, and shortly thereafter the base I had just left vanished too. The cockpit windows were transformed to opaque sheets of reddish brown. My navigation must now be entirely by instrument. Even wireless communication quickly degraded and then became useless due to the static charges of the uncountable dust particles.

This was a far mightier storm than the previous two. Time and again during the hours that followed I felt my vehicle tilt to one side as the wind lifted half its wheels off the ground. The wind was blowing broadside against me, but my course and my sense of urgency dictated that that would continue, not allowing me the safer tactic of zigzagging to drive first into the wind and then with it. Only luck and the car's wide, low design kept it from rolling onto its side. I kept my eyes glued to the compass, heading straight for New Way City and Lily, and oblivious to the danger of the storm, to the high probability that, driving blind, I would simply blunder into some crater or rille and drop to my death, and to the constant susurrous of the sand against the exterior of the car. I cared only that Moriarty was due and that he would surely appear on Mars.

It was purely good fortune that the path was clear all the way to the rim of Valles Marineris. I sat glued to the seat in the cockpit for two days and two nights, utterly unaware of the need for food or sleep or other physical relief. I had entered something akin to a trance by the time my car ran up against the solid stone wall of the transmitting station on the valley rim, for I sat stultified at the controls for some moments, the wheels spinning futilely, digging themselves into the sand, before I came to my senses.

Sheltering myself in the lee of the car, I stumbled into the transmitting station. Here, an elevator took me down to the floor of the valley on the outskirts of New Way City. The dust was thick even in the valley. Those who had no choice but to be outside their homes hurried through the streets, scuffling along in the gathering layer of fine, red dust that blanketed everything, wearing respirators and blinking red-eyed at each other through the pink haze.

I ran all the way to the Union Party offices. I'm sure that my body was weakened by hunger, thirst, and the constant tension and lack of sleep to or beyond the point of exhaustion. However, I was unaware of any fatigue, unaware of anything beside my driving, growing, overpowering need to reach Lily before . . . Before what? I could not have said, only that something threatened her and that the evil was upon us. My intuition was correct, but I was too late.

At the office building where Philo Tremusson's party was headquartered, I found both Sherlock and Mycroft Holmes awaiting me in the hallway outside the door to Philo's office. A crowd stood about with that combination of long faces and eager eyes common at disasters. My alarm grew even greater. I would have pushed into the office, but Sherlock Holmes grasped my shoulders, his thin fingers digging into my flesh with desperate strength. His face was haggard and drawn, his eyes anguished, his voice pleading. "For God's sake, Watson, don't go in!"

"A cliché, Holmes." And of course, he could hardly have chosen a cliché more likely to make me eager to enter. I pushed him aside and went in. Lily was not there. Philo Tremusson, however, was. He was behind his desk, leaning backward in his armchair, looking at the ceiling and wearing an expression combining amazement with agony. My greeting died on my lips. The desk, the carpet, Philo's clothing—all were soaked with blood. There was a still oozing hole beneath Philo's left eye, and his throat had been torn out. I must confess to my shame that, horrified as I was at what had been done to this man of peace, this saint, my concern was all for Lily.

I spun about to find Sherlock Holmes behind me. "Where is she?" I demanded. "Where's Lily?"

He licked his lips. "She's all right, I believe."

"You *believe!* Where *is* she?"

He turned away from me. When he brought himself to speak, his voice was filled with pain. "Watson, I can only tell you what I saw. But come away from this awful place first."

I turned back to look at Philo. Suddenly I was overcome by nausea, and even more by the realisation that this man in whom I had placed so many hopes was dead, swept from the stage of human activity with shocking, senseless brutality. Numbed, my worry about Lily's safety beginning to be swallowed by bewilderment, I followed Sherlock Holmes from the room and down the hallway to another office. Here he produced a chair for me and, as if by magic, a bottle of whisky and a glass. He poured me a generous helping and waited until I had swallowed most of it before he spoke.

"Lily called me from her office, adjacent to Tremusson's," Holmes said quietly. "She was plainly terrified. She could hear Moriarty's voice from next door, ranting at Tremusson, and Tremusson's replying calmly, trying to soothe his visitor. He could of course have had no idea who Moriarty was or what a threat he represented. I told Lily that I was coming immediately and that she should lock herself into her office. Apparently, she chose not to take my advice."

He paused and looked at me with concern, but I said nothing. The power of speech had left me. Indeed, the power of active movement, of conscious control, had departed. I felt unable to do anything but listen and absorb passively, to be acted upon by the callous universe.

Holmes continued. "I arrived too late to save Philo Tremusson. Lily had entered his office a step or two ahead of me. The door was open when I reached it, and Lily was inside. Moriarty was there, too." He paused and licked his lips again. "Moriarty . . . was there, too. He . . . he didn't see me, but he did see Lily."

As he spoke, the image sprang to life before me as if I had been there. I scarcely needed Holmes' description to see and hear what had happened.

Moriarty towered over Lily, leaning toward her. Two spots of color glowed high on his cheeks. His head moved back and forth in its hypnotic, reptilian manner. "You!" he hissed. "You *did* survive! And you betrayed me in America, didn't you?"

Lily, unable to speak, could only nod.

"And because of you I failed and Holmes and Watson live." He would have said more, but he felt the faintest beginnings of the compression, and the hint, the echo, of the onrushing atomic blast, closer behind him than ever. With a cry of mingled fear and fury, Moriarty leaped forward, flinging his arms about Lily and holding her captive against him.

At that instant, Holmes at last willed himself to move. "And at that instant," he whispered, "they vanished. Lily and Moriarty vanished together. For just an instant, I thought I saw a brilliant light and felt a flash of heat, but it must have been an illusion. And yet I *do* have something like a sunburn on my face." He laughed nervously. "Watson. Watson . . ."

I had risen painfully to my feet and stood swaying. "I don't blame you. None of this is your fault."

He put his hands on my shoulders. "Work is the only salve for such a loss, my friend. I need your help. Mankind needs you. We have less than a hundred years left to build our mountain."

"Build a mountain, Holmes! Good God, build a mountain!" I sagged back into the chair, my arms dangling without strength by my sides, and I wept helplessly. How could this madman speak to me of building mountains when I had plunged to the bottom of the pit?

Interlude

WHAT WAS this place?

Lily looked about her in bewilderment. She stood next to a curving, rising street. On the other side of it was a park, quiet and graceful, and beyond that the sea. The sky was hazy, white mist on the horizon, and the sea calm and blue. In the park, the leaves of the trees stirred suddenly to life, and moments later Lily felt the sea breeze herself on her face and bare arms and legs. She shivered suddenly in the cool, moist air: It had been warm in New Way City. *New Way City . . . Then where am I now?*

Behind her were the well-kept lawns of a peaceful, prosperous residential neighborhood. It was naggingly familiar. Lily frowned, trying to pin down the memory.

Old photographs. Yes, that's it. She had seen family photographs of this very scene. Those had been ancient pictures of San Francisco, of the house her ancestors on her mother's side had lived in before they'd moved to Illinois. As far as she could remember the story, the ancestress after whom she had been named had lived with cousins on this street, perhaps in one of those very houses. *Unless all of these have been built since that time. The style looks right for the late nineteenth century, though. They've been well preserved,* she thought admiringly. How could she possibly have travelled the intervening millions of miles from Mars? Lily shut her eyes, trying to remember.

Moriarty! That was the first memory, and as it emerged, she shivered violently. *He grabbed at me. No, he caught me.* Another shudder, this one of revulsion. She remembered being pressed against him, full length, the hold of predation, not love. *And then there was that flash of heat and light, just the way John described it that time Moriarty attacked him. And then, and then . . . What happened then?* Frantically she clutched at fading memories of a grey place and time, lasting interminably. She recalled Moriarty's face looming over hers in that greyness, glaring demonically with the joy of vengeance achieved, mouthing words she couldn't hear. Then she had been torn away from him by something immense and implacable, and her last memory of him was of his clutching hands and scrabbling fingers sliding off her and of his face contorted into a howl, a shriek, an inhuman scream of frustration, but with no sound coming from him. And then she was here.

"There was a man," she muttered. A mental image of one old snapshot had come sharply to her, and she could see in it a man standing just about where she stood now. He was rigid and unsmiling, and his clothes were those of the late 1880s. How little this neighborhood had changed since those photographs were taken! Lily had always meant to visit here some day but had never found the opportunity.

I'll have to find a communications center somewhere and call Mars. John can transfer enough credit and I'll book passage home. Or he could come and join me here for a vacation, if it wouldn't be too painful for him. For she knew that San Francisco must inevitably remind him of that other Lily Cantrell he had known and loved in this city in the mid-1880s. He had returned to England, saved his money, and then sent for her as prearranged as soon as he could afford it. Only to be informed by a letter from her relatives that his Lily had left home on a shopping trip into the city and had vanished without a trace. *Why, what a coincidence! It never even occurred to me before that both my great-something grandmother and John's Lily Cantrell were in San Francisco at about the same time.*

Just then she noticed that one of the houses nearby was not yet complete. It had not been apparent at first glance, but now she could see that the topmost section of its walls and the roof were little more than wooden framework. *But—But it was complete in the photograph.* For an instant, the world reeled, but then she discovered solid ground again. *Oh, it's being renovated, of course. That's it.*

At that moment, a man came around the curve of the sidewalk, toiling up the hill toward her. He stopped as soon as he saw Lily, and they stared at each other in matching open-mouthed amazement. Lily stared because it was most certainly the man of the old photograph, complete to the many layers of clothing of 300 years ago. His face and bearing were almost as stiff as she remembered from the photograph. A suspicion began to grow in her that made her heart race and robbed her legs of all strength. Those very legs, well exposed by Lily's shorts, were what had made the newcomer's jaw drop—and her short-sleeved, open-necked shirt and sandals. Suddenly he whipped off his jacket and flung it to her. "Cover yourself!" he said harshly.

Top or bottom? Lily wondered. She decided that legs must be the most offensive to a Victorian gentleman, so she wrapped the copious garment as best she could about her lower half. She affected an air of injured, bewildered innocence; under the circumstances, that came easily to her. "Kind sir, perhaps you can help me. I'm looking for the house of my cousins, Thomas and Eliza Cantrell." *Thank heavens for family histories.*

The anger vanished from his face. "Why, *I'm* Thomas Cantrell. The house is just over there, and my sister is at home. But who are you?"

Oh, God, it's real! I'm really in the 1880s. And John . . . is 300 years in the future. I don't have the pills. I can't live that long. The sudden flow of tears was not feigned. "No, uh, Thomas. You didn't know about us. We lived in Illinois. We were all moving out here, the entire family." She licked her lips and thought quickly. "We were almost here when the Indians attacked. I'm the only survivor." She elaborated, "I played dead, but they stripped the corpses."

"Good gracious, what savages! You poor child. Come inside, quickly."

She hobbled after him as quickly as she could, her movements constrained by the need to keep the borrowed jacket tightly wound around her legs. How very fortunate that Cousin Thomas was too horrified by and taken with her story to ask how she had managed to complete the long journey to San Francisco and then across the city clad only in those curious undergarments.

Entering the house, being given into the maternal arms of Eliza

Cantrell, Lily had the most curious feeling of propriety, of fit-tingness—of inevitability. Something important lay ahead of her, though she could not have said what it was; but she knew it would be something good, even wonderful, and elated anticipa-tion cut through her despair.

Six months later, in January 1885, Lily was introduced to a young doctor fresh from England who had just opened a practise in San Francisco. His name was John Hamish Watson, and now she knew what it was she had been anticipating. So there *was* only one Lily Cantrell, after all, and it was she.

Only one question remained: How much longer would her contraceptive shot, already a year in the past, last? By the time John Watson left for England in the late summer of 1886, having promised her earnestly with many a hug and a kiss that he would be sending her money for a passage to England as soon as he could, she had the answer to that question also.

25

Meesian

ARMIES MARCHED through the streets of Mars.

Scarcely a single physically able resident of Mars between the ages of fifteen and forty-five was not in the army. Daily life continued in a normal enough fashion, but the possibility of being called to active duty was always present.

Other armies, also largely composed of Martians, marched regularly in the streets of Earth's major cities, a demonstration to keep the populace from forgetting where supreme authority lay. The so-called War of Reconquest of 2148 had been bloodless and shortlived. With the ever-deteriorating, fragmenting state of Earth, little more had been required than a demonstration of Martian strength and unity; Earth had succumbed within a day of the official start of war. Now, after twenty-two years of Martian rule, one would be hard put to find anyone on Earth who was unhappy with the situation: The Martian armies had brought with them order, peace, and an everyday security for the ordinary man that had been absent for a century.

And there were new outlets for Man. Mars was settled almost to its limit, but new colonies were springing up on the moon and Venus and in orbit around all three inhabited planets. Each colony was controlled by the inevitable complement of Martians. The total human population hovered near fifteen billion happy, prosperous, well-fed people. Of all the essentials for total satisfaction, they lacked at most one.

All those people, all those armies, all those colonies owed allegiance to one man: Meesian IV, isolated from his subjects on icy Europa, an inner Galilean moon of Jupiter. Europa was the nerve centre and headquarters of his empire and he the only living being on it. It was whispered that he trusted no one else so close to him and that was why the only other residents of Europa were robot servants and vast computer and communications devices of almost human intelligence. What was not whispered, what was most certainly true, was that there had never before, in the history of the human species, been so much power centred in one man, that never before had so many people looked to one place and one individual as the source of all power and all law.

In 2170, on the tenth anniversary of his accession to the throne that was not called a throne, Meesian IV made a speech to his fifteen billion subjects. As was the case with his three predecessors, each of whom had borne the same name, Meesian was called simply Number One. It was an apt enough title, for Number One each of the four had been, without a doubt. What need for more grandiloquent titles, such as King or Emperor? For the four of them, the similarity of governmental style and the family resemblance were equally remarkable.

Meesian IV's speech was broadcast into every human habitation. It was filled with ringing phrases and moving sentiments. Patriotism to the human species, to its glorious future, and above all to Meesian IV figured high in it. Throughout the teeming cities of Earth and Mars, the Venusian colonies, and colonies in space, a busy, industrious populace turned aside from its work to watch and listen to Meesian IV.

Martian history was a required subject in all schools, so that he could be quite sure that the vast majority of his audience knew all the important names, dates, and events in Mars' past. Nonetheless, Meesian recounted it for them.

He reminded them of the death of Philo Tremusson in 2071, ninety-nine years earlier, and of the resulting landslide victory by Meesian I and the Mars First Party over the Union Party in the elections of 2073. A most pleasing tradition had been established then, Meesian pointed out with a twinkle in his eye. Meesian I had been reelected to the highest office on Mars repeatedly, by ever-growing margins. Within a decade of its founder's death, the Union Party had disappeared from the scene, but its principles of a grand union of the human race, cutting across all the old political and physical boundaries, had at last been achieved by Tremusson's political enemies. "And that is why," Meesian intoned unctuously, "I have ordered statues of Philo Tremusson, shown looking at the stars, to be erected in parks everywhere in time for the twenty-fifth anniversary of the War of Reconquest, three years from now. At that time, all history texts will be changed to reflect a new name for that great event: the Reunification. How Tremusson, the old warrior-philosopher, would have loved that!" He beamed at his invisible audience.

Meesian turned abruptly serious. "Now, I know quite well that there are those who say that the failure of the government to hold elections for the past seventy-odd years marks me and my predecessors as tyrants. Nothing could be farther from the truth! Compare our present peaceful, industrious society, with its infinite variety of opportunities available to everyone, to the anarchy that prevailed a century ago. Anarchy, my friends, that is a true tyranny, when no man may be sure at sundown whether he will still be alive by the next sunset, when children starve and cities burn and women are given into slavery." He shook his head sadly. "Ah, my friends, *that* is tyranny indeed, no matter what political system it may call itself."

Some in his audience agreed loudly with what their leader had said. Others muttered to their friends that there must be a third alternative, a path somewhere between anarchy and Meesian. The vast majority had no opinion at all: Things are, of course, as always, just as they are, and that's how they will remain.

Meesian IV went on in this self-congratulatory tone for some time, smugly giving himself and his three predecessors many a sound pat on the back. If the vast audience, scattered across the billions of cubic miles, had begun to nod and yawn drowsily by the end and their attention to wander, Meesian's enigmatic closing lines brought them back to full alertness.

"In an unbroken line, we have ruled now for only three years short of a century—four men with the same name, the same blood, and the same policies. Each of us has deemed his absolute rule to be a better thing than its alternative, anarchy. But what if there were another alternative? Picture yourself, each of you, as a citizen of a democratic, parliamentary republic of interplanetary dimensions, replacing my . . . Well, let us not mince words: my empire. That day must come, must it not? The line of Meesians will end, perhaps with Meesian the One Millionth, perhaps with Meesian IV. Perhaps the day I speak of will come sooner than we imagine, and then it will be the turn of those who preach the democratic, electoral alternative to my reign to prove themselves. Good day, my friends."

As his image faded from the screen, his billions of subjects turned to each other excitedly in some cases, nervously in others, and fell to loud discussions of the meaning of those closing remarks. Was Meesian about to give up power, to leave, to die, to abdicate? They all had the sudden sense of forthcoming change, of an end to a way of life and a security that had lasted for almost a century on Mars and for almost twenty-five years on Earth. To some, the idea brought with it exhilaration; to others, only foreboding and terror.

As soon as the speech was over, Meesian called his assistant, the man who handled for him the day-to-day details of administering Mars and Earth and the settlements elsewhere. "Well, Number Two," he said, "what did you think of it?"

The moustachioed man on the screen grimaced. "Ghastly. One of the very worst political speeches I have ever heard in my long life."

"Hmph. Thank you very much, I'm sure. I can always depend on you not to be a sycophant."

"Always and ever," Number Two agreed. "By the way, do you really think it was wise to hint at what's coming?"

"What we *hope* is coming," Meesian corrected. "I thought I ought to drop some sort of hint, forewarn them somehow. After all, what *will* come after Meesian? The opposition needs some encouragement now, so that they can start organising themselves in a serious way."

"That's all very well for you to say," Number Two grumbled, "sitting up there in your regal isolation and being Olympian. As for me, though, I'll have to handle your opposition over the coming months, as they start to feel their oats."

Number One shook his head. "Dear me. You poor chap. Heal thyself, etc. I have confidence in you, as I always have. You don't fool me, you know. *I* know you're really on their side. *I* know

[187]

you've never really believed it was necessary to do what I've done."

Number Two sighed. "The proof of the pudding, of course. If you succeed in the end, I'll gladly say you were right all along. Less than a month now, isn't it? Oh, by the way, I thought I recognised most of that speech of yours."

Meesian laughed and shook his head. "I might have known you'd remember! It was essentially the tenth anniversary speech of Meesian II, suitably revamped and updated. I really didn't feel like writing another one. Added the ending, of course."

"Ah, yes, I remember now. It was just as ghastly fifty-nine years ago, when Meesian II gave it."

"My loyal comrade. Come up here as soon as you're able. We must make final preparations."

Number Two nodded. "Tomorrow, perhaps. Certainly before the end of the week." He leaned forward and broke the connection. Then he arose and stretched and strolled over to the window, unconsciously twisting his right moustache spike with one hand, making it sharper and smoother. He became aware of what he was doing and stopped with a guilty start. He had been delighted when moustaches had come back into fashion, not least among his reasons being the occupation the style provided for his idle hands. He leaned on the windowsill and stared up at the pink sky and sighed. Yes, he did think the whole Meesian thing had been a mistake, and perhaps the worst mistake had been his participation in it. But then, he knew full well that without it he would have become an automaton, or perhaps simply a vegetable, numbed by grief into a state of absolutely no contact with the world. *But enough of this*, he told himself. *Hollow regrets and pointless reminiscence.*

Besides being Number Two to Meesian's Number One, he was also organiser and head of a secret opposition cell, the first one on Mars but, by now, far from being the only one. Not surprisingly, the Martian police forces had never been able to track the cells down or infiltrate them. Number Two drew his mask from its hiding place. A cell meeting was scheduled for tonight; he foresaw that he would have much to do before he could join Meesian in his Olympian retreat.

Interlude

MIDWINTER, HE JUDGED from the cold drizzle and the grey sky and the chill, damp breeze. The red brick walls lining the street glistened with oily wetness in the light of a nearby street lamp. During the summer, he knew, it could be quite sunny and cheerful; but dreariness was typical of winter in this town. It was all so disturbingly familiar. How could he have come here?

Footfalls broke the silence. A tall, slender figure came into view at the farther end of the pool of light cast by the street-lamp. The stranger's appearance was camouflaged by a woolen scarf and a hat pulled low against the weather, but the gait was the gait of youth. Watching him approach, Moriarty smiled suddenly. *How could I not have seen the connection?* For so many years he had puzzled over that mysterious visitor on that momentous night in 1868. *How very fitting!*

The younger man came up to him and paused in surprise at finding someone else out late on such a wretched evening, and moreover seemingly waiting for him. Professor James Moriarty stepped forward and said, "Good evening, Professor James Moriarty. I have many things to tell you which I know you will find of extraordinary interest."

Later, in the academic's cramped quarters, the young professor asked his visitor, "How much longer can you stay?"

The older man thought for a moment. "My total allotted time is approximately six hours." He drew out his watch and looked at it. "We have used better than two hours of that already."

The younger man looked at him half in thought, half in fear. He could not say, even though he bent all of his powerful intellect to the task of analysing the phenomenon, why this mysterious visitor so awed and mesmerised him. Nor could he understand why this man was so hauntingly familiar. He had refused to give his name or any other information about himself, and yet he possessed a minute and remarkable knowledge of Professor Moriarty's past and, so he claimed, his future.

"Sir," young Professor Moriarty said at last, "you have painted for me an extraordinary picture of my future should I turn aside from my present course into the path advocated by you. But that is a path from which the vast majority of my fellow men would recoil in horror."

The older man smiled at him benignly, paternally. "Oh, yes, the common mass of men would recoil, as you have said. But what care we for them? *You* have not recoiled, so I notice. And tell me truly, Professor: Has not the path I have shown you already been known to you, and has it not always . . . intrigued?"

The young academic sprang to his feet, angry and confused and filled with shame. He strode to the apartment's small window and stood staring out into the darkness, his hands clasped behind his back and his head thrust forward and oscillating slightly from side to side. His visitor looked on with considerable interest but no anxiety, remembering clearly what thoughts were running through the young man's mind and remembering too what would be the resolution.

"Yes," the young man admitted, "yes. It has always appealed to me. Even in childhood, it was a fascination I sometimes fought, sometimes succumbed to. But I have chosen my path, and it is not the path of evil. The beauties of mathematics will be all I'll need. That and a career devoted to opening young minds to those beauties."

His visitor smiled at his back but still said nothing by way of counterargument. Within seconds, he knew, the counterargument would present itself.

Drunken voices penetrated from the outside, young voices raised in riotous song. Three young men stumbled into the light cast by the lamp over the building's front door, arms linked, clothes awry, faces flushed. One of them looked up, noticed the pale, austere face staring down disapprovingly, and made an obscene gesture at the window. The three of them laughed loudly and passed on into the darkness.

Moriarty snarled in anger and spun about. His visitor noted approvingly the clenched fists, the tightened jaw, the blazing eyes. "Three of my students," young Moriarty hissed.

The visitor nodded in sympathy. "You are like that idle king: By this still hearth I mete and dole logic's laws unto a savage race that hoard, and sleep, and feed, and know not me. I invite you instead to drink life to the lees." He stood and gripped the young man's arm and stared intently into his eyes, which were precisely on a level with his own. "Listen well. You've known the beauties of mathematics intimately, but you've only sampled that other beauty. I have only hinted at it to you. Drink deep of it tonight. Only then can you judge fairly between your present path and that other one.

"Listen to me. Not only do your students ridicule and revile you. No, don't try to pull away. Listen! Your colleagues, too. Remember their reception of your book? And when you were offered the position here on the basis of your treatise upon the Binomial Theorem, there was one old man here—"

"Harrington! Yes!"

"Yes, Harrington, who dismissed your brilliant work as—"

"Trivial. Harrington, who has never produced any work of importance and never will." The young man stood deep in thought for a moment and then asked, "But what am I to do about it?"

"You already know the answer. I cannot stay past this night, but before dawn, you and I can pay old Harrington back in fullest measure for his insult. Here the ways divide, James Moriarty. Choose!"

The younger Moriarty said, "Perhaps I had already chosen years ago but denied it until now." He smiled, a smile of eagerness and evil. "Yes," he hissed. "Teach me what to do to Harrington."

"I will help you to do it," the older Moriarty replied, matching his smile.

26

Time Will Out

MONDAY, 11 MAY, 1812. Spenser Perceval, the Prime Minister of England was at the zenith of his power. He dominated Parliament and the country to a degree his contemporaries considered remarkable, one of them writing to another that he saw no reason why Perceval's star should not remain in the ascendant for another twenty years, at least. His enemies despaired of ever being able to remove him from office.

On that day, however, as Spenser Perceval walked through the lobby of the House of Commons on his way to attend the Commons committee examination of witnesses in the matter of the Orders in Council, he was shot dead by John Bellingham.

Bellingham was a trader and merchant who had seen his business wither away to nothing and who had himself been imprisoned for some time in Russia. He blamed these misfortunes on England's wars against Napoleon and against the United States, and he blamed the Prime Minister for the wars. A large body of opinion in England, after the assassination, held that, whatever small justification Bellingham might have for these opinions, he was surely a madman. To what extent these ideas of his, this fixation on Perceval as the author of his woes, was his own and to what extent he had been influenced by another, would never be established.

Sixty-five thousand four hundred and one days later, on Monday, 3 June, 1991, Mrs. Letitia Chalmers, "Lettie" to her circle of friends, and to the rest of the world the Prime Minister of England, was working late as was her usual custom in a small office adjoining the Cabinet Room at the rear of the ground floor of Number 10 Downing Street. The room had originally been intended as the office of the private secretary to the Prime Minister and had been quite large and handsomely appointed. Mrs.

Chalmers, demonstrating that aversion for ostentation which remained from her childhood in Jamaican slums and which had endeared her to the voters, had had the room divided in two to provide an office both for her and her private secretary. Her own office she had decorated only with books, stuffed into bookcases which were in turn crammed into every available space along the walls.

At a noise, she looked up to find herself no longer alone. But it was not her private secretary, a young man named Wilford, as she had expected. A stranger stood before her, a tall, thin man with the face of an ascetic. He stooped slightly, his shoulders hunched, his face projecting forward and oscillating from side to side in a repulsively reptilian manner. She thought his pallor ghostlike, as if he were indeed the spirit from the preceding century his clothes suggested. How he had entered, she could not imagine; perhaps the policemen stationed outside the house had fallen asleep. Clearly, though, she was faced with a madman and must treat him gingerly until help could arrive.

And indeed, this strange man ranted at her for some minutes, and even her sharply worded order to him to leave had no effect. She was reluctant to press the button beneath her desk that would bring help, for she had detected the bulge of a gun in his pocket, and she hoped she could soothe him with words. Thus, when Wilford knocked at her locked door to ask if she were in trouble and needed help, she answered that she was not.

The visitor's blazing eyes had had an almost hypnotic effect. How else explain that she had not previously noticed the machine that stood behind him, a glittering, metallic framework, a thing of brass, ebony, ivory, and translucent, glimmering quartz, but squat and ugly nonetheless? The Prime Minister gasped in astonishment and blinked her eyes.

Her visitor laughed harshly at her bewilderment. "It is nothing but a device for travelling through time, dear lady," he said, with an affectation of old-world chivalry that filled her at last with the terror she had been staving off until now. "A simple device from my point of view, I assure you."

"And you invented and built it?" the Prime Minister asked, hoping to humor the lunatic.

He scowled. "No, I did not. But I could have, had I put my mind to it earlier, instead of spending my efforts on profitless pursuits. Well, well!" he suddenly exclaimed. Darting forward, he snatched from her bookcase a small volume bound in red morocco. Mrs. Chalmers recognised it as one she had picked up on an impulse in an antique bookshop some years earlier.

"There, now!" Moriarty said, well pleased. "The unappreciated fruit of my first life, fruit indeed of a wasted youth. And yet *you* appreciated it. For that alone, I am tempted to modify my plans."

The Prime Minister's fear and patience vanished together. "It's an antique book, nothing else, and it's at least a hundred years old. Obviously you're only fantasising about having anything to do with it. Now take yourself and your . . . your gadget out of my office and out of this building, or I will call a policeman and see that you're shut away for life."

Moriarty snarled like an animal, cast the book onto the desk, where it fell open in the middle, drew the gun from his pocket, and shot Mrs. Chalmers precisely through the heart. He then returned to the Time Machine and both vanished.

Sixty-five thousand four hundred and one days later, it was Monday, 25 June, 2170.

Meesian IV sat at his desk in his office in his complex of buildings on Europa. Little of the original surface of the tiny world was still visible: Almost everywhere, pressurised buildings housing Meesian's computers, Meesian's communications devices, and Meesian's robot servants covered the ground. At the center of this vast complex sat Meesian IV, his fingers playing over the console that was his desk with blurring speed, his eyes scanning a dozen small screens set into the desk as he absorbed data, processed it, and sent out orders in response.

Suddenly all this frantic activity halted. Meesian IV's fingers froze in the air above the buttons of the console. He raised his head and stared into the camera that faced him eternally over his desk. "He has arrived," he said calmly. "He comes this way."

Motion resumed, and for some moments the blurred fingers and scanning eyes were as before. An observer could not have told that Meesian IV was issuing orders prepared long in advance to terminate a thousand different projects.

Again his fingers stopped moving and he looked up at the camera. "Now I can hear the footsteps. Human, beyond a doubt. Well over six foot, I would judge, with a light frame, and in rather a hurry." A faint, ironic smile flitted over his thin features. "It has been most fascinating to serve you." Unhurriedly, he resumed his work.

The two men watching the image relayed by the camera facing Meesian IV leaned forward simultaneously, each holding his breath. Now, through the sound pickup on Europa, even they could hear the hurrying footsteps Meesian IV's far more sensitive ears had picked up minutes earlier.

As the eager footsteps approached his doorway, Meesian IV swept his hand lightly over his desk, blanking the screens and cutting off the arrays of insistently blinking lights. It was a gesture of finality. Then he pushed his chair back from the desk and looked up at the doorway expectantly.

Professor James Moriarty stalked into the room, his hands outstretched, fingers curved to rip and tear, fingernails grown long and sharp, his face contorted into a beast's ferocity, with lips drawn back to expose long, yellow canines. The two distant observers gasped involuntarily. Suddenly Moriarty stopped in amazement, staring at the ruler of fifteen billion human beings, The feral grin disappeared. "You!" he said hoarsely. "YOU!"

Before Moriarty could move, faster than the limits of any human reaction, Meesian IV leaped across his desk and wrapped his arms and legs around the intruder. Moriarty's expression changed from predatory anticipation to dawning understanding and terror. He shrieked. And Meesian IV exploded.

27

Time for Sherlock Holmes

THE CHEMICAL EXPLOSIVES packed into the body of Meesian IV, the atomic explosion pursuing Moriarty through time, and the awesome temporal energies built up by his repeated oscillations all combined into one gargantuan release. Europa was vaporised. The two watchers looked out their window to see a new star flare and slowly fade above the crater of Olympus Mons.

The taller and slenderer of the two relaxed from an unconscious tension that had been with him for decades. "Over at last. What a long, long century it has been. Eh, Number Two? Watson, rather."

I laughed. "Yes, Watson from now on, please. And Number One can revert to being Sherlock Holmes."

"Well, Watson, tell me: Is this not the proof of the pudding?"

"Oh, indeed. I can scarcely argue with you any longer. You had to change human history to do it, but you managed at last to build a mountain great enough to draw Moriarty to you."

"In the person of Meesian, the most puissant ruler in all history, yes. Yet you know, Watson, that you provided the germ of the idea."

"I! How?"

"Long ago, you made me see how impossible the task of chasing Moriarty would be, how improbable it would always be that I should find myself in the right time and the right place merely by coincidence or a fortunate guess—and moreover prepared to deal with him. Taking that argument to its logical end, I saw that I must make him come to me. That reasoning and the fervent nationalism then growing on Mars led to the invention of the Meesian persona."

"And eventually to the explosives-packed robot isolated on Europa. I still hold, though, as I always have and always shall, that you were unwise to give him your face and general appearance."

Holmes chuckled. "Credit that to an indulgence in my old theatrical impulses. I foresaw that last encounter between Moriarty and the robot in fairly accurate detail, and I chose Meesian's appearance as my final little trick on the professor."

"Harmless enough, I suppose, as it turned out. Almost, I feel sorry for him."

"Moriarty, or the robot?"

I smiled. "Both, perhaps. That machine you created to handle governmental details and trap Moriarty demonstrated a sudden flare of independent humor at the very end. A quirky and cynical touch, that last remark of his."

"Yes, indeed. Wasn't that remarkable?"

"How strange to think that it's all over at last, after all this time." I sighed and shook my head. "Almost three hundred years for you. One hundred for me. And now, whatever shape human government assumes after Meesian, our part is done. We have no rôle to play, you and I. The purpose was so overriding for so long, and now . . ." *And now*, I thought, *after a century of distraction, I am forced at last to face up to an eternity without Lily.*

As if he had read that thought, or at the very least sensed the return of my old grief, Sherlock Holmes put his arm over my shoulder and said, "My oldest and dearest friend, the pastimes for us will be endless, infinite, and eternal." He led me back to the window. "There will be a period of unrest, certainly. But I doubt if the disruption will reach serious proportions. Assuredly, your ingenious suggestion that you start an underground opposition movement dedicated to parliamentary democracy will deserve credit for that. With the organisation of your cells and their dedication to the principles of order and liberty we both hold dear to act as a balancing force and a substratum for the future society, the transition to the next stage will surely be quite peaceful. And with the iron hand of Meesian withdrawn, Mankind will explode with creativity and exploration. Soon we will see men travelling to the stars at faster-than-light speeds." He waved his hand toward the mighty, silent sweep of the Milky

Way. "The stars, Watson! There will be vast emigrations, colonisation on an unimaginable scale, settlements spread across the light years. New and remarkable societies will arise out there, dwarfing in scope and diversity everything you and I have yet seen in our long lives. And where there is civilisation, there will soon be new and ingenious crime. And where there is clever crime, can Sherlock Holmes and the faithful Doctor Watson be far behind?

"Time," he murmured, gazing at the stars, seeing into the infinite distances. "All the time in the Universe. Time enough for anything you could ever dream of doing. Time for Sherlock Holmes."

Postlude

GIVING UP her baby was a wound to which only her forced sep-
aration from John Watson compared, but Lily knew she had no
choice. For months, the intuitive knowledge had been growing
that she would not be here for much longer. There was no logic
to it, but she found herself accepting the feeling as reliable. What
it would be, she could not tell. Disease? Accident? Murder? San
Francisco abounded in all three. She knew only that it was coming, and now it was only minutes away, and she wanted the tiny
girl well and safely cared for.

"I've been called away for a few days," she told her cousins,
standing before the window and staring at the blue horizon. A
carriage toiled up the curving, rising street outside. Lily stood
motionless by the window until she felt sure she could keep the
tears from flowing. Even so, she feared her cousins could see
that her eyes were brimming when she turned toward them. She
had no idea what she'd say if they asked why she was crying.
She smiled brightly at them. "You won't mind taking care of
the baby, will you?"

"Of course not!" Thomas harrumphed. "We'll be delighted to,"
Eliza said softly. Lily knew they meant it and silently blessed
them. She hesitated, wanting to give them detailed instructions,
wanting to hug the child fiercely to her for that one last time,
but she couldn't let herself do anything that would arouse suspicion. And so she kissed the tiny face only once, lightly, smiled
again all around, and walked quickly from the house, a beautiful
young woman with scarcely a care in the world.

They watched her walk rapidly down the street. "That damned
Englishman," Thomas Cantrell said feelingly. "Running out on
her like that."

"*And* after taking advantage of her, ruining her," his sister
added fiercely.

"Hmm." *Can't say as I blame him, though. Cousin or no cousin . . .*

"Tom!" his sister said sharply. "Go upstairs and get me some clean underthings for the baby."

As the house disappeared from sight around the curve of the road, Lily paused to look out at the sea again. She felt unaccountably strange, as if the ground beneath her feet had become fluid, alive, in motion, and the air was pressing upon every square inch of her skin. The pressure increased. Her vision blurred. *Then this is what I've foreseen for so long. But what is it! What's happening to me!*

And then the greyness of intertime began to gather about her and she realised what was happening. Her gloom vanished, giving way to elation. She was going back! With that understanding came another, no less certain: The baby she was leaving behind would have grandchildren who would move to Illinois, and one of them in turn would eventually have a granddaughter named Lily Cantrell after her, the young woman who had walked out into this warm and lovely San Francisco day and never again been seen. . . .

But she *would* be seen again! She didn't know when it would be and certainly not where, but some day and some time, perhaps in a thousand years or a million, perhaps on Earth or Mars or some unimaginable distance away from either, she would appear again and rejoin John Watson, for he was her *idée fixe*.

As the bright, sunny day disappeared and the grey space of the time between all times wrapped itself comfortingly around her, Lily Cantrell laughed aloud with delight and anticipation.